Andoshen, Pa.

ALSO BY DARRYL PONICSAN

The Last Detail
Goldengrove

Andoshen, Pa.

a novel by
DARRYL PONICSAN

Authors Choice Press

San Jose New York Lincoln Shanghai

Andoshen, Pa.
a novel

Authors Choice Press
an imprint of iUniverse.com, Inc.

For information address:
iUniverse.com, Inc.
5220 S 16th, Ste. 200
Lincoln, NE 68512
www.iuniverse.com

Originally published by The Dial Press

ISBN: 0-595-18252-6

Printed in the United States of America

Dedicated to
Ann and Frank Ponicsan
(Mom & Pop)

"Everybody who ever lost a finger, practically, lost it by one way and one way only. They had it where it didn't belong."

—*Thunder Przewalski*

Andoshen, Pa.

Dear Son,

Isn't it too bad you didn't think about all these things when you were growing up here. A boy lives in a town all his life and has no use for it until he's in the city and then he remembers and wonders about it all.

Remember the cave-in, when we lived on Coal St. and I jumped up on a chair and tried to hold our ceiling from coming down but it came down anyway right on top of us? And our store was destroyed? When we received your letter we began to remember the funny things that could only happen in Andoshen. You just ask whatever comes to mind and if Pop and I can help any, we'll write and tell you.

Love,
Mom & Pop

Chapter One

Thunder

Brolly's Bar had only two signs. One lamenting,

The hurrier I go,
The behinder I get

and the other inviting patrons to

Join the Pistol Club.
Drink til midnite,
Pistol dawn

There was no closing time at Brolly's Bar. He closed only when no more customers were left, though he did for the sake of the state law draw his curtains and lock his doors at the legal time, opening them only for anyone with sense enough to tap lightly on the window with a quarter.

Brolly had no specific closing time, but for specific customers he reserved specific points of departure.

Thunder Przewalski's night was quickly coming to its conclusion.

In Thunder's case his exit usually began with losing his pants (and ceremoniously hitching them up again) and ended with his falling off the bar stool. Somewhere in between he would sing his Song.

He would lean his short, hard, brutish body against the bar, keeping at least one empty stool between him and the next drinker, lower his head and sing to the puddles and the ashes on the bar in a raspy whiskey bass, painfully enunciating each word:

> *"There's poTAToes in the OV—en,*
> *They are ROASTing nice 'n BROWN—*
> *There's a JUIcy waterMELon,*
> *When the SEAson rolls aROUND—*
> *In the PANtry there's a CHICKen,*
> *In the SMOKEhouse there's a HAM,*
> *And I'd ruther be Monsignor O'BRIen*
> *Than a poooor WHITE man."*

Someone would buy him a beer for the song; someone else would buy him another not to sing it again.

"In my opinion, Thunder Przewalski is a misanthrope, and no one in America today really understands Noel Coward," said Doc Rice, the dentist, in the way he had of expressing an opinion of general interest in conjunction with an opinion of no interest whatsoever.

"He's a miss 'n throw up, all right," said Gunner Walsh, a retired sailor, Gunner's Mate Second Class, "but he ain't no coward. He justs boozes more than he's entitled to."

"To kill the taste of his fellow man," said Doc Rice.

"He's more off than he's on, work," said Boss Mahoney, the iceman.

"He soweth not much, neither doth he reapeth much," said Doc Rice.

"He lets a lotta blood in the alley behind the Majestic Pool Hall," said Stump Bonomo, who had been a miner, lost his leg in the Oak Hill cave-in, was given a wooden one, and now worked topside in the Blue Mountain Coal Breaker. " 'Course, there's been others done the same for him."

"Pool shooting and blood letting," said Doc Rice. "The one is the head of the beast, the other the ass."

Thunder growled.

"Some day he will commit a dastardly deed," said Doc Rice. "Dastardly" was one of his favorite words.

"Oh, I wouldn't say that exactly," said Gunner Walsh.

Standing patiently by the kitchen door was Kayo Mackey, of professional pucking fame, who was unable to hear their conversation clearly because his sense of hearing was on the decline, and his mind was elsewhere. Brolly reached into the kitchen, his wife gave him a greasy brown bag full of leftovers, and he gave the bag to Kayo Mackey. As Kayo left he said to the patrons, "Youse wanna play the pools? I'm be on me way home now." He pulled from his hip pocket a sheaf of papers.

No one answered, and Kayo left Brolly's with food for tomorrow.

"He's not a man one can talk to," said Doc Rice, still on the subject of Thunder Przewalski, talking about him as though he had already been shown the door.

"His neighbors call him the Ruin of Rattlin' Run."

Thunder growled again, slid first on his arms, then on his chin along the edge of the bar and fell to the floor, staring at the ceiling. Brolly routinely made the circle to the other side of the bar, helped Thunder to his feet, made sure he left nothing on the bar, and put him out on the street.

As he staggered down the long narrow road to the colliery patch, Rattlin' Run, Thunder cursed aloud everything between him and his miserable mattress, from goats and garbage cans to Most Holy Reverend Fathers.

The squad car pulled up next to him and he recognized Shakey the Cop, who leaned toward the passenger's window and said, "Get home and shut up your mouth and get off the street and be keeping quiet 'cause the birds be's tryin' to sleep in the treetops."

"Dis ain't your shift, copperhead," growled Thunder.

Thunder was not unknown to Shakey the Cop, Chief Red Sweeney, Justice of the Peace Malloy, or the gentlemen of the county court. In fact, several unsolved burglaries of long standing were still attributed to Thunder, though if true the take must have been small indeed, for he lived as poorly as any other wretch. His known M.O. was assault and battery, pure and simple. The drunk and disorderlies did not count.

It was even rumored by some wags that Thunder, in spite of his Polander name, was the actual Mick who, in fact, threw the overalls in Mrs. Murphy's chowder. And when the righteous preached against "plumbing the depths of human degradation," Thunder was the plumber they had in mind.

"Who are you to be carin' how the police force works?" barked Shakey.

"Works!"

"Shut up your mouth and have some professional

courtesy or I be's layin' the wood on your puss just for drill."

"I'll shove that billy down your yonko throat and make you eat it like a kiski, you dumb flatfoot."

"One of these days, Thunder Przewalski, you're gonna push old Shakey the Cop too far 'n I'm gonna plug you, and the ladies from Rattlin' Run will have a block party and they'll gimme all the proceeds and the leftover eats."

"Yeah? Well, one of these nights I'm gonna lay for you, and if you ever move your fat ass from that dumb squad car I'm gonna cut off your head with a double-edge ax and for the rest of me life they'll let me drink free at Brolly's and shoot free pool at the Majestic."

"Oh, boy, Thunder Przewalski, a big shame on you for talkin' such a way to a policeman officer. I should be runnin' you in the jug for that."

"Go fart in the bathtub," said Thunder.

"Boy, are you ig'nernt. If it wasn't near time for me to go home, I'd run you in for drill. I'm lettin' you go dis time, but let it be a lesson to you."

"And bite the bubbles," said Thunder as the car pulled away.

When Thunder did get to his neighborhood he made sure to wake up the ladies who would throw a block party for the yonko who killed him. He sang his song and belched loudly and recited at the top of his voice, "Oh, 'tis better to belch the belch and bear the shame than squelch the belch and bear the pain."

All of which was done to protect him from the finer nature of human beings.

Rattlin' Run was crowded with ladies, not only the

wives of the men who lived there, but also the mothers and daughters of these women, plus some old widows who lived alone. Thunder annoyed them when he came home late at night, and they annoyed him in return early in the morning by slamming their screen doors and going about their chores like shrill chattering birds. It was a joke of life to Thunder that those who bear men later burn them. As for the women, they cursed their sex that one of their number should give to Rattlin' Run and the world a brute as bad and as ugly as Thunder Przewalski.

He took off his clothes and fell into a bed that had been turned down by stray dogs.

Next morning the ladies were in their adjacent backyards, hanging up the wash. There were seven of them in a row, like an accusing finger, pointing to the eighth house, Thunder's. It was another joke of life that women should wash early in the morning, the same time that men suffer from flannel tongues, gritty eyeballs, and pulsating skulls. Thunder turned on his stomach and covered his head with what passed for his pillow but could not block out their torturous chirping.

It had rained for three days, but now was clear and bright. The women wore galoshes because their yards had turned to mud. Each had a flat stone to slide along before her, to protect the bottom of the wash basket from the mud.

Except for the yard in the middle, Mrs. Grotzki's, a seventy-four-year-old widow, the yards belonged to married women, and as they hung up their wet sheets, pillow cases, and underwear they discussed the conditions of home and country.

"Didja notice the Wowak girl ain't at Newberry's no more?"

"I never even noticed. Where'd she go?"

"Would you believe it, to New York."

"Well, they're all going now, the young ones, out of town. There's nothing here for them."

"Ah, but she came back again the same day. The grass is always greener, ain't?"

"But nobody can tell you when you're young. You know it all when you're young."

"Well, so did you. We all did."

"So what does she do, the Wowak girl, now she ain't at the five and dime?"

"She's at Savannah Hand-Made Cigars. I give this to her: she ain't lazy. Lotsa girls would take advantage and sit on their *dupas*."

"She's a good girl. I never bought a chocolate-covered pretzel when she was at the candy, that she didn't smile for me."

"But those awful smelly cigars, *Woi Yesus*, how can she stand it?"

One of the women held a pair of undershorts in front of her and above her head and said, "I think my oldest is a man already."

The others squealed and one said, "Oh, the little divil!"

From Thunder's house came a low, long, mean growl.

"It's himself, registering a complaint, you."

"Suffer, suffer, you bring it on yourself!" yelled one of them.

"Oh, what a terrible specimen of a man."

"No, he's a perfect example. Are the others so much better?"

"They can't be any worse, can they?"

"Did you hear about Ella's Lunch? She's havin' awful trouble with her brother-in-law, or his wife. Both, I guess."

"I heard they're not going to be partners no more, that they'll be two places instead of the one big place. That's what happens when . . ."

This gossip would have continued except that Mrs. Grotzki was swallowed up by the earth.

She had been fastening a clothespin to one corner of a dish towel. The other clothespin was held ready in her toothless mouth. There was a *swooooosh* and she was gone.

"Jesus, Mary, 'n Joseph!"

Almost immediately they realized that a mine must be below and that the rain must have softened the layer of earth above it.

They screamed and looked at their own galoshes and tried to will the weight off their feet, afraid that they too would be swallowed by their own backyards. They screamed almost in chorus, which gave them again the power of motion. They took tentative light steps across their yards, and, courage returning, they finally went into Mrs. Grotzki's backyard and gathered around the hole in the ground. Their wailing brought men, women, children, and dogs from the street, but all were careful to stay well away from the perimeter of the hole.

Aware of their own brashness now, the women themselves began taking backward steps away from the danger. One of them stopped and leaned forward and said, "Old Myra, oh, are you alive or dead?"

Everyone heard the faint cry, like the squeak of a broken sparrow.

They wailed anew.

Into this scene came Thunder Przewalski in bare feet, hitching up his pants and extending and working his tongue outside of his mouth, trying to make it respond to the demands of his brain. "What's the goddam noise? *Bęnda bida!*" he growled, shaking his fist at them. "Somebody's gonna get a puck in the snotbox before I leave here."

They moved aside so that he could witness the sacrilege he was committing.

From deep in the pit came the feeble squeak.

"Well, ain't nobody gonna go down and get her?" asked Thunder, but the others turned their heads away.

Thunder took his knife from his pants pocket and cut down two of Mrs. Grotzki's clotheslines, dragging the freshly laundered whites through the mud. The women gasped and covered their mouths or held each other's arms. After he tore the clothes off the lines he tied the two ends together and fastened one end around his waist. He gave the other end to three husky men and said, "Do youse tink the three of youse can hold dis and do what I tell youse to do in English?"

The three of them held the end of the line and lowered Thunder into the hole. The spectators held their breath as they watched the knot that marked halfway, twenty feet or more, go over the side and into the darkness.

When he reached her she was in mud almost to her chest. She was unconscious, which made it more difficult for Thunder to pull her free. He finally managed to clear enough of her so that he could take the line from his own waist and tie it around hers.

"Okay, youse yonkos, pull her up slow and careful 'cause I tink she's be hurt bad."

Thunder watched the woman being hoisted above him. Her galoshes had come off in the mud. Her muddy head dangled as though she were on the gallows. Mud dripped from her as she was hoisted. He heard the siren of the ambulance. She would be taken immediately to Peddler's Hill Hospital, to Thunder's mind only one short step above being in this muddy pit. He looked down and saw that he had sunk to the knees.

He tried to rub some mud away from his eyes with his arm and tried to remember what he had done last night, or the night before, to rate the condition he was in now. The base of his skull was throbbing painfully and he kept his head erect, neither turning nor bending, so that the bowels of his head would not list. He felt pressure at his crotch and knew, because of his extra weight, that he was sinking much faster than Mrs. Grotzki had.

"If I'm not bein' a bother . . ." he yelled. He could hear noise and confusion above and began to adjust to the fact that he was probably forgotten by those above him and would lie in a muddy grave under all those squealing women and their dripping wash. If only he could have a taste of wine now.

The mud rose to his waist.

"I don't mind the people down here in this fancy resort, but the weather be awful cold and awful wet!" he yelled.

He sighed and thought, well, there's no livin' forever

↰ 12

and if there was, who'd take it up? He felt the mud roll over his belt.

Before his eyes fell the end of a stout rope, not the clothesline he had used for Mrs. Grotzki.

He reached out for it and yelled up, "I wouldn't take up the rest of the day about it, lovin' neighbors!"

They hauled him out of the hole. The mud, trying to hold him there, kept his pants, so that when he surfaced he looked like the most terrible naked beast God ever gave life to. Someone wrapped one of Mrs. Grotzki's muddy sheets around his bottom and the photographer from the *Call* took his picture. Men pushed each other aside to shake his hand and the women patted him on his muddy back and ran inside to wash their hands.

He walked away from them, puffing like an old parade. It took two tubfuls of water to wash away all the mud, after which Thunder Przewalski fell back on his mattress and tried to get the sleep his body ached for.

It seemed he had hardly fallen asleep before there was a knock on the door. He pulled on a dry pair of pants and opened the door to see one of his seven neighbor ladies.

"What do you want, you won't let me sleep?"

"I'm sorry I woke you up. It's the middle of the after'. I brung you a potato cake."

She handed him the pan, still warm, covered with wax paper. He held it away from his body, confused. No one had ever made him a potato cake.

"What are you up to?" he asked. "I don't have anything for you."

"Some people would say thank you and let it go at

that. You're a bad man and I'm glad you ain't mine. . . ."

"Me too."

". . . but what you did out there today was a brave thing. That's what I'm sayin' with the potato cake, if a person had the ears to hear it."

Thunder grunted and lowered his eyes. When he lifted them he saw another of the ladies and the two of them were pushing their way into his house. He backed up, still holding the potato cake. He put it on the chair and turned to order them out when the second woman put a large covered bowl in his hands.

"Pierogies," she said. "I was makin' them anyway."

The third woman brought leftover scrapple.

The fourth and fifth brought their cleaning gear because, "We always knew you lived in a pig sty and now that we're inside we can see we were right. My God, it's a miracle you don't catch a sickness."

Thunder sat with his rewards around him, trying to look sullen and disturbed, as the women scurried about cleaning up his hovel. Someone made him hot coffee and it tasted better than his own.

The sixth woman finally showed up carrying a five-quart crock covered with a dish towel.

"Mrs. Grotzki that you life-saved has they think a broken hip," she said. "But she don't complain. I brung you a crock of dandelion wine. It ain't gonna be ripe for another three, four weeks, if you can keep your hands off of it that long."

Thunder carried the crock lovingly to his dirt cellar where it was cool.

"I'll give back all the empties," he said to the ladies as they were preparing to leave.

They stood in a line, waiting. Thunder looked at his grimy fingernails as though reading from them and said, "Thanks for the good eats . . . and all."

The *Evening Call*, known to the locals as the *Mackerel Wrapper*, carried the story on the front page. There was a big picture of Thunder with the caption: LOCAL HERO. He was the talk of the town.

That night Thunder could not even go out for a beer because he knew what would happen the minute he walked into Brolly's. Everyone would buy him a beer, and clap him on the back, and expect him to display all the characteristics of a hero for it. Someone would be sure to say, "Hey, Thunder, say something in hero for us." He stayed home and watched his wine ferment.

The next day old Mrs. Grotzki died.

The evening after, the *Call* reported on the last page of the issue that Gerald "Thunder" Przewalski was arrested in the alley behind the Majestic Pocket Billiards on a drunk and disorderly charge. Reportedly, he had smashed a back window with his fist, sustaining a gash that required several stitches to close. He was treated at Peddler's Hill Hospital and later appeared before Justice of the Peace Malloy, who reprimanded him and sentenced him to five days in the local lockup.

The ladies of Rattlin' Run read the report and shook their heads silently like philosophers.

Dear Son,

Who knows why they called him Thunder, probably because he sounded like it. He was one old dog whose bite was as bad as his bark, worse. He worked as a miner, mechanic, hauler, anything he could get, like most people around here. Before the Blue Mountain breaker came down, he used to come into the store and never had a cross word for me, lucky for us both, because I know a couple myself. The one he really went round and round with was Shakey the Cop. They knew each other since they were kids and were so much alike they had no use for each other. Both miserable, that no decent woman in her right mind would marry, and none ever did. Once Shakey saw Thunder standing in front of Sol Levit's jewelry store window and he went up to him and said, "Move along, yonko, let the sun shine on the diamonds." Thunder spit on Shakey's shoe and Shakey wiped it off on Thunder's pant leg. Could this ever happen in Los Angeles?

You've got some memory! Do you also remember when our store was across the street and it caved in and our ceiling in the house buckled and I stood up on a chair to hold it up and yelled for you to get Mrs. Murphy next door, like she wouldn't be worrying about her own ceiling, and there we were, covered with plaster. You give something enough time and it becomes funny. Already they're making jokes about Abraham Lincoln.

They still talk about how Thunder saved Mrs. Grotzki. I don't remember if this was before or after he lost three fingers when he caught them under the eccentric rod of a fan engine. The next day she was dead and he was in jail. So one day you're a bum, the next you're a hero, the next you're a bum again. Remember that.

Love, Mom & Pop

Chapter Two

Shakey the Cop

A place was reserved for the squad car on the corner of Main and Center. The slot was across the street from the Majestic and up a few doors, hidden from the vision of approaching cars because the squad car was parked parallel to the sidewalk while all the other cars behind it were parked diagonally. Likewise, a car headed north on Center Street could not see it until it was too late.

There were three men on the force in addition to Red Sweeney, who sat in police headquarters above the Good Friends and Neighbors Volunteer Fire Company and manned the new two-way radio the boys were crazy about using, or played pinochle with a prisoner, if they had one. Red never left headquarters unless a bona fide crime involving the loss of a large sum of money, a valuable piece of property, or a life had been committed, regardless of whether or not detective investigation was necessary. The last time that happened was the winter before, when Eggshell Oechsle took a shotgun to his father and his uncle. When Red was not at the headquarters he left one of his three teen-age sons in charge.

Shakey the Cop worked the four-to-midnight shift. At

least two generations of Andoshen children grew up terrified of him, and countless children gave up a life of malicious mischief and went straight after ringing a doorbell and running away right into the knobby backhand of Shakey the Cop. Whenever a child thought of Shakey the Cop he thought of the billy he was reputed to have broken over Matt Weston's head for beating his wife and of the thirty-six stitches it took to pinch together the two halves of Matt's scalp. Later, when "police brutality" became a rallying cry, these same children remembered Shakey as their first example of it, and the memory was oddly one of love for the direct, simple, and almost kindly application of Shakey's violence. It was never planned, enjoyed, or denied, and thus was not brutality at all.

But even those citizens of Andoshen who had reputations as dumb Polacks called Shakey the Cop a dumb Polack.

One night, just before dusk, Shakey was sitting in his squad car, finishing a take-out coffee from Ella's Lunch. A few boys were loafing and snapping their fingers in front of the Majestic, and traffic was light, and the air was calm and warm. He made up a little song and sang it softly, "Oh, I'm goin' to the Lakie, for the Polish Picnic, cookin' up halupkes . . ."

A fancy Packard passed beside him and went through the amber light. Shakey was sure that part of the Packard did not make it through the intersection before the light turned red. He started up the Nash and called to headquarters on the new two-way radio.

"Chief Red, Chief Red, this here's Shakey the Cop, come in, Chief Red."

"Okay, Shakey, what's on your mind?" replied Red Sweeney. "Over."

"Roger. A big Packard from outa town just went through the light. Pennsylvania license, number Edward, Stanley, Two . . ."

"Okay, okay, Shakey, give 'im the ticket and collect the fine if he's from outa town and cut the crap."

"Well, can I be puttin' on the flasher? Over."

"Jesus, don't make a three-reeler outa this, will you, Shakey?"

Red Sweeney waited for an answer, then said the forgotten "Over."

"Roger, I be's pullin' the bugger over. Roger Wilco, over and out."

Shakey put the squad car into gear and caught the Packard as it was about to climb Peddler's Hill out of town. Shakey hit his horn three times and the Packard pulled over to the side.

Shakey picked up his citation book and then threw it back on the seat in disgust. "*Woi Yesus,* I'm outa tickets!" He considered issuing a ticket on plain note paper, but doubted the legality of this. Besides, he did not have any plain note paper. He would have to let the Packard go, but "Not before I chew him up a little, the sneaky wise guy."

Shakey strode up to the driver, who was with his wife and two children, and lowered his head to the window to say, "You know, youse went tru a light there on Center."

"I thought it was on caution, officer," said the driver.

Clearly from out of town. No one in town would call him "officer."

"Well, that's when you're suppose' to use caution."

"But you can go through," said the driver. "You only have to stop on the red."

"Say, are you tellin' me me business?"

"No, sir, I just . . ."

"Say, where are youse from?"

"From Pittsburgh, we're . . ."

"Oh, *yeah?*" said Shakey, indicating he had caught them in a lie, and flashing what locals called his shit-eating grin.

"Yeah," said the driver, "Pittsburgh."

"Then how come youse got a Pennsylvania license plate?" said Shakey the Cop, straightening up triumphantly and putting his fists on his hips.

The road goes up and all seems normal rural Pennsylvania, not as pleasant as the Lehigh Valley you've just passed through, but still green with healthy deciduous trees and huckleberry bushes and mountain laurels, the state flower. Then the road drops down hard and you are aware of something changing rapidly. The houses are tight together and dilapidated, and they seem to be slanting, clutching each other as they sink. Though they may have had color originally, they are all now in varying shades of gray. Huge trucks heaped with coal slow your progress and you feel the need to hurry through. Street signs, stop signs, and traffic signals are covered with a black dust you can almost taste and you imagine it getting under your fingernails even as you drive.

You drive under a long tube leading from a black mountain to a coal breaker one hundred feet high and as big as a city block, with tiny satellite buildings around it, all connected each to the other by conveyor belts encased in tubes. The main building has hundreds of windows, like stamps on an important package, most of them cracked or broken. More trucks are lined up at a coal chute. The breaker vibrates and makes the jarring noise of industry.

On a Sunday afternoon, from a distance, a coal breaker looks like something you might see in an elementary classroom, made out of papier-mâché and placed on rumpled black felt to serve as a model for a distant and little-known industry, but close up, everything is coated with the blackest of all dirt. Puddles of black water are all about. Acres of smooth black silt surround the structures like miniature deserts on the moon. A stream of brown water runs out of a hole in the earth. You see a little brown animal scurrying along the bank of this brown stream and at first you think it's a squirrel, but squirrels do not venture into mining operations. It is a rat.

Incredibly, a few trees grow naked around the perimeter of the breaker pit.

Now you go up another hill and next to you, on the right, is a wide clear dirt road on which the trucks rumble along, chunks of coal bouncing out over their sides. The trucks travel on the left side of the road because when the dirt road winds away from the black-top to the mine strippings drivers must be wary of driving off the road and into a pit.

Next to you on the left is a flat, perfectly smooth field of black. Squint your eyes and it looks like a pool of black water. It is coal dust, three hundred feet deep.

The road dips again and now you know for certain that you have left a reasonable world behind, because smoke rises from the earth on each side of the road. If it is dusk or night, you can see the earth glow where the blue haze rises. When it rains, of course, the smoke is much worse. You wonder if you have driven into hell, because you can smell the brimstone, an odor of damned and dead entrails. It is a fire in the mine below where thick veins of anthracite have been burning for fifteen years, and although you may hold your breath and think it hellish and find yourself nervous to be driving on such a road, to the residents of Andoshen, Pennsylvania, this is simply the Kimberly Run Fire, the unofficial welcome to town.

. . . at least if there's a war they won't bomb us. The planes will look down and think we've already been bombed.

Love,
Mom & Pop

Chapter Three

Estelle

Estelle Wowak graduated from Andoshen High School
without any particular honors or skills. She knew how to
type, but would never gain distinction in that department, because carbon copies made her nervous and she
often found herself making the same error she had just
erased on an original and four. She knew a little shorthand, as long as the one dictating spoke slowly and
clearly, but beyond that could be of little service to the
business world, even though she had completed satisfac-
torily the "Business" course of studies at A.H.S., as opposed to the "Academic" course, the only other course of
studies available.

In spite of her few thin secretarial skills, when the
yearbook came out she was named "Miss Girl Friday,"
and when she opened the book and saw that title next to
her picture she cried. It didn't mean anything. Oh, she
was familiar with the term, but applied to her it was at
best meaningless, at worst a bad joke. The others were
"Miss Good Looking," "Miss Personality," "Miss Eyes,"
Miss *Some*thing, something that could be understood im-

mediately, but hers was senseless. She tore that page out of her yearbook and gave it to the dog.

She went to work as a counter girl at Newberry's Five and Dime, first at the candy counter, then at notions, by her own request because she was getting fat from eating the few pieces always left in her hand after weighing a pound on the scale for a customer.

It made her mother sad to see Estelle begin her working life at the five and dime store in a town that could hold only the worst of its young men, the dreamers, the rowdies, the pool shooters, boys destined for nothing but varying degrees of self-deception. The other boys were gone to colleges and jobs in the cities, to return only on weekends with their suitcases full of dirty clothes for their mothers to wash. They were eager to date those local girls who had remained at home, to impress them with their new ways and knowledge, and to take them parking in the cemeteries as though it were their right. Even with her own daughter this could happen, until when she did marry, she would have to marry a hard man, an old man, a drinking man, any man.

Her anxiety was Estelle's as well, especially after two years had passed and she was still behind the notions counter. To think of it made her blood ripple. The girls in the present graduating class were two *years* behind her. In high school, she had hardly known them, and now they were out and off to adventures, while she spent her days imagining breaking in a new girl to take over her job.

As she went about her work, she could picture the new girl beside her and gave her her own physical characteristics but made her slower and not as pleasant. The new girl never smiled. *The one thing you have to remember,* said Estelle, as she broke in the imaginary new girl, *is to be nice to the customers. A woman spends a dime with you, she feels she deserves some pleasantness. All you got to do is smile and say thank you. They like that. Shoplifting you never have to worry about 'cause this is the last counter the kids want to hit. Once in a while one of 'em will try to get away with a pair of scissors, though. If you're not busy you should just watch some of the other counters after school when the kids come through looting.*

A customer handed her a "Chic Fashion Accessory," a twenty-nine-cent belt buckle. She dropped it into a bag and took the woman's exact change.

She took the imaginary new girl up one side of the rectangle of notions and down the other, pointing out the merchandise. *It won't take you long to remember where everything is. When you sell satin ribbon you measure it right on this yardstick bolted to the front of the counter here so the customer can see you. Always give a couple extra inches when you sell a few feet of the stuff. Here's the buttons, there's thousands, enough to drive you crazy, but remember there's a number under each stack of buttons, so all you do when you run out is look for that number in the cabinets under the counter. Same goes for the spools of thread. If they want a color that's not there, all you can tell 'em is if it's not on the rack you don't have it. Here's the iron-on patches, they go pretty good. The zippers, arranged by numbers, more in the cabinets. For the dress patterns they have to look through the catalogue here and give you the number, then you just find it in these drawers. Everything is by number, and everything has the price already on it, or the price is listed on the bin, so it's not so hard. But you gotta remember to be pleasant. Also, you gotta be careful with the register. If you make a mistake, write "void" on the tape with your pencil and ring it up again. Don't try to balance it out with the next sale because nine times out of ten you'll make a worse mistake and then you'll really be in the soup. Remember to smile once in a while. It's not a hard job. It's easy to learn. What makes it rough is you're on your feet all day, and also any job where you're dealing with the public is pretty demanding.*

Some public. No matter how hard she tried to put some zip into it, it was still the most useless job in the world. Well, what did she care? She didn't have to impress the girl she was breaking in with the demands of the job; she would find out for herself soon enough. The job demanded nothing but good feet.

Estelle ran the scene over and over again in her imagination because some day soon she was actually going to break in a new girl. She was going to go to New York. She was going to get a room right in the city and find a job as a secretary, and if she couldn't find one, she would go to the five and dime, there must be fifty of them in New York, and with her experience she would have no trouble getting a job. Working in the five and dime in New York is not like working in the five and dime in Andoshen. There you're really dealing with the public. You probably never see the same customer twice.

She would get a room in the middle of the city, and every night she would walk down Broadway and once a week she would go to Radio City Music Hall, on Saturday, and to the zoo on Sunday. After a while she would be like any other city person, and strangers would stop her on the street and ask for directions to the Statue of Liberty. She would tell them (because she would know) in a clipped, familiar way, and measure the distance in minutes instead of miles, like a city person.

This is what she was planning on, this is what she prepared for when she repeatedly broke in the imaginary new girl.

This is what happened:

She quit on a Monday, at closing time, explaining to the manager, "I'm sorry, I can't put it off any longer. I've got to get going to New York before I have even one more day to think about it."

"It happens like that. You should get it out of your system."

"I feel bad about not breaking in a new girl for you."

"Oh, don't worry, we can take care of that."

Estelle knew that it would take all of ten minutes for him to break in a new girl. I have wasted two years of my life, she thought.

"Would you like me to give your pay to your mother, or should I mail it to you?"

Estelle looked at the notions counter and saw herself gone from it.

"Do you have all your stuff with you?"

Over her arm she carried her smock, the name pin still attached.

The manager looked at his watch. "Then I guess I'll wish you good luck."

He shook her hand, took a "Girl Wanted" sign from the file cabinet, and walked her to the front door. He propped the sign against the window, locked the door behind them, and said, "Bye."

The next morning she boarded a Trailways to New York City, and the driver assured her that the bus stopped right in the middle of the city.

She disembarked at Port Authority, her heart full of

adventure, but on the street she clutched her bags and looked around, frightened. Where was Ella's Lunch? Where was the Capital Theater? Wadden Park? The brewery? Where was the five and dime? Where was Kayo Mackey and his pool sheets? Where was Duncan from the Majestic?

A colored man approached her on the street in front of Port Authority. His clothes were dirty and he smelled.

"Can I get you a cab? Where are you staying? I'll carry your bags for you."

Her breath was caught in her throat. She forced it out and said, "No, thank you, no, thank you. I'm waiting for someone. My husband's picking me up here."

The man went away.

She stood on the sidewalk at the station, clutching her bags, feeling the force of the city against her body, the air in her nostrils, the noise against her ears like the hammers of hell, the tall buildings pressing down on her head. She stood there in the New York City summer for fifteen minutes, until her clothes were wet with perspiration and her panties clung to the fold of her body.

She turned around, went back into Port Authority and waited six hours at the boarding gate for the next bus to Andoshen.

Her job at Newberry's had been filled by a young widow, recently made, named Donna.

The following day a cigar roller died at the Savannah Hand-Made Cigars factory and she got that vacant job.

Dear Son,

I can't guess why you'd want Estelle Wowak in your book, with all the characters around here. What can I say about her? She's not homely, she's not pretty. She's friendly, a hard-worker. She's kind of colorless. Father's a miner. Mother's a single-needle operator in the dress factory. She gets home from time to time for a visit. I don't know where she's living now, somewhere in the city, but I hear they're living on love. Her husband's a dreamer. There's a lid for every pot.

Love,
Mom & Pop

Chapter Four

Donna

Donna, motionless beneath the blanket in her slip and housecoat, counted five low bongs of the St. Mary's bell. The individual peals carried well on the chilly air that evening. She pulled her eyes open a crack, the act a struggle against dried tears. All she saw was the soft pale green of the bedroom ceiling. She did none of the things a waking person does when ending an afternoon nap, but simply opened her eyes, saw the ceiling, and wished that she could be waking up to a new day rather than reawakening to this day.

In the morning her husband had sung a song on his way to breakfast, robustly slapping the sides of his stomach as he sang,

> *"Our wages, John, grow beautifully less,*
> *And if they keep on growing thus, I guess,*
> *We'll have to put on magnifying specs,*
> *To see the little figures on our checks. . . ."*

"Is that a homemader?" she asked.

"That's an Irish ditty from the days of the Molly Maguires, when miners weren't the millionaires we are today."

"You're not any Irish, are you?"

"No, I don't think so, but I'm a miner anyway." He sat down to the table. "A lovely breakfast, Donna darlin'. What's in my bucket?"

She laughed and said, "You haven't even started breakfast yet and you're already worried about what's for dinner."

In Andoshen one ate breakfast, then dinner, then supper.

She put his lunch pail on the table and kissed the top of his head. "There's ham in your bucket," she said.

"God bless you, Donna, if that doesn't bring back memories. My mother used to wake us all up with that call. Long before the sun came up, she used to holler up the stairs, *Wake up, wake up, there's ham in your bucket,* . . . whether there was or not—and there usually was not."

Donna loved his recollections of the past. It was one of the advantages of marrying a much older man. An older man has a history and a deep feeling for it, and though she wasn't part of that, it belonged to her because she delighted in a oneness with her husband. Once she put it into words and it came out, "I am what he was," and although she did not comprehend completely her feelings, she knew that in saying it and believing it her twenty-two years of life need not be meager.

John finished his breakfast and holding his pail in his left hand squeezed her with his free arm, kissed her lustily, and left for the mine. On that morning he sang a song, he kissed her lustily, and he left her a widow in her twenty-second year.

Her sister Louise had told her in plenty of time, "Don't marry that man. He's old enough to be your father." Donna had told her not to be ridiculous. He was only twenty years older. "In ten years he'll be an old man," Louise had told her. "He'll die and leave you a young widow. Pick a young healthy man."

But Louise didn't know that Donna would not pick a man; Louise didn't know that Donna would wait and hope for the right man to pick her, and when he did, she knew it, and years and other numbers meant nothing.

Donna turned her eyes from the ceiling and saw his shoes in front of the open closet, saw his desert boots, old and worn, a part of his past. They looked pathetic lying there, as if they knew he was not coming back. They were soft and gray with splotches of shiny sections where the outer layer of material had worn off. One shoe was upright, the other on its side, touching toes with its mate. Like exhausted arms, the shoestrings lay on the floor. She could see inside one shoe and found it shaggy inside as well.

He had a brother named George, the mysterious one, the one who had escaped the grip of anthracite in Scranton and Wilkes-Barre to go—where? There are so many places, some where coal is unknown. How does she notify this next to next-of-kin that his brother is dead? She knew nothing of George except for the stories John told of their boyhood adventures in the strippings, in the fascinating world of giant trucks and deep gouges in the earth, where John paid his dues in bloody noses and bloody heads. Donna could remember and feel one of his earliest sensory memories—the touch of caked blood in his hair.

She pushed back the blanket and sat for several minutes on the edge of the bed, staring at the shoes. She went to them, fell to her knees, pulled them to her breast, and as quietly as possible cried.

"Donna, put them down, dear," said her sister, holding her by the shoulders. "Come back to bed."

"I can't, Louise. The bed is too big for me. I feel lost. I feel lost alone on that bed. I can't."

"Maybe a cup of coffee? Come on, we'll go in the kitchen. Nice hot coffee."

The choke escaping her throat was faint. She was helped into the kitchen and put at the table. Louise held her momentarily, then took away her hands to make sure Donna could sit alone.

"I've got it brewed strong."

With her forefinger, Donna made triangles on the plastic table cloth. "Remember when Ed Novak was killed in the Oak Hill cave-in? Emily kept saying over and over again, *I can't believe it. I can't believe it.* But it's not like that. What's hard to believe is that he ever lived. Isn't that funny?" She rubbed her forehead and tried to stop blinking. "When we got married, I couldn't remember ever *not* being his wife. Being his wife was such a thing. Do you know what I mean, Lu?"

"Sure I do, honey." Louise poured the coffee. "Now, here, you drink this. It'll make you feel better."

Donna put her hands around the cup and welcomed its warmth.

"Where's Stan?" she asked.

"Down to the colliery to pick up . . . well, to get Johnny's stuff, Donna, out of his locker."

She sipped some of the bitter coffee. When she first met

him, she had been drinking coffee. He was with Stan at Ella's Lunch, and she was with Helen, after the movies. When John looked at her that night, she *had* to look back. His face was as true and impelling as the face of a deer or a mountain cat or some other wild thing, hunting or hunted. When he reached across the table to light her cigarette, she could see his muscles harden underneath his shirt, and yet later when he held her face between his massive hands, he was as gentle and as soft as the mountain laurels she loved so much.

It was Saturday and Stan and John had been drinking. Donna didn't mind. She knew that miners drank a lot, there was so much dust in the throat to be washed away. She had grown up with it. A hard-working man, in her opinion, was entitled to get drunk on Saturday night, and the woman who complained about it had no right to a hard-working man.

Stan knew Helen well and teased her, leaving John and Donna to amuse themselves.

"Have you been working with Stan long?" asked Donna.

"No, just a few weeks. I'm new in town."

"New in town" was a big-town expression. People somehow were never new in town to Andoshen.

Donna was only twenty-one and had expected John to treat her like a child, as Stan had always done, but he treated her from the first like a mature woman, someone he might desire today or tomorrow.

"Do you have your family here?" she asked.

"I'm not married," said John. "Who'd have me?"

Donna laughed, but knew that she would have him if she could. She wasn't flighty or man-crazy and never had been. She merely recognized something in him that struck a response in her. The knowledge was simple.

In as long as it takes to drink a cup of coffee, they were talking and laughing like old friends. When they were leaving, he drew her aside and said, "Tomorrow is Sunday. What do you do for a Sunday?"

"Nothing. I hate Sundays."

"Don't say that. Every man's his own man on a Sunday. It would make me happy to have you take a drive with me tomorrow. I may be my own man on Sunday, but I admit I'm my own lonely man. If you think people will talk or anything, don't be shy of saying no. I'm probably out of line anyway."

By Sunday night Donna knew she loved him and could say it out loud. They had driven over the hill and all around the Valley and felt good in the midst of the green hills and lush farms. The smell of the air was heavy with the richness of growth. Then he took her out of the Valley and to a small abandoned bootleg coal mine, little more than a hole in the side of a mountain. The sides and top of the cave were supported with rotting old timbers. But he saw no great contrast between the bleak, played-out mine and the fertile farms they had just seen. Each in its own way was beautiful.

"Both are a man and the earth, top or bottom," he said. "If I wasn't a miner, I'd have to be a farmer."

They ventured far enough into the shaft to feel the cold of the underearth and to feel the wet walls of the cave.

"Farther back, the water drips from the top and falls onto your neck and your back," he said. "It's a less than average feeling. When I was a little kid, I used to get up early in the morning with my father and go down to the kitchen to watch him dress. He would take his clothes down from the rack by the coal stove and they would never be dry from the day before. My skin went crawling when I'd watch him cringe as he pulled on those wet clothes. You could hear a *zap* when he rammed his legs into the pants. But I couldn't wait until I was old enough and my body was hard enough so that I could do it too. God bless him."

"Is he dead?"

"Yes, Donna. He was lost in a cave-in. There were fifteen of them lost. Never could recover the bodies. They closed the mine and put a stone on top with all their names on it. Well, I had to take care of my mother, didn't I, and she passed on last year. That's when I left to try other towns." He pressed his hand against the wet wall. "How come you never left Andoshen? I thought the young girls always left for jobs in the cities."

"I like it here," she said. "Most of the girls leave because they have to prove something. I don't have to prove anything."

"But the boys leave too, I'm told. They say there's nothing here for them."

"Then they should leave. For me, there's something."

"I guess you know how glad I am you didn't leave," said John.

"One month," Donna said to her sister in the kitchen, "one month and eleven days later we married. He's no sooner found me and I have him than he's gone forever . . . forever . . . oh, no, Lu . . . I'm all right."

She pulled her housecoat more tightly around her.

"Where's Stan?"

"At the colliery, like I told you."

To hear colliery whistles blow. They made up a song
for their only Christmas together:

> *I'm dreaming of a black Christmas,*
> *Just like the ones I used to know.*
> *Where the coal hills glisten and children listen,*
> *To hear colliery whistles blow . . .*

It seemed hilarious that their existence, their home,
and their fate revolved around ugly, hard, black coal. It
was more hilarious by virtue of being a free choice.

Her finger toyed with a loop in the housecoat sash.

"There was such a lovely silence about him. You just
never heard him. He used to pad around in those soft
shoes so that one minute he was here . . . the next he
wasn't . . . and you never even heard him. So gentle . . .
so quiet. Did you ever hear him raise his voice? Did
you?"

Louise said she never did.

"Neither did I. I'll tell you, he didn't have to talk. He
could look at you, and you could see what it was he
wanted to say. When you have something like that,
Louise, it's better than having rubies and pearls for play-
things." Donna covered her eyes. "Oh, Lu, how will I
live without him? How will I?"

"First you got to burn those shoes."

The answer startled Donna.

"They're a dead man's shoes, Donna. No one can wear
a dead man's shoes. Don't you remember when Papa
went? Don't you remember burning the shoes? They're
good for nothing except remembering and that's no good.
Burn them."

Donna was eight when her father died. After the funeral, her mother, Louise, and she carried her father's shoes down the narrow rough wood steps to the dirt-floor cellar. By the light of one dim bulb, her mother opened the furnace door. The bed of live coals glowed and stung Donna's face with its heat. Her mother took a shoe and threw it into the furnace and watched it burn. She scattered the ashes with a poker and threw in the other shoe. The shoe, according to her mother, alone among all articles of clothing retains something of the man who wore them. They are like little leather ghosts. They cannot be kept or passed on, they can only be burned.

"That's a silly superstition and it doesn't bother me," said Donna. "No particle of anything he had will ever be burned. Everything he had or touched or was is *me*. Without him I'm not much. Without the memory of him I'm less. I don't think you understand. I don't think you know what I mean. Well, I don't either. Inside of me it's clear, but when I try to say it, it gets all garbled on me."

"I know, honey, you're going to miss him, sure, but we have to go on living."

"Yes, Lu, but nobody's ever said why."

"You're young and pretty."

"That takes care of it, huh, to be young and pretty?"

"It helps."

Donna walked into the living room, dropped wearily onto the couch, and said, "Let's not talk any more."

The door opened an inch and Stan could be seen peeking inside. He put a ragged cardboard suitcase on the floor next to the door and advanced uneasily.

"Donna?"

"Hello, Stan, what have you got there? Is it Johnny's?"

Stan ran his fingers through his hair, but said nothing.

"Sit down," said Donna. "I want to thank you. I wouldn't know what to do without you both."

"He was my best buddy."

Donna took a deep breath and said, "Tell me what happened."

"What's the good?"

"I deserve to know. It wasn't a cave-in. They knew right away. They just came and told me he was . . . I was washing clothes. After they told me I put in another load of his laundry. Why did I do that?"

"At a time like that who knows what to do?"

"Did he go through pain, Stan?"

"No pain at all. It was the black damp. He only had time to pull his shirt to his face."

"They say it's . . ."

"Black damp is what happens when the shaft is full of carbon dioxide. He shoulda checked it out with a canary first, but it's the old story. The best swimmer's the one always drowns."

Donna ran her hands over her eyes. Stan sat down in front of her, leaned forward on his chair, his forearms on his knees, his hands together, and said, "Donna? I hate like the fires of hell to say this. I'm afraid I got more bad news for you."

"More bad news? Still more?"

"About John," casting a look aside at the suitcase. "That case there. It was in his locker. What's inside it, none of us really knew that man."

Donna jumped to her feet.

"No! I won't hear it! No more, please. Don't tell me I didn't know the man I loved."

She pressed her sides with her elbows and weaved to the bedroom, her open hands in front of her, warding off whatever it was Stan wanted to tell her.

"He was my husband. He was the one I loved. No one knew him if I didn't."

She went into the bedroom and sat at her dressing table, staring into the mirror. She had left the door ajar and was conscious of their voices.

"Are you crazy? What are you talking about?" asked Louise.

Stan released the latches of the suitcase. In the momentary stillness of the apartment, they were equal to two rifle shots.

"We didn't know that man," said Stan, his voice cracking. "Look here. Papers. Documents. Letters. He wasn't even named John Krubeck. He was named Edward Caravage! The letters! You should read. It's all here in black and white. There are savings bonds here, three of them. Hell, you look for yourself. Your sister was married to a stranger."

"We're all married to strangers."

"Don't get fancy. This man, none of us really knew him."

Donna heard but could not accept these words. They could not be trying to destroy the only thing she had left. They could not be trying to make her less than a widow. She staggered to the closet and slipped her bare feet into his shoes. The way the wide gray rims of the desert boots encircled her tiny white ankles made it seem as though the shoes were devouring her. Like a child in oversized shoes, she shuffled back to the center of the room and stood there, her shoulders rounded, her clenched fists held under her shaking chin.

"Jesus, Mary 'n Joseph!" she heard Louise cry. "Who was he?"

"I told you!"

"I mean, he must of been on the run. What did he *do*?"

"That's a good question. It can't be anything good, can it? Look, what we should do is get on the phone and . . ."

"Shhhhh, Stan, look."

Louise pointed to the door.

"Do you think she heard?" whispered Stan.

"I think she was listening."

Stan pushed the door all the way open. Donna looked at the two in the doorway but spoke beyond them.

"Nobody's going to burn his shoes, I've made up my mind to that . . . do you hear? Nobody can take them away from me. Got that? He may have left me only these old shoes when he left, but I'm holding onto what I was given . . . holding on for dear life."

"Sure, Donna," said Stan. "Anything you say."

"You can wear those shoes if you want to. It'll be all right," said Louise.

"It doesn't matter," she said. "Not at all. Nobody's going to destroy his shoes. They're mine now."

Pigeon-toed, she turned and started for the bed. Her first two steps took her out of the shoes and left her in naked feet.

Many days later she put on her own shoes and went out for a job, securing a position behind Newberry's notions counter, replacing Estelle Wowak who had just quit and gone to the city.

Dear Son,

I agree. Donna Krubeck is a sad girl. But she has something to be sad about. She was your brother's age, maybe a year older. All these years she is still at the five and dime, but is now an assistant manager or something. She never' remarried. Her husband was divorced so they could not bury him in the Catholic cemetery. They pulled the same stunt with Tommy Dorsey. They buried him in the Valley. Donna said he liked it there when he was alive. The headstone says "EDWARD CARAVAGE also known as JOHN KRUBECK." They said he used that name because when he was a little boy they had a neighbor by that name that he liked.

He had a son who was almost as old as Donna and he is still in Scranton I think. The story was that he was married to a very awful woman who drank and ran around but was smart enough to have him committed, who knows how. He was not crazy but this is a favorite trick for getting rid of people. He escaped the hospital and came to Andoshen.

You asked about burning shoes. A superstition, who knows where it came from, that all the dead man's shoes must be burned. The rest of his clothes can be handed down. Only the old people worry about it nowadays.

Black damp—when they find the victims they have their shirts pulled over their faces which is all they have time to do it gets them so quick. They sometimes have a canary that they fly into a shaft they are not sure of. If the canary comes back alive, it's o.k., if not then there's probably the black damp. They also use a candle on the end of a long pole or something. If the flame goes out they run like heck.

Love,
Mom & Pop

Chapter Five

Ella

The Cleveland Lunch was in a good location, and that was one of the reasons why Ella and her mother were willing to mortgage their house to buy the place after its original owner Rudolph Wiekrykas died. His name alone explains why the place was called the Cleveland Lunch. Actually, Mr. Wiekrykas was born in that city and came to Pennsylvania with his parents when he was twelve.

It was located around the corner from the Majestic Pocket Billiards and was right next door to the Trailways Bus Station, or rather right next door to the Glide Hotel, in whose ragged, stuffy lobby the Trailways business was transacted and the passengers waited for their bus. Hardly anyone ever stayed at the Glide Hotel, except for the very rare occasion when a clan gathering for a wedding or funeral overflowed onto its dingy beds.

The Cleveland Lunch had become a landmark over the years. Usually it was the last stop before boarding a bus and the first stop upon leaving a bus. People were pleased that Ella and her mother effected very few changes when they took it over. Nothing, of course, could be done with the outside, except for a coat of paint, an investment Ella wisely chose not to make. It was still the short, squat, blocky place it had always been, with one long window and a door facing the street. The name of the place was changed and people accepted this bit of self-indulgence on the part of a new property holder as they watched the new rectangular sign put into place above the window.

breakfast		hot dogs
dinner	ELLA'S LUNCH	hamburgers
supper		peanut butter pie

The sign was erected courtesy of their Coca-Cola distributor, who included at each end of the sign large red medallions suggesting what people should drink with the food Ella served.

She had installed two gooseneck lamps above the sign so that it could be seen as easily at night as during the day.

Inside, there was a counter seating twelve. There was room for only two tables, each able to seat four. Between the two tables was a decrepit jukebox. On the working side of the counter everything was huddled close together: the cereal rack, the milk dispenser (*Drink Cold Milk, Pasteurized-Homogenized, Cream in Every Drop. Grade "A"*), the meat slicer, the four coffee pots on their burners, the steam table, the bun warmer, the cold table, the grill, the French-frier, the Grape-Ade dispenser. At one end of the counter, near the door, sat the cash register. At the other end was the entrance to the kitchen proper, where the big stove and the sinks were located.

The menu was posted on the wall, with a special place for Today's Feature (Beef & Noodles, 70¢, for instance). Right above the menu Ella's mother had taped two hand-lettered signs that she composed herself:

EAT HERE
DIET HOME!

OUR CREDIT
MANAGERS NAME
IS HELEN WAIT . . .
SO, IF YOU WANT
CREDIT
  GO
    TO
      HEL-
        EN
          WAIT

Ella believed her mother wanted to own a restaurant just as a gallery for those two signs.

There was a small fan built into the wall at each end of the room, and these were constantly in motion trying to clear the place of greasy odors, a job too large for the two small fans. But the atmosphere was pleasant and the food good, and the partnership between Ella and her mother prospered. Their specialty was peanut butter pie and few people in town could go many weeks without having a piece of it. Naturally, the women in town wanted the recipe, but it was a secret and Ella guarded it jealously. All attempts to duplicate it were unsuccessful.

Ella's mother died, having run out of her "borrowed time." It was in consideration of this eventual certainty that her mother had insisted the place be called Ella's Lunch. Any sign that included her own name would soon have to be replaced, an unnecessary expense for ego's sake.

Soon after the death of her mother, Ella married Bill Bistricky, a miner. Even though they had been keeping company for some time and even though Ella could hardly manage the lunchroom herself, which required her attention from seven in the morning until nine, sometimes ten, at night, Bill was afraid that people would say he had married himself a good job. He kept on at the strippings and helped out at the lunchroom only after his regular shift or during the periods in which he was laid off.

It was a hard life for newlyweds, or for old married people, and often when they fell into bed at the end of the day they were too tired even to squeeze each other's hand.

But they prospered. After a few years Bill quit the strippings and devoted his full time to the lunchroom, and no one faulted him for this. Life became a bit easier. Ella was able to take off for a few months to have a baby boy, and the following year she took another few months off to have another. Then she went back to work and the children played or napped in their playpen in the kitchen, and business was good.

Then, like a telegram in the night, R.K. came into the lunchroom carrying a pawn-shop suitcase and pulling behind him a shy and sickly young pregnant wife. He wore a flowered shirt and a gaudy ascot.

R.K. was Bill's younger brother. He had left Andoshen for California five years before, on some sort of dare. During that time there had been an exchange of only two letters. In the second letter R.K. told Bill that he was in "the hotel business," and asked him to come out to California if he wanted to be shown a royal good time.

"Easy for him to say," Ella had said, "now that he knows you're married with a family and in a business."

Bill was happy to see his brother again and to meet his new sister-in-law. He sat them at the counter and made them some ham and eggs.

"What happened to your hotel?" asked Ella, not attempting to purge the sarcasm in her voice.

"The hotel business is great, but out there in Hollywood the movie stars and rich bitches expect you should kiss their ass because everybody knows their name."

"Did you cater to the movie stars?"

"Hell, I'm so sick of movie stars. This is where I belong. Dianne is gonna love it here. We're gonna have a kid, you know."

"What are your plans?" asked Bill.

"Just stepped off the bus, brother," replied R.K., eating the ham and eggs.

"You can stay with us," said Bill. "We can make up the attic for you."

"I was just about to ask if you'd like a visitor or two," said R.K., smiling.

They stayed rent free in Bill and Ella's attic for six months. R.K. got a job washing rags for the sheeny, to whom he had sold rags and newspapers every Saturday of his boyhood for the price of a pomegranate and a matinee. Dianne did not take well to pregnancy, and even after the baby girl was born she seemed incapable of caring for it. Ella was forced to assume the extra work of making sure her little niece lived until they were able to move into a place of their own, but she didn't like it. She didn't like Dianne's out-of-state airs, she didn't like standing in line at her own bathroom, and she didn't like R.K. parading around in his underwear and bare chest, with his silly tiki charm hanging from his neck. Grief was in the making.

Dear Son,

R. K. Bistricky was a wild kid like the rest of you, older than you and your brother. Everybody thought he straightened out after he came back from Calif.—had a wife, kid, worked hard. But then there was much trouble, family stuff that causes rumors which shouldn't be paid attention to. Some of it was funny because of the arrangement. You remember?

The Calif. business was always a great mystery around here. He bragged a lot about being in the hotel business out there and he used to dress like a movie director, but nobody would believe a word he said because they all thought he was a bit off. I never did. There are lots crazier. It's funny you remember the Rita Hayworth thing because you were just a kid. I don't know how she's in the story. Maybe it was Susan Hayworth, who I think is even better or even somebody else but it did have to do with a movie star—that he was supposed to go out there to see in person or something. I don't remember it because he was a wild kid and acted peculiar sometimes, but nice when you talked to him. I don't think I would like to talk to him about the Rita Hayworth business. Maybe you should leave that chapter out.

Love,
Mom & Pop

Chapter Six

Estelle and the Reader

Savannah Hand-Made Cigars was a tiny place on North Main Street and was one of the few places left in the country where people instead of machines made cigars. Estelle Wowak went to work there and soon became one like the others in the humid silence, though she was paid by the hour and would have liked some conversation to make the time go by, and could have afforded some, unlike the rollers who were paid by the cigar and sat intense and speechless in their carrels, some of them establishing a rhythmic rocking motion to carry them through ten hours a day.

There were twelve rollers, four to a bench, and the three long benches faced a raised platform against the wall and often they looked up wistfully at the empty platform. There were eight women, all of them middle-aged and beefy, with huge arms pressing tightly against the short sleeves of their working blouses, wearing babushkas to keep their hair from falling into the tobacco; and there were four men, too old for standing labor, as thin and wiry as the women were fat. As the men reached into the seemingly disarrayed sections of tobacco and brought fingerfuls to their blocks and rolled the cigar, one could see the veins pop out in their skinny arms under the pressure of rolling.

She went to work in the cigar factory and became a stripper, sitting from seven to five in front of a large wooden tub, a plank across the tub, on the plank a coffee can full of water. She sat off in a corner, away from the rollers, in her smock, a cloth over her knees. From the tub she took a bundle of broad "wrapper" tobacco leaves, moist from the spray of the unbaling room. She untied the twine that held the leaves together at one end, like an old-fashioned broom, and hung it over the edge of the tub so that it might be reused on a future bundle.

One by one, she took a leaf and with a backhanded twisting motion, wrapping one end of the tough center vein around her forefinger, stripped off the vein and threw it on the pile of them on the floor. She put the two halves of the leaf on one of four stacks, according to size. One stack was draped over her right knee, the other three stacks were draped over the edge of the tub. She did this with her head lowered, seeing only her knees and the tobacco leaves and her brown stained fingers, and wondering, "What can I accomplish in this world?"

The smell of tobacco made her nauseous for the first few days and followed her even after quitting time. It lingered in her hair, in her clothing, on her skin. But in time, like tanners and fishmongers, she got used to it.

"What can I accomplish in this world?"

There was an awakening of spirit in the rolling room the Friday of her second week there. The reader, who had been sick in bed with a sore throat, returned to work. She had heard of this reader when she was first hired, when the foreman roller informed her that she would have to pay half a dollar a day to the reader. She did not question. One has expenses in holding a job.

The reader was warmly greeted on his return and chided for his porching, a malingerer's activity. ("I don't feel good today, I think I'll just lie here on the porch and watch the street.")

The reader wore blue jeans and a sweater and a scarf wrapped around his neck in spite of the humidity, to protect his tool of trade. He carried a shopping bag, obviously heavy with its load. One of the rollers placed a chair on the raised platform facing them and the reader ascended, brushed the dust off the chair, and sat down. He put the shopping bag on the platform next to him and took from it the day's *New York Times*. He leaned his back against the chair and crossed his legs.

Seven o'clock. They went to work immediately.

The reader cleared his throat and said, "Headlines: SENATE EXPECTED TO VOTE INCREASE IN AIR FORCE FUND, Democrats Ask Billion Above President's Goal—Wilson Calls Rise Plan 'Phony.' "

"Sure it's phony," said Mrs. Demalis. "If they give the Air Force a billion more, that's a billion less for the foreigners."

"What's phony about that?" asked Mrs. Griffiths. "Better to put bread in the mouth of a hungry foreigner than bombs in the belly of an airplane."

"Charity begins at home," said Vitold Minduirsky.

"Whatever that means," said Mrs. Palino.

"First you feed the hungry here, with what's left you feed the hungry over there," said Vitold Minduirsky.

"Ike is against it, and he used to be a general even," said Joe Yuschock.

"It's that Senator Johnson from Texas that's pushing it. He wants to cut the foreign aid."

"He wants to cut Eisenhower."

"You can't beat Ike, so forget it."

"Not if his health holds out."

"You ask any farmer in the Valley. When the Democrats are in power the annual rainfall drops off somethin' pitiful. They're hard on the crops, those Democrats."

"But what about the working man?"

"Should I go on or can I go get a cup of coffee or something?" asked the reader.

The cigar rollers became silent.

The reader continued: "PRESIDENT TAKES FIRST WALK OUT OF HIS HOSPITAL ROOM."

"That's a good sign," said Mrs. Piencowski.

"Just so they're not rushing things," said Mrs. Bernicky.

"TRUMAN CAUTIONS WEST ON DANGERS IN SOVIET TACTICS."

"Truman don't trust nobody," said Fred Robb, "that's how he got to be president."

"Would you trust a Red?" asked Raymond Przytulski.

"When a man holds out a hand to you, you shake it," said Vitold Minduirsky.

"It's what's in the other hand you got to worry about," said Raymond Przytulski.

"Sometimes you gotta live with people."

"That don't mean you gotta love 'em."

"DULLES CHARGES PEIPING NEGLECTS TO DISOWN STALIN."

"They're the ones you gotta watch," said Mrs. Maglosky, "those slanty-eye divils."

"At least the Russians gave old Stalin a kick in the ass," said Mrs. Thompson.

"The chinks loved him. He was their idea of kindness."

"You can't put all the blame on one man like Stalin, like they put all the blame on Hitler."

"Dulles is willin' to bury the hatchet with the Russians."

"Well, just remember the story of the eagle and the bear from the Bible."

"The more things change, the more they stay the same."

"Oh, Christ!"

"SENATE OUTRAGED BY HUNT FOR BUG, Security Check on Lehman's Office Is Protested."

"Hey, read that. That sounds good."

The reader read the story involving two Pentagon security agents who searched the senator's refrigerator closet to determine if a bug had been planted to eavesdrop on top-secret testimony on defense that was taking place in an adjacent committee room. The Democratic senators demanded an explanation from the Secretary of Defense and an apology from the Pentagon. Senator Lyndon B. Johnson accused the Pentagon agents of "typical bureaucratic flatfoot stupidity."

"There goes Johnson again," said Mrs. Stanikis. "He sure gets his name in the paper."

"Uh-oh," said the reader dismally. "Here's a headline: ARTHUR MILLER ADMITS HELPING COMMUNIST FRONT GROUPS IN '40s."

"Go on!" cried Mrs. Griffiths. "Remember *Death of a Salesman*? What a lovely play! I can still see it from when you read it to us. None of Joe Stalin's boys could ever write something like that."

The reader read, "But Playwright Denies Being Under 'Discipline.' "

"A poet or a playwright signs a petition and right away he's a Red," said Vitold Minduirsky. "You think I wouldn't sign a petition, like to put out the Kimberly Run fire or to lower taxes, I don't care if it's a commie carryin' the petition, as long as the petition is right. If Jesus Christ himself carried a petition for higher taxes and less benefits, I wouldn't sign it. But if Joe Stalin gave me a petition that said hungry kids should be fed, what am I gonna say?"

"He probably went to a meeting or something," said Joe Yuschock. "How else is he gonna get stuff to write about? Ever notice how politicians like to jump all over writers? It's enough to get on your damn nerves."

"Hey, hey, hey," said the reader, "get this." He read each word slowly and distinctly, "To Wed Marilyn Monroe Soon."

"Now you know why they're out to get him."

"More power to him."

"I like to see a beautiful woman with a homely man."

"She can get all the beauty she wants. That's why she wants brains now."

"They're all jealous of him 'cause he can do something they can't. Boy, oh, boy, can he ever do something they can't!"

Everyone in the rolling room, including Estelle,

laughed. The reader went on to read the entire front page and the rest of the paper, stopping at sections to solicit approval or rejection.

"Society?"

There was no affirmative response. There never was.

"Want-Ads?"

"What are they getting for a '41 Chevy?"

The reader looked for it and said, "None advertised."

"Who the hell would bother with an old car like that? Run it off into Fetter's Lake," said Nancy Stanikis, berating the little man for owning such an old car.

"Run *you* off into Fetter's Lake," he replied.

The reader finished the morning paper, and the rollers felt the satisfaction of being informed and part of a larger world than Savannah Hand-Mades and Andoshen, Pa. He put the paper on the floor and said, "What now?"

"How about a nice juicy O'Hara novel?"

"We read all of O'Hara," said the reader.

"All? How the hell can you read *all* of O'Hara?"

"Ten hours a day, five days a week, and six hours on Saturday," said the reader.

"What do you have by Steinbeck?"

"I've got *Sweet Thursday*. It's a follow-up to *Cannery Row*."

They agreed they would like to hear that, and the reader began. The rollers were delighted to meet again the characters they had enjoyed so much before, characters who reminded them of people they knew in town. It was like visiting after a long absence, and the hours sped by, the rollers hardly conscious of their drudgery until it was done and time to tally up the cigars.

The reader finished the book with some minutes to

spare, and during those waning minutes of the workday he exercised his prerogative to read what he wanted to read.

"Time for a poem," he said.

"Ahhhh," sighed Bertha Griffiths, "I love the read of a good poem. Read something by someone Irish."

"I'm going to read something by someone English."

"Oh, Jesus Christ."

"This is called 'A Slumber Did My Spirit Seal' by a wonderful man named William Wordsworth, who was born in England in 1770 and died in 1850."

"He's the Westminster Bridge guy."

"Very good, Raymond, that you remember these things."

Raymond shrugged his shoulders, pleased with himself.

"Here goes," said the reader.

"A slumber did my spirit seal;
I had no human fears:
She seemed a thing that could not feel
The touch of earthly years.

No motion has she now, no force;
She neither hears nor sees;
Rolled round in earth's diurnal course,
With rocks, and stones, and trees."

"Ahhhh, what a sad poem. They're all so sad, poems," said Mrs. Griffiths. "He's missing his dead sweetheart."

"What does *diurnal* mean?" asked Mr. Yuschock.

"Ahhhh, what does it matter?"

"Daily. Day by day," said the reader.

Mr. Yuschock nodded.

Estelle was sitting at her stripping tub, still rapt in the funereal waves of his voice. She was motionless, her finger wrapped around the end of a vein. The reader announced, "Five o'clock," and put his paper and books back into the shopping bag and emptied the jar into which his employers had dropped their half-dollars. It was then he seemed to notice, for the first time, the new stripper.

"Where's Mrs. Lupatsky?" he asked Vitold Minduirsky.

"She died," he replied. "While you were out sick."

"Died!"

"What do you expect? She was almost eighty years old."

"What did she die of?"

"The *ich,* it's been goin' round."

"No one ever mentioned it to me. I didn't know a thing about it."

"An eighty-year-old wrapper stripper dies ain't exactly a tragedy that everyone knows about like Hamlet, Prince of Denmark, outa Shakespeare that we read."

"Damned disheartening. I wish someone had told me first thing this morning. I could have read something appropriate."

"She's in the Annunciation Cemetery," said the roller, as if the reader might want to read something over her grave.

Estelle was next to them now trying to get out of the room and into the cool dry air outside.

"Here she is, the new stripper," said Vitold Minduirsky, by way of introduction. "Youngster, ain't she?" The roller walked away.

"Hello," she said.

"You are awfully young, you know. The others here are far away from their youth."

"I have to work."

"I can understand that. I suffer the same temporary, I hope, problem. Is this the best you can do?"

"Is this the best *you* can do?"

"Touché."

"Huh?"

"You win."

"It's not too bad. At least not now. I worry a lot about doing something. That is, getting something done, accomplished. Today is the first time since high school that I read a book and a poem, and the first time ever that I read a whole newspaper, practically a whole newspaper, all the news at least. But I guess you couldn't really call it reading, listening."

She found herself talking quickly and excitedly. She stopped, ashamed.

"It is a good use of time that could drag, isn't it?" said the reader. "The people who work in this room are much better read than the average college graduate. Ironic, isn't it, since it won't raise their income by a penny and when they go home tonight there's no one there they can talk to about what they've learned. But it makes the time go by."

Mentioning time made him think again of the old stripper.

"The woman who had your job? She was eighty and

had read, listened to, all of Shakespeare's plays and Mickey Spillane's novels, and could quote both."

"It's beautiful the way you read. You feel like you're almost there. Almost like you're there."

"Thank you. Even when I'm doing some of the crap that they occasionally like to be read, I try to give them their fifty-cents' worth."

"Have you always been here?" she asked.

"There's always been a reader here, if that's what you mean. The last one died four years ago and I've been here since then. They tell me I'm better than the old reader."

"Well, you're just . . . in my opinion, I think you're about . . . the best reader I ever heard."

The reader laughed.

"You're making fun of me," Estelle said.

"Please, I'm not. I was only thinking of how many readers you've heard."

Estelle smiled. "You know what I mean," she said.

"Do you have a car?" he asked.

"No."

"Neither do I. I'll walk along with you if it's all right. Which way do you go?"

"Down to Oak, down Main. I live on Oak Street . . . with my parents."

"What's your name?"

"Estelle Wowak."

"I think I know your father. Is he a Rum-Dum?"

Estelle laughed. "Yes, but it's all a mystery to me."

"I've been to a couple of their parties. I know him from there."

"What's your name?" she asked.

"Anthony Taylor."

"What an elegant name!"

"Then call me Reader. Everybody does."

"Okay. I'm afraid of elegant names."

In her mind she said *Estelle Taylor, Estelle Taylor, Estelle Taylor, Estelle Taylor. . . .*

They left the cigar factory and walked down Main Street.

"Where do you live?" she asked.

"Down on East Coal Street. Near the First Ward . . . with my mother."

"But we just passed Coal Street."

"I have nothing better to do. It's a nice day and I've been in sick."

"What I can't understand is why I don't know you," she said. "Did you go to Andoshen High? I don't remember you. I graduated two years ago . . . Tyra Bernard, Mary Kay Lepis, and Billy Buddusky were in my class."

"I went to A.H.S., but how could you remember me? When I was a senior you were only in first grade."

She looked at him walking beside her and said, "Can that be possible?"

"Not only possible, it's a fact."

"That's amazing. What is a fact now would have been impossible a few years ago."

She felt ashamed again because she was talking fast to someone older than she, and she did not know what she was talking about.

The police car turned the corner in front of them.

"There goes Shakey the Cop," he said, "in pursuit of the forces of evil."

"What a funny way to say it! Did you hear about him and the guy driving through from Pittsburgh?"

"Who hasn't? The guy from Pittsburgh stopped at a bar and told the story. Good old Shakey. I wouldn't trade him for a dozen Mike Hammers."

They crossed Center Street and he asked, "Are you in a rush to get home?"

"Only to get the smell of cigars off of me."

"Well, let's go over to Ella's for coffee or something cool. No one will notice the smell of cigars there."

They went to Ella's and the next day everyone had an opinion on the new pair: he was too old for her, she was too nice for him, he was too smart for her, she was too ambitious for him, he was too fast for her, she was too old-fashioned for him. These opinions meant nothing to Estelle and the reader, who fell in love.

Dear Son,

The cigar factory is still there. They are waiting for the cigar rollers to die and then they'll close up and go out of business because no young person nowadays wants to learn how to roll cigars. It's too bad too, says Mr. Daniels the owner and manager because machine-made cigars are no good. One of his favorite tricks is to cut open a machine-made cigar (not cheap ones, either) and show you the paper and the crap they put inside. It's true too because he showed me. He also showed me the inside of the hand-made cigar and it's nothing but tobacco. You can really see the difference. Thank God Pop has stopped smoking them, though.

Mr. Daniels says that he is the one who started the idea of a reader. He said when he was no more than a boy his father who was also in the cigar business sent him to Cuba to visit the cigar factories and see what they did. This was before the time of Castro. They all had readers down there and that's where he got the idea. It keeps the rollers from going crazy and usually turns them into philosophers. Which everyone is today. Also, the reader is useful because he settles all arguments. If anyone gets in a beef about something, he looks up the facts and settles it, which is more than I can say about our store where the arguments can give you an earache.

Love,
Mom & Pop

The Majestic had been there for so long that only a stranger in town would notice that it had once been the Citizen's National Bank. Those words were chiseled deep in stone high above the doorway and were also part of the sidewalk in front of the entrance, placed there in brass ages ago when the sidewalk itself was constructed.

The changeover could have occurred during that year when the unthinkable thing happened to banks, when so many of them became poolhalls and other unsophisticated institutions. Or, simply, the Citizen's National Bank could have done so well that it moved to more prestigious quarters, though a branch of this bank was not to be presently found in town.

Entrance is provided by two tall wooden doors, one of which is always open from June to September. Once inside, you find yourself in a front lobby between two parallel glass counters. Only one of these two counters is manned. Here you buy your cigarettes, cigars, magazines, prophylactics, and here you pay for your game and your Moxie, a particularly bitter soft drink, the consumption of which reflects the intense self-discipline of a good pool shooter and a man.

The other glass counter is inexplicably devoted to the display of bows, arrows, and other archery equipment. Bows and arrows *hardly describes what is on display. The weapons here are so highly developed, with their curves and colors and sights and optional accouterments, that they become grotesque, and to look at them would traumatize an Apache of 150 years ago.*

Five steps across the front lobby and you encounter a pair of old-fashioned swinging doors, over and under which you see or sense what awaits you beyond them. You push them open and you are in it, and the life a step behind you might as well be a continent away. You are in a cave, in the heart of the Majestic, where the atmosphere is constant: a gray smoky twilight, smelling of felt and talcum powder and old oily wood. It is both restful and terrifying, a cave of pool tables, so close together that shooters must cooperate in order to have an unencumbered shot. Each table has above it a light and a metal shield over the light, upon which has settled a heavy layer of dust, until a shooter swings his cue in anger, striking the shield and causing dust to rain down upon the table and the ivory balls.

The floors are oiled wood and creak in many places. There are tall benches with arm rests and back rests against the walls, and under these benches are stored the cases of empty Moxie bottles. Two pin-ball machines occupy one of the dim corners of the Majestic, but they receive only slight action. There is a pay-telephone somewhere in the shadows, but it never rings.

Chapter Seven

Duncan

There is a back room in the Majestic for illicit poker, and beyond that another back room, or closet, and this is where Duncan sleeps, in a niche off the hollow off the cave, having made his spiritual home his only home.

In a town this size there are always two or three kids who live alone with mothers whose husbands died before the children were born. Everyone understands that the two or three kids are in fact bastards, but nothing is made of it until there is a fight in the Majestic during which an angry enemy will identify the nameless son by the cruelest synonym.

These two or three kids generally stay around to reach self-knowledge, then drift out of town to Standard Pressed Steel of Philadelphia, or General Motors of Jersey, or the Army of America. Years later they come back to town to bury their mothers. They timidly go into the Majestic for a pack of cigarettes and slip into the timelessness of the heart of it, beyond the swinging doors, to see if they are remembered. Usually they are, and someone will ask the inevitable question put to all returning sons to determine their measure of success: "What are you driving now?"

Duncan in his time was one of these two or three kids, but unlike the others he stayed on after his mother, who had worked at the dress factory, died when he was seventeen. By that time he had already worked a year in the mines. Since he spent all of his off time in the Majestic anyway, he just moved into the back-back room. Their house had been a rented one, and after the burial of his mother, who doubtful of the mental capacities of her son had arranged the details herself, he cleaned out the place and other tenants moved in.

All that remained of his mother were personal women's things—underwear, dresses, shoes, bits of cheap jewelry—which made Duncan feel uncomfortable. He gave them to the neighbors, sold them the kitchenware and tattered furniture, and took from the house only a box of his own clothes (they never owned a suitcase) and a thin deck of family photographs that he had trimmed so that they would fit into an empty Band-Aid can, which he carried in his hip pocket, where most men carry their wallets.

In his teens and early twenties Duncan had by nature what others must cultivate through the years: he could make that cue ball go wherever he wanted it to go. He even impressed Willie Mosconi on one of the champion's swings through the anthracite fields. Mosconi finished him off easily enough but told him that he held exceptional promise and gave him his personal Zippo cigarette lighter as a keepsake.

It became Duncan's prized possession. He valued it

and cared for it and used it with the special attention most men save for the finest of mistresses. No one in the Majestic ever had to light a cigarette when Duncan was around with his infallible Willie Mosconi Zippo.

Some months after his 110 points against Mosconi, he suffered a mine accident and the first three fingers of his left hand returned to the earth. He accepted the loss stoically and was thankful that he still had the little-finger-thumb opposition, without which he would be crippled. Even if he had lost only the thumb, he reasoned, he would be in worse shape.

Though the little-finger and thumb provided a workable bridge, he felt off balance. Instead of his usual unity with the stick, he found himself fighting it.

His fingers and his confidence were gone and he never shot another rack of pool.

In addition, he lost his nerve, not only for the table and for the cold wet bowels of the earth, but also for many of the everyday encounters that require even a modicum of courage.

Before long he was the resident derelict, an object of distant pity, who lived in a closet at the Majestic and racked balls for tips, in an area of the country where giving tips for small services was considered an experience only of those long accustomed to gracious living.

He fared well during the summers when parties returning from the groves would give him their leftover bean soup, franks, and specialty of the particular ethnic group that had been celebrating: Sons of Italy, St. Pat's Lads, the Polish Hook and Ladder Volunteer Fire Company, The Lithuanian Ladies, and the Rum Dums, not an ethnic group but a jolly society of men dedicated to one night a week of good draft beer and good food and good fellowship in the woods, with only three rules: no women, no whiskey, and no card playing. Duncan could count on at least half a dozen ears of corn and a gallon of Columbia beer late every Tuesday night from the returning Rum Dums.

He was able one May to salvage an ice box from the dump to save what he could not eat of the leftovers he received. Every morning he would go down to the ice house by the railroad tracks and bum broken pieces, which he would wrap in his burlap bag, and run back to the Majestic before the small pieces melted away.

One night a foursome from Gibbsville came into the Majestic and acted tough, as though they would not mind hustling a money game, but the regulars there could tell they were no more than another band of punks, each a hero of his own meager fantasies, so they ignored them. The punks began to play pill pool, which is what they really wanted to do anyway.

Duncan racked the balls for them and took a seat on the bench against the wall, watching the game and jumping forward with his Zippo whenever one of them reached for a cigarette. Sometimes he would hang back and give the smoker a chance to try his own lighter. If it failed to light on the first try, Duncan would be there with his gleaming Zippo before there was time for a second try.

It was clear that one of the four had through some previous chemistry risen to dominance and the other three were used to his assuming the role of spokesman. As it happened, he was the smallest of the four. It is not unusual that the slightest man in a small band of punks will assume leadership. He may have the money, the car, the skill at the table. More often, he simply has the brains and the gab, the natural weapons of the small man. When a small punk feels he has the muscle of his gang behind him, he may become insufferable, and unfortunately this was the case with the small punk who led the band of punks from Gibbsville.

He was a sixteen-ounce shooter with a twenty-ounce cue.

Wheezer, they called him, probably because of the annoying sounds he made in the process of breathing. He was no more than five-four and quite thin and pale. A head of curly black hair made him look top-heavy and he did, in fact, seem to bend forward, to be falling forward.

Duncan had lit no more than three or four of their cigarettes before Wheezer saw in him a potential victim.

Wheezer was new in the Majestic and thought that the rack boy there suffered the same status as rack boys everywhere, and in this regard he was half right. The other half of being half right, however, can often do one a serious misfortune.

When they finished a game, instead of hitting the floor twice with the rubber base of the cue as everyone else did to call for a new rack, Wheezer would intrude upon the steady and predictable sounds of the Majestic by yelling, after he had learned his name, "Rack 'em up, Dicky Duncan!"

He used the name in an insulting way to indicate what there was no time for when the frost was on the pumpkin: "When the frost is on the pumpkin/That's no time for dicky dunkin' . . ."

No one in the Majestic thought it cute.

Duncan would flick on the Zippo two or three times in Wheezer's direction, as though shooting him, before racking the balls. "Name happens to be Duncan, but it ain't no Dicky," said Duncan good-naturedly. "Duncan already *is* my first name, that's all the more you gotta know."

Once between games Wheezer went up to him and said, "Open your mouth wide and I'll show you a trick."

Duncan liked tricks, and when he opened his mouth, Wheezer brought something up from his throat and pretended he would spit it into the open mouth. Duncan ran away laughing at his own naïveté, turned, and fired off a few shots from the Zippo.

"Sure are ape about that crummy lighter, ain't you, Dicky?" said Wheezer.

"Never fails," said Duncan. "And it's Duncan, like I said. No Dicky."

"The Japs make 'em, those lighters, outa old beer cans. They ain't worth a crap."

"Willie Mosconi give me this Zippo years ago for givin' him the best competition in the coal regions."

Wheezer and his friends were momentarily impressed by the revered name of Mosconi, but no one believed Duncan until another patron of the Majestic confirmed that what he said was true.

Forced to accept it, Wheezer said, "I bet he gets 'em two for a nickel from the Japs and drops them wherever he goes. They all do that, for publicity."

"I'll buy all the Zippos you can get like this, two for a nickel," said Duncan, smiling, and rubbing the lighter against his thigh, although even at those prices he could not afford one lighter.

"I say it's a cheap Jap lighter and I'll give you ten bucks if you can light it ten times without it fails on you once."

"Oh, man, oh, man, I got me ten easy bucks now," said Duncan and flipped open the Zippo. "A buck a light."

He stood at the long side of the pool table and was about to begin lighting. Wheezer was next to him. Duncan looked at him and said, "What if it does fail once?"

"Thought you said it was never-fail?"

"Yeah, but what if it does? I can tell you it won't. But I don't got no ten dollars to pay if it don't. Even though it won't."

Wheezer looked down at Duncan's hand.

"Notice you got a two-prong claw there," he said.

"That's my business," said Duncan.

"Well, put your little finger up here on the table."

Duncan held the lighter in his right hand. He put the little finger of the other on the table, the thumb pointing in the opposite direction with nothing but space between. In an instant Wheezer had the blade of his knife against the little finger, and Duncan could feel its sharpness and froze to avoid a cut.

"Well, if it fails once outa ten, well . . ." said Wheezer and looked down at the little finger under his knife.

Wheezer's heart was galloping. He had seen the premise on a TV show and was won by it. Money against a finger, the lighter as the contest. He had been on a constant lookout for the opportunity to spring it, like a great gag line that called for perfect circumstances.

Duncan looked at the finger too, the little finger without which his left hand would be useless. His own ability and the ability of the Zippo were suddenly the same thing. His confidence in the Zippo transferred to himself, and there was more at stake now than ten dollars and a little finger.

He sniffled and blotted his nose with his sleeve. He coughed and could taste his chest cold breaking. The thumb of his right hand flipped open the Zippo, he brought it down hard upon the wheel, and the wick ignited. He closed the lid again.

One. A contract had been made.

Duncan knew that the Zippo could light indefinitely, a hundred times without a miss, a thousand. But what if he had forgotten this morning to replenish the fluid? Now he could not remember doing it. It was what he did first thing every morning. This was why it was so easy to forget having done it. What if the flint was worn out, something that could happen without warning? For the wick, he did not worry. He could see enough of that for at least ten lights. But what if his thumb should slip?

He hit the wheel again. *Two.*

Again, *three.*

Both Duncan and Wheezer had runny noses now, both were sweating visibly at the foreheads and under the noses, and both were developing glassy, watery eyes. When his own friends drifted to the walls, sorry to have been indirectly included in this display, and the Majestic crowd gathered around him, Wheezer knew he should fold his knife and walk away that instant, and when the instant passed and he was still there, he knew that he was a loser: a loser if the lighter struck ten times straight, for he did not have the ten dollars to pay up; a loser if the

Zippo missed because he knew now that he would actually have to cut off the little finger and he did not want to do it, did not know if he had the stomach to do it, yet knew that he would have to do it if the lighter failed because everyone in the Majestic had gathered around him. The perpetual sound of billiard balls cracking together had stopped, and all the players stood holding their cues in front of them, leaning on them.

Wheezer wondered if it were even possible for the switchblade to cut cleanly through bone. On the TV show they used a meat cleaver or a guillotine or something.

The Zippo lit. *Four.*

Again, *five.*

Wheezer had never expected him to go for it, and here they were, halfway down the road.

The three who had come with Wheezer slipped inconspicuously out of the cave-like Majestic and into the fresh open night outside, to make their way back to Gibbsville and the safety of their own turf, to construct a face-saving story, to continue as before.

The scrape of steel against flint. A flame. *Six.*

Again, *seven.*

Duncan's hand was shaking and he interrupted the rhythm of the contest to calm it. He could register the nervousness of Wheezer by the movement of the blade against his little finger, a movement not visible to the eye of an onlooker.

He hit it again and it lit. *Eight.*

This time, before Duncan could shut the lid on the flame, someone from the crowd poked his head toward the lighter and lit his cigarette from it. Everyone laughed. Others had been dying for a smoke too but were afraid to torch up in the midst of so much tension. Duncan laughed with the others as he watched the intruder draw deeply from the cigarette and inhale like a man who really needed it. Even Wheezer tried to laugh, but it came out a feeble childish whine that bothered those close enough to hear it.

Silence fell again as Duncan stroked the Zippo for the ninth time. A tear was working its way out of the corner of Wheezer's eye. In the TV drama, at this point, an interloper called a halt to it.

Duncan struck the Zippo for the tenth consecutive time.

The crowd cheered. Everyone tried to push close to pat Duncan on the back and razz Wheezer. Duncan kissed the Zippo and held it above his head for everyone to see and admire.

Wheezer folded his knife, put it into his pocket, and said, "I knew it would do it all the time. I was just kidding you."

"Give him his ten bucks!" yelled someone from the crowd.

"I said I was just kidding him."

"You owe him ten."

Wheezer searched the crowd for his three friends.

"Okay, okay," he said, "but it's a gyp 'cause I was only kidding."

He opened his wallet and took out the dollar bill that was inside.

"Hell, man, I thought I had a sawbuck here but it's only a lousy singleton." He put it on the table in front of Duncan. "I'll have to owe you the rest."

"Pay up!" yelled the crowd.

Wheezer dug into his pockets. He took out the change and put it on the table.

"That's every dime I got. Here, you can even have my knife. That's worth it."

No one touched the money or the knife on the table.

"You owe him ten bucks. You better pay him ten bucks," said a voice in the crowd, but the tone of the voice made it the voices of all.

"I don't got it!" cried Wheezer. "You want my goddam shoes? You can have my shoes even."

Duncan put his foot next to Wheezer's. It was three inches longer. No one laughed.

"I don't got the money," said Wheezer with resignation.

Several grabbed him and held him as dispassionately as a fisherman holds a flopping trout. One opened the knife, another stretched Wheezer's little finger on the table, and another said to Duncan, "You want his little finger? He was gonna have yours."

In answer, Duncan smiled and held up two little fingers, showing that, of those at least, he had the full quota.

"You want an ear?"

Duncan laughed, amused at the uselessness of what they offered.

Wheezer was whimpering.

"What about his nose? You want that? This punk woulda cut off your finger."

Duncan laughed still louder. The punk began to cry.

"Take a tooth at least."

Duncan thought for a moment and said, "Okay, I'll

have a tooth," as if refusing a free shot and a free beer and finally agreeing to a bag of chips, just to be social. He planned to attach the tooth to the Zippo as a reminder of the two best nights in his life.

Someone got a pliers from under the front counter of the Majestic and said, "Which one do you want?"

"The front," said Duncan.

Wheezer cried without shame.

They took him, his legs dragging, through the back door to the alley behind the Majestic. Duncan stayed behind to pocket the dollar and the change and the knife on the table. They returned without Wheezer, and the one with the pliers held it in front of him, a huge central tooth in its grip. His knee was blood-stained.

"Had a chopper as big as a horse's."

He dropped the tooth into Duncan's open hand. Duncan pocketed it, and the Majestic Pocket Billiards gradually returned to normal.

The next day Duncan washed and polished the tooth and gave it a coat of clear shellac. He was reluctant to use glue to attach it to the shining Zippo, and even if he did, it would make the lighter awkward to carry and handle.

All that day he looked at the tooth, trying to determine how best to use it. He finally dropped it into the Band-Aid can with his mother's pictures and carried it in his hip pocket, and sometimes when he racked the balls at the Majestic, one could hear it rattle as Duncan moved.

Dear Son,

They can dress them up in tuxedoes and call them by Christian names, but pool shooters are pool shooters.

I'll never forget taking you and your brother to Ella's Lunch and you both almost fainted and said to me, "Mom, do you see who's sitting at that table?"

Who?

"Willie Mosconi!" you and your brother whispered. You were so upset you couldn't touch your bean soup. You started stuttering.

He looked like a school teacher to me, sitting quiet in a suit and drinking a cup of coffee and reading his newspaper.

"Who's Willie Mosconi?" I said.

Until that day I didn't know I was an ignoramus. Only in Andoshen, Pa., can a pool shooter get the key to the city.

We didn't try to keep you out of the Majestic because how could we and where else would you go if not there? We just crossed our fingers that you'd get over it somehow.

Nobody knows what happened to Duncan's famous Zippo. Somebody probably helped himself when they found him, the poor boy, too young to be coughing up so much blood and then laying down to die in the back room of a pool hall. I don't think he had a breath of fresh air in his life. First the mines, then the smoky Majestic.

Pool shooters! On some subjects I'll always be an ignoramus.

Love,
Mom & Pop

Chapter Eight

The Holy Concrete

It was eight o'clock and Shakey the Cop sat in the squad car at Center and Main, tapping his fingers on his knees. He had a good job, relatively free from danger and totally free from hard physical exertion, and because of this he sometimes felt guilty and he often felt bored.

He had too much time for reverie, technicolor waking dreams in which he pursued gangs of criminals in trench-coats who held bank bags in one hand and barking pistols in the other. He was constantly being plugged dead center in the stomach and miraculously surviving to capture or gun down desperate and despicable thugs. Then, flat on his back on the sidewalk of Main Street in front of the Miners National Bank, he lay with blood oozing from his wounds, his smoking revolver gradually falling from his grip. With cloudy vision he looked at the crowd of townsfolk gathered around his bullet-ridden body saying things like, "They don't make cops like Shakey anymore . . . with no thought for his own safety . . . to risk your life for that kinda pay. . . ." And of all the faces he saw above him, faces he had known for so many years, not one really belonged to him. No wife, no child, no family, no one to miss him in a personal way.

Shakey the Cop was incomplete.

It's too late and I'm too old to be lonely, he told himself and wished for some action.

But another half-hour passed before he received a call from headquarters.

"Shakey, this is Red, over."

"Roger, dis here's Shakey, over."

"Got a call from old Mrs. Fagan. There's a bunch of kids hangin' around the Holy Ghost Church again, makin' noise, and she got a bug up her ass about it. How 'bout goin' over there and chasin' 'em away. Over."

"The little rascals, I'll give 'em what for."

"Don't go whackin' any of 'em, Shakey."

"Don't you worry, Chief Red, they don't deserve it, they don't get it. Over."

"Roger," said Chief Red with a sigh.

"Is dis be in the Holy Ghost Polish National or the Holy Ghost Russian Orthodox Greek? Over."

"Polish National. Over."

"Oh, those heathen little buggers. I be's givin' 'em the fear of God in a minute. Roger Wilco, over and out."

The Holy Ghost Polish National was Shakey's church.

The church was on a corner. He parked the car a block away and sneaked toward the corner slowly, keeping close to the porches that lined the sidewalk. When he was within twenty yards of the corner, he was spotted by a pre-teen boy who screamed in undisguised terror, *"Shakey the Cop!"*

There were around twelve of them, boys and girls, and they raced down the street with Shakey twenty yards behind them. One of the boys, seeking to make his reputation in the group, yelled back, "Eat the bird, Shakey!"

Shakey stopped running and shouted after them, "Next time I be's comin' from both ways and then we'll see who gets away from Shakey, youse mean little brats!"

He walked back to the church and there, sitting on the stoop, was Thunder Przewalski, whittling a figure with his pocket knife.

"Oh, a big shame on you, Przewalski, messin' up the holy concrete."

"I ain't no buncha kids you can chase, so turn it off, copper."

"We been havin' complaints at headquarters of sacriliges goin' on in front of the church. I shoulda knew it was you was the ringleader. I should throw you in the jug."

"For what?"

"For contribution to the delinquencies of the minors."

"I was showin' 'em how to whittle, you dumb yonko."

"Who needs a church for this to do in front of?"

"It's a free country."

"It ain't a free church."

"You're tellin' me."

"I should get the father out here after you, that's what I should do. Why don't you stay at your own church?"

"This *is* me own church."

"Oh, yeah?"

"Yeah."

"Then how comes I never see you in it?"

The reason Thunder was never seen at the Holy Ghost was that he had done something beyond redemption within its walls. He and the other boys his age were not long past their confirmation and every month four of them were chosen by the father for usher duty, which included collecting the offering. During the time between seating the parishioners and collecting their money, Thunder generally organized wheelbarrow races for the ushers behind the church, but one day he gave in to the devil's urge, just to see if he would be noticed, and how he would be noticed. He tried to make the other three ushers join him, but they were horrified and couldn't believe he would attempt it. When the four ushers marched to the altar with their bountiful plates, to give them to the father, Thunder Przewalski marched there and back with his penis hanging out.

"You're seein' me here now," he said to Shakey. "On the front steps."

"And I'll be seein' you clean up your garbage. Whaddaya whittlin' there anyway? Lemme see," said Shakey, grabbing the figurine. "Hey, dis is a naked lady!"

"So why's everybody say you're so dumb? You knew right away, just like that, without no help from nobody."

"Oh, a big shame on you, Thunder Przewalski. In front of children and in front of the church. You're gonna go to hell for this."

"Save me a place at the table, yonko."

"Okay, you got the jug."

"For what?"

"For indecent exposin'," said Shakey, grabbing Thunder by the back of his collar.

Thunder kicked his heel against Shakey's shin, but it was a glancing blow. Shakey gave him a punch in the stomach and as Thunder was trying to catch his breath put him in handcuffs.

At headquarters, Chief Red Sweeney gave Thunder a beer, played a hand of pinochle with him, and sent him home with his figurine of a naked lady.

Chapter Nine

R.K.

R. K. Bistricky was shooting pool when the idea was given life. He was shooting French pool, buddies with Gyp the Blood against Jake the Fake and Lemonears Behind the Brewery. Duncan was racking for them, lighting his famous Zippo and staying pretty much out of the way because Jake the Fake made him look bad, inasmuch as Duncan was missing only three fingers of his left hand and could not shoot pool whereas Jake the Fake was missing his whole left arm and shot a fairly decent rack by handling the cue with the hand he had and balancing the end of the cookie cutter on his left knee to serve as the hand he did not have. Of course, originally, when everyone had all his fingers and arms and legs and eyes, Duncan was the best at the Majestic. Mosconi said so.

Gyp the Blood missed a hanger and made his displeasure known.

"Don't cry on me shoulder and gimme pneumonia," said Jake the Fake.

"You ain't got no shoulder to cry on," said Gyp the Blood, which was true. There really wasn't much else of him either.

"You cry more than any human being I know shootin' pool," said Lemonears Behind the Brewery.

Jake the Fake made the hanger and ran out the rack and laughed and said, "That makes me feel better all over than anywhere else!"

R.K. and Gyp the Blood had to buy the Moxies. They sat on the high benches against the wall, smoking and drinking the Moxies, the wet bottles causing the blue chalk on their fingers to run. Duncan racked the balls.

"I went to the Capital this after'," said Lemonears Behind the Brewery.

"How was it?"

"Rita Hayworth," he replied.

They sighed appreciatively.

"Somebody's doin' it," said Lemonears Behind the Brewery. "That's what gets me. Somebody with the same standard equipment I got is doin' it while I be sitting in the Capital gettin' hot rocks."

"There's only one reason why somebody's getting it from Rita and you ain't," said R.K. "Besides that you're ugly and would make her throw up."

"Oh, yeah? What's that?" he asked, ignoring the second possibility.

"Proximity," said R.K., who could occasionally throw a big word into the game.

"Huh?" said the others.

"That means nextness," said R.K. "If I bumped into Rita Hayworth every day at the Cleveland Lunch or Wadden Park, chances are I'd wind up takin' her parkin' at the cemetery."

"If you bumped into her knockers three times a day,

she still wouldn't give you the directions to a bottle of ass-burns."

"That ain't true," said R.K. "I bet you if I put my mind to it, and planned it all out, and was willing to give up everything else to do it, I could take Rita Hayworth out on the town. I'm not sayin' she'd come across, because there's no way in hell to second-guess women in that department, but I sure as hell could spend some time with her, and all it would take is a little money, a little time, and a little brains."

"Well, you got plenty of time," said Gyp the Blood. "Let's shoot pool."

They never spoke of it again, but R.K. was off his stroke because he kept running the idea around in his head, as though he had already accomplished it and was now remembering how it had been. That night he could not sleep for thinking how simple it would be once you got yourself in the same town. All you had to do is find out where she lived, which shouldn't be too hard if you don't give in. Then you just hang around the house and bother her until she goes out with you to get rid of you. It had worked for him any number of times before. But it probably wouldn't work with a movie star. She probably had guards all around the joint to rough up characters like that. Well, if you had the coin and was willing to spend it, you could bother her in a nice way. Send her a dozen, two dozen, *three* dozen roses every day, twice a day. Hell, send her an orchid. What woman in the world doesn't go ape for orchids? Twenty or thirty orchids should arouse the curiosity of even Rita Hayworth. With the orchid you include a card: "A Secret Admirer." No, that's what a jerk would do. Sign it, "R. K. Bistricky" and write below it, "Will call you soon." That way she's curious and hanging in there for the call, just to see what it's all about. Then when you call her you tell her, no, she don't know you, but what the hell, you been sending her orchids all month and will a date with a guy who isn't in the movies kill her? What's she gonna say? Oh, all right, I'll go out with you, but just once. Then when she meets you she sees you're not a bad guy. She might even go for you a little. She might consider you a diamond in the rough, as they say. She'll take you around the next day to meet all her friends and before you know it half the dames in Hollywood are crazy for you because they know Rita is, and you live the rest of your life like a king.

All of this could conceivably happen, and *did* happen, in the imagination of R. K. Bistricky.

He would not get a Rolls, as everyone would expect him to. He would get a simple El Dorado, no need for ostentation. Rita would be pressed close against him as he drove down Main Street, honking the horn (horn, hell, *chimes*) in front of the Majestic.

By dawn it had become an obsession. He did not even consider it a long shot. It was a good bet.

The first step was to acquire a large sum of money, and his first thought was to steal it, but for the amount of money he needed he would have to hit a bank, a league for which he would never be ready.

He could try to borrow the money, touching many people for a small loan, but anyone lending money wants to know what it's for, and once he told them it was for a trip to Hollywood to date Rita Hayworth, well, that would be that. It's not that they would consider it a waste of money; they just wouldn't lend money to someone who plans on taking it three thousand miles away.

The horrible solution was that he would have to work for it, and he went down into the mines. He stopped smoking, drinking, and playing pool. He took as much overtime as he could get and handle. When he was out of the shaft and free, he went about scheming of ways to pick up extra change, and he was not above searching for empty bottles or collecting paper and rags to sell to the sheeny. He began to watch the pools and run against the high school kids, and sometimes even the younger ones, for tips.

First his friends worried about him, and soon the entire town began to notice the awakening of ambition, tantamount to avariciousness, in R. K. Bistricky. But he told none of them of his obsession, because to reveal it half-baked was to invite scorn and ridicule that in Andoshen, Pa., might follow him to the grave and then go after his children.

He worked long and silently and often he said to himself, "This is almost too hard for a human being to do."

It went on for more than a year and every part of his body, not excluding his mind, ached from the effort. But finally he had it, two thousand dollars, and he packed a box and got into his old Dodge, which for a year had been run only enough to keep the battery charged.

He waited until evening and stopped at the Majestic on his way out of town. Gyp the Blood and Jake the Fake were sitting on the bench, smoking and idly watching a contest.

When they saw him, Gyp the Blood said, "You look like a friggin' ghost. You quick better have a Moxie."

"Hyuh," said R.K. "Where's Lemonears Behind the Brewery?"

"He ain't in yet. I think he had to take his mother to a wake down by the patch."

"Well, you can tell him when he's in that old R.K. is on his way to take out Rita Hayworth, and any yonko who wants to put money against it will be covered by me personally."

He put his hands into his pockets and smiled at them.

"Huh?"

"You heard me."

"What the hell are you talkin' about?"

"Remember we talked about it right here? It was only a little over a year ago. Youse said it couldn't be done, and I said I could do it."

"Do what?"

"Lemonears Behind the Brewery was the one brought it up. He just saw a Rita Hayworth movie."

"Look, R.K., do you be all right?"

"Christ, don't tell me you don't remember. I was sayin' if a guy wanted to, he could plan it careful and not give up and sure as hell get to take out Rita Hayworth."

They did not remember the discussion.

"Well, Lemonears'll remember, I can tell you that. You just tell him when he's in I'm off to do it, and watch the columns for, 'A dream queen with the initials R.H. has been seen hand-holding at one of the local joints with a handsome young newcomer from Pennsylvania, down by Andoshen.'"

"Now, wait a minute," said Jake the Fake. "Lemme get this straight, you're on your way to California, right?"

"Right!"

"And how're you gonna get there?"

"Well, I got a damn Dodge, don't I?"

Jake the Fake roared and said, "That damn Dodge ain't gonna get you to Whistlin' Run! You better hope so anyway, 'cause there's deserts on the way to California. You'll be frying your ass on one."

"We'll see."

He hadn't thought about the deserts.

"Wait a minute," said Gyp the Blood. "The idea is once you get there you're gonna shack with Rita Hayworth?"

"That's the general idea," said R.K.

They laughed and slapped their legs and slapped each other's legs. Gyp the Blood had an annoying way of laughing soundlessly, his mouth wide open, all the teeth showing, and his body jerking forward and back. They called the others away from their games to hear R.K. the maniac.

"He who laughs last, buddies, he who laughs last," said R.K., who walked out of the musty twilight of the Majestic and drove off into the night.

. . . you want to know whatever happened to Gyp the Blood, Jake the Fake, and Lemonears Behind the Brewery? What do you think happened to them? They're still sitting around the Majestic, only now Lemonears's brother sits around with them. They call him Little Lemonears Behind the Brewery. Little! He weighs over 250 pounds!

Love,
Mom & Pop

*In her younger days she did not give a damn about the posses-
sions she retained, could she have cared more about those she discarded? Yet in her old age trash cans and the droppings they caught
from the nameless strollers in Wadden Park became her work, and
as surely as the women from the dress factory and the men from the
junk yard and the gassies quit the park at one o'clock to return to
their jobs, she arrived and walked the paths they had walked, now
lined with the old and the unemployed, inspecting every trash can on
the way. Not that the lunch-timers kept her in business. There were
others. Oh, yes, there had to be others, in the evening after the col-
lection or in the morning.*

*She crossed Oak Street every day at one o'clock. In spite of dreary
hand-me-down housedresses, she kept the touch of flamboyance that
had been her trademark in the early days. She wore red bedroom
slippers with big white pompons. In her hair she had placed hap-
hazardly a matching rag of a ribbon, found for free on another day
like this. Though the temperature was in the mid-nineties, she wore
dingy white gloves and carried in one hand a frayed beaded evening
purse, in the other hand a five-cent shopping bag, which had cost
her nothing.*

*She passed The Sour Greek, a victim of the Oak Hill cave-in, in
which he had lost both legs, one at the hip and one four or five
inches above the knee. From Petroni the shoemaker he was given a
metal device used as a footrest in shoeshine parlors. This he attached upside down to the longer stump, and by using a child's
crutches he was able to touch the ground with one metal footrest.*

"Afternoon, Greek," she said to him.

He turned his sour face and mumbled, "Hyuh."

*He had worked hard to stand like a man. He did not like the old
lady.*

She dipped into a can, rummaged about, and came up with a

good find: a four-snap red leatherette key case with only one snap missing. It had a black "L" embossed on it.

"L," she said to Wadden Park. "L, for Lois, my sister's youngest."

A man with a fiddle sat and practiced in his stocking feet, right next to the second can on her route. The man lived with a daughter who would not let him play in the house. He played good songs like "Summertime," but he played them badly. Still, he played them well enough for the melody to be recognized.

As the woman approached, he played the National Anthem, and although a few felt inclined to sing or hum along, no one thought it necessary to stand.

The woman heard the cry of a wounded bird behind her and turned, thinking at first that it was a competing fiddler.

A skinny old woman sat next to the fiddler, and she made herself look like his girlfriend. She glared at a young man who sat across the way, his brown chest bare to the sun, his eyes shut. He was of an alien generation, one of the crowd from the Majestic, loafing around in the sun and inviting the resentment of those whose youth had gone.

Up to the elbow, the scavenger dug into a trash can.

"Pick a winner, dearie," said the fiddler's girlfriend.

"Never you mind."

"What do you expect to find in there? A free trip to Paris, France, all expenses paid? Act your age."

"Never you mind."

"Hush!" said the man with the fiddle as he went into a chorus of "Red Sails in the Sunset."

Chapter Ten

Wadden Park

Estelle Wowak and the reader passed the woman digging into the trash can and sat on a bench and watched the old people: with their goiters, their empty bottles clinking together in grease-stained shopping bags, their canes that they lifted and let slide back down through their fingers, studies in boredom or resignation. One of them leaned over and shouted into his friend's breast pocket, where the hearing-aid pickup was located, about a mutual friend who recently discovered he was landlord to a tapeworm.

"I used to like to come sit here," said Estelle, "with the old people, so that when old age happened to me it wouldn't come as a shock. I would know what to expect."

"Used to?"

"Like isn't what I meant. Felt compelled to, because the only thing I would ever accomplish is growing old."

"Used to?"

"Oh, I like to come here now for different reasons. I'm with you now, so I don't care about growing old or accomplishing anything."

"I'll grow old before you and I'll tell you step by step what to look out for."

"Oh, won't that be fun!"

"It's fun to think how much fun it would be."

"Why so sad?"

"Why don't you care about accomplishing anything anymore?"

"Because I love you."

"I love you too."

"But you still care about accomplishing something."

"Yes."

"That's because you're a man."

"Awful, isn't it? And becoming an older man with every passing season."

"But you've accomplished an awful lot."

"I make thirty-six dollars a week, counting the three I get from you."

"But you're so bright and your head is filled with so many books and things."

"I wish you'd let me give you a free ride and you can keep your money."

"It's the best three dollars a week I've ever spent, and besides, the others would be jealous."

"They would expect it. Everybody knows we're in love."

"Isn't it wonderful! And there I was in first grade while you were going to the Senior Prom."

"With Ella Bistricky, Ryan then."

"Ella Bistricky! But she's much too old for you!"

"Classmates."

Estelle shook her head and said, "I'm having lots of fun finding out these secrets you've been keeping from me. Don't worry, soon I'll know it all. Ella Bistricky, huh? Amazing."

"I wish we had a car," he said. "Or a place to go to."

"I know what you're talking about, Reader. When it's time we'll have a place to go to."

"Estelle . . . when will it be time?"

"Please, Reader, I'm such a baby. Give me a day to grow up in and then it will be time. I promise."

"Don't make it a long day or I'll have grown old."

"Sometimes I wonder why you put up with me. How can I be of any interest to you?"

"You're the queen of the cigar factory."

"Some queen. Some court of princesses."

"Ah, signs of dissatisfaction."

"I wouldn't mind being the Duchess of Windsor."

"For me it's not so bad, but for you to be a stripper in the cigar factory is somehow doomful, like the Kimberly Run Fire . . . burning away underground."

"I tried New York once," she confessed.

"Didn't you like it?"

"No. Why is it not so bad for you but is for me? Why aren't you like the Kimberly Run Fire, too?"

"I also tried New York once," he said.

"Didn't like it?"

"It scared the pants off me," he admitted. "I sat in a dark and dirty room and drank cold beer as fast as I could before it got warm. For three days. Then I came home and wanted to kill myself. But instead I went to work at the cigar factory."

"I was going to be a big city secretary," she said.

"I was going to be a poet," he answered.

"Go on!"

"What's so funny about that?"

"It's not funny, it's terribly interesting. I never met anyone who wanted to be a poet. Where do you go to do it?"

"New York, I think. Maybe Paris."

"But not Andoshen?"

"Oh, Christ!"

"What kind of poetry did you want to write?" she asked.

"I wanted to shake the world. I wanted to do a couple thousand lines on America: the working people, the politicians, the leisure class, the fields, the rivers, the deserts, the mountains, the past, present, and future. I wanted to say it all."

He stopped himself. He was getting too excited.

"I wish someone would write a poem about that stinky old cigar factory. I'd love to see that."

"I was talking about shaking the world, Estelle."

"I'm sorry."

"It doesn't matter. Just so I can keep from getting sore throats. That's all I think about."

"It would have to be a funny poem, as I see it," she said. "Why break people's hearts like so many that you read us? Especially when it can be funny or heartbreaking, take your pick."

Chapter Eleven

Rita Hayworth

R. K. Bistricky picked up every hitchhiker he found on the road to California, asking that they chip in for gas. In this way he conserved most of his own money for its sole purpose.

He had never been farther west than Altoona, and so did not become aware of what the West meant until crossing the Texas Panhandle. So much wide-open space made him nervous after a year in the ground, and he kept telling himself, "Uh-oh . . . there's no turning back . . . I'm coming, Rita . . . Rita, here I come."

He could not find a rider through New Mexico and had to travel the Land of Enchantment alone. He drove conscientiously, as though trying to cross the great expanse without calling attention to himself, so that the huge imposing rock formations would not notice him. At one point he was so overcome by the land that lay natural and undisturbed, so unlike the gouged black earth of Pennsylvania, that he had to pull to the side of the road and sit quietly with his hands folded in his lap. He wished to be back within the soothing, smoky confines of the Majestic Pocket Billiards.

His resolve was strengthened upon entering the State of California, and he landed on the Hollywood Freeway as solid as a citizen. The sign said *Hollywood—Next Seven Exits*. R.K. took the fourth exit, saying, "I'm coming closer, Rita, closer."

He explored on foot the streets of Hollywood and slept in his car that night. The next day he found a garage for rent, four dollars a month. He thought that as a necessary living expense that was not too much. He moved into the garage and slept there in his car. Four gas stations were close at hand and he used their conveniences, shaving and taking a sponge bath daily, just in case he should bump into Rita by surprise.

On a corner he saw a small boy in a sandwich sign as big as he was: "Maps to Stars' Homes." The boy held a map in his hand and waved it at the passing cars, signaling them to pull over. R.K. did pull over and paid the boy thirty-five cents for a map. He rushed back to his garage and spread it out on the driveway. He found her in the index and with a trembling hand landed his forefinger directly on her house.

Proximity.

He immediately drove to Beverly Hills, following his map. It was the only house on the dead-end street, *court* they called it. My God, he thought, to be the only house and have the street all to yourself. He could not see the house itself because of the high walls and rolling landscaped grounds. He stopped his car at the front gate, on which was posted a sign telling who was responsible for electronically protecting the place against burglars and other trespassers.

R.K. got out of the car and stood at the front gate and

said, "Am I really here? Can Gyp the Blood and the others be down by the Majestic and me here in the sun on Rita Hayworth's stoop? Is life such a miracle?"

He wondered how he would be able to prove it all to the others at the Majestic, short of driving down Main Street in an El Dorado convertible with Rita at his side, though even this was not out of the question, not if he could really be standing now in the sun on her stoop.

That day he stopped at the florist's and ordered an orchid to be delivered every day for a week. If the florist could be so curious, could Rita ignore it? R.K. winced as he counted out the cash for seven little plants. He wrote seven cards, each with the same message: "Will call soon. Love, R. K. Bistricky."

He went back to the garage to wait for a week. He sent a picture postcard of Hollywood and Vine to Lemonears Behind the Brewery and The Boys, c/o Majestic Pocket Pool, Andoshen, Pa.

"I'm working on it. As the monkey said when they cut off his tail, won't be long now. See you soon. R.K."

That week he loafed around coffee counters and got to meet many of the unemployed people "in the industry," actors mostly. He told them that he was an actor too, but stayed out of their trade conversations because he knew nothing of "central casting," "atmosphere work," and the other things they discussed with such ease. He told one of them that he thought he could get a job if he could only get Rita Hayworth's telephone number.

"Anything in it for me?" asked the actor.

At first R.K. thought he meant money, but then understood that the actor was talking about what he valued more than money, a role.

"Gee . . . yeah, there might just be."

"You got a property to show her?"

R.K. did not understand and said, "Hell, man, I live in my car in a garage. All my property is on my ass."

The actor thought it was a good joke and laughed with R.K. He called up the Actors Guild and got the name of Rita's agent.

"This is the biggest agency in town," said the actor. "Now, there are a couple ways of doing it. Watch, I'll show you."

He called the agency and said, "Hate to bother you but I'm just in from St. Paul, waiting for a flight to the Islands. I wanted to give Cousin Rita a call but . . . Rita *Hay*worth. I'm her cousin from St. Paul. My mother told me to be sure to call, but damn, wouldn't you know it, she forgot to give me the phone number. If you could . . . well, having her call me back won't do much good because I'm in a pay booth and I'm waiting for a flight . . . well, damn, I *am* her cousin you know. Freddie Schwartz, what the hell do *you* care what my name is? Screw you, Mac."

The actor hung up and said, "Doesn't surprise me. Wouldn't give the number. You sure there's a part in this for me?"

"I'm no damn director, but I would sure as hell say so."

They went to the agency. The actor took a manila envelope from a waste basket, stuffed it with paper and put it under his arm. He took R.K. to what he called "traffic," and leaned toward a secretary and said, "Sweetheart, I tried to get this script to Rita Hayworth, but damned if there isn't something wrong with her gate buzzer or something and I didn't have her number. Look it up, will you, and let me use your phone."

The actor leaned closer and made circles on the secretary's elbow with his forefinger. She never said a word to him. She looked in a roster and gave him Rita Hayworth's number. He wrote it down and said, "Thanks, I'll call from downstairs."

Later, R.K. sat in his car and looked at the number and rearranged the digits and added them and invented number games to play with them and said to himself, "I have done something that no one in Andoshen, Pa., has ever done. I now have the power to talk to Rita Hayworth. I must be a genius."

When he dialed the number on the seventh day and dropped his hand to his side, he felt warm water in his hand and looked at it and saw it was wet from the sweat that had rolled down his arms from his armpits. Whoever answered the phone had to say it twice. "Miss Hayworth's residence."

R.K. coughed and said, "Is this you, Miss Hayworth?"

"No, who is calling please?"

"This here's R. K. Bistricky."

That should get some action, he thought.

"I'm sorry, sir, I didn't get the name."

"Bistricky, R.K."

"Would you spell it, please."

"B-I-S-T-R-I-C-K-Y," his heart shrinking further inward with each letter.

She left the phone and when she came back said, "I'm sorry, can I take a message?"

"Yeah, just tell her I called. Hope she likes the orchids. More on the way. I'll call next week this time."

He went back to the florist and doubled the order for the next week. Still, he could not speak to her. He tripled the order on the third week, and on the fourth week he bombarded Rita Hayworth with twenty-eight orchids. This time when he called she came to the phone. This is good, he thought, for he was running out of money, and failure now meant that he would have to get a job and start all over again.

He could hardly manage his tongue. His eyes were wet and ready to overflow.

"At last," he said, "at last. I hope you like the flowers."

She said she did, but why was he sending them?

"Miss Hayworth, I'm not a bad guy. I ain't crazy. I live in a little town in Pennsylvania and I never had any ambition. All I ever did was hang around the Majestic. Then this idea came up, that even though I'm just a coal-cracker if I had some proximity with you and could talk to you maybe you would like me and maybe I could take you out . . . to supper."

She said it was out of the question.

"You see, just setting myself on this goal has made a different person out of me. I can work and earn and save money. I can go to a strange place and live on very little and make friends, and I can even get the number of a famous star like you and talk to her on the phone. For a guy whose whole life was just hanging around, this is really something."

She said that was very nice but she really couldn't go out with a stranger.

"Why not? I'm not crazy. I won't hurt you. Look, would a crazy man buy you all those flowers?"

She said it was sweet of him, but really, he must stop

now. And don't forget, the house is always under guard and she has policemen and detectives at her disposal.

"Listen," he said, "I might not be in the movies and I sure as hell ain't a rich man, but I ain't a maniac either. I got, *had,* two thousand dollars nearly. You get two grand for smiling once, but, lady, I was in the *coal mines* for over a year to get it. And working on my off-time. You know what it's like to be in the mines, always wet, always cold, always scared, chewin' tobacco to keep your mouth lubricated, breathin' soot, jumpin' a mile every time you hear a funny sound? I did that for *you.* It was a very stupid thing I did. My mother raised a very stupid son, but I'm here now. Would it hurt you to see me in some way? Would it make your life worse? Would it spoil up your future? You live in a different world. You can't know what mine is like. You can't know how far it carries a guy like me to be able to say, 'When I met Rita Hayworth . . .' Something like that can carry me a lifetime. Even talkin' like this to you on the phone is the highlight of my life, the most important thing ever happened to me. Funny, ain't it? Tomorrow I'll meet somebody and I'll say, 'When I talked to Rita Hayworth yesterday . . .' and then the next day and the day after that I'll meet someone and I'll say, 'The other day when I called up Rita Hayworth . . .' That's the kinda life *I* have. I ain't even gonna be able to go home if you don't see me."

There was a long pause and finally she said, all right, she would see him at her home briefly to say hello, but she would not go out with him.

He became gelatinous.

With the last of his money he bought a suit and a pair

of shoes, got a haircut, shave, and manicure, and rented a car, just in case she met him at the gate. He did not want her to see the beat-up old Dodge.

He drove there, proud of himself, having proved the point that a man can do what he sets out to do if he refuses to give up. Wait till the boys at the Majestic see him. In Andoshen, for the rest of his life, he will be known as "The Boy Who Had Coffee With Rita Hayworth In Her Living Room."

There were other cars there when he arrived at the end of the *cul-de-sac*. What if she'd called the police? What if she truly believed him to be crazy? What if she invited a bunch of her friends over and R. K. Bistricky was to be the afternoon's entertainment? They would make fun of him, of his foolish quest, of his rented car, of his tie, his suit, his shoes, his haircut, his soul. He looked at his fingernails and imagined the coal grime still underneath them. They would laugh at the way he talked. They would call up columnists who would write items about the vulgar clown from Pennsylvania who wanted to be able to say he had taken out Rita Hayworth. It was a stupid goal. Why hadn't he put out the same effort to get a Harley-Davidson, something he had once wanted as much? The best thing to do would be to turn around and forget the whole thing. Let them find another sucker to make fun of.

He sat in the car a long time, rendered immobile by anxiety. Finally, he told himself, let them make fun of me. They never seen me before and they won't see me again. But he waited another twenty minutes.

When he was able to get out of the car and stand erect, he felt the cool air against his sweat-soaked body. His shirt stuck to his skin. Even the jacket was wet. He reached down to his crotch and pulled at the sticky garments. He lifted one arm and put his nose against his armpit, making a face at what he discovered there. He got back into the car and returned it to the rental office.

Some men were not meant to meet Rita Hayworth.

Five years later he peeled away the last layer of his shame and was able to leave Los Angeles and go back home. By that time everyone had forgotten exactly why he left in the first place.

Chapter Twelve

Manny

The fiddler hit a particularly sour note, and Manny opened his eyes involuntarily to see the fiddler's skinny girlfriend glaring at him as if to say he had no right to take off his shirt and sit on a bench in the park and give himself up to the sun, unproductive, unearning. When he looked back and said with his eyes, "Give me one reason why not," she had no answer and turned her attention and scorn to an old woman gainfully self-employed in rummaging through a trash can.

On the bench next to him lay a copy of last night's *Call*, folded at the Classified Ads. He picked it up and looked at it again, more for the benefit of the fiddler's girlfriend than for his own. He knew what it said. There were three entries in the Male Help Wanted section. Only three:

> WANTED: TV and refrigerator
> repairman. For Gibbsville
> and vicinity.
>
> HIGH SCHOOL graduate inter-
> ested in retail selling career,

in Lehigh Valley store. Will
train. Salary and commission.

ENERGETIC MAN interested in
department store retail selling
career. Will train if necessary.
Salary, commission, other benefits.
Lehigh Valley.

Three men were wanted, and all of them for out-of-town jobs. There wasn't anything to work at at home. Forty per cent of the people there were on Social Security benefits. While the population was increasing practically everywhere else, Andoshen had fallen from 30,000 in 1920 to 9,000 today, now that its essence had been raped to the point of exhaustion, now that very few had any use for what was left between her legs and inside her belly.

Why do I stay here? he wondered. Why don't I go away and get a job? I have some abilities, he thought, though he sometimes felt guilty that his youth had been spent on youth, rather than in sweetening the record so that his later life might be comfortable.

There were ways for him to earn a living. He could always pick up a day or two in the mines, but he would not like to walk with a limp, to see out of only one eye, to be lopsided with only one ear, to line up with the others for Black Lung benefits from the Commonwealth. Most of all, he wanted the distinction of living his entire life with all of his fingers, as though this were a fit challenge for a young man.

He could remember on his hands the thorny handshake of men with less than five fingers. In the Majestic they struggled with cues or sat broken, like Duncan, the boy who once impressed Willie Mosconi. Perhaps it was not an admirable goal to a young man from Denver, but to Manny fingers were very important and very vulnerable.

There was a gas station job that could have been his, it could have been anyone's, but how many tanks can you pump full, how many windshields can you wipe clean, before you realize that one more will drive you crazy? Manny knew it would not be many. The problem, as he saw it, in taking the gas station job was that in short order he would be*come* a gas jockey, and that job would *be* him in spite of himself. That was a way of dying. It was the problem with any job he could get. He would cease to be Manny and would become instead The Gas Jockey, The Salesman, The Helper.

His first and only job was to be himself, with all his fingers, simply, though he knew there was nothing special about that. He knew also that there was something in him that was pure, something that would be gone the moment he wore the company's uniform and spoke the company's words, something that would be missed when it was gone.

The worst thing about not having a job was that his father kept offering him one. It would be especially bad today because his father was firing Ed, which meant he honestly would need someone. It wouldn't be a matter of routinely taking junior into the business.

For days his father had talked about firing Ed. It kept him awake nights. He could not adjust to the fact that he, a seventh-grade dropout, was going to have to let go a college graduate who certainly needed a job.

The fiddler's girlfriend began to glare at him again. He threw his newspaper into the trash can, put on his shirt, and went home.

It was not the first time Manny went home to find the television on and the house empty. Often his mother would squeeze her marketing between two soap operas and would not bother turning off the set before leaving. Manny opened a bottle of beer and sat down in front of the TV.

Platter Party, a teen-age dance show, was on the air. The show was emceed by a high-spirited young man about Manny's age. He wore a checkered sportcoat. He would clown a bit with the kids, who seemed to like him well enough, then introduce a record, and they would all dance to it. Manny did not understand why they wanted to dance on TV, but that was their business.

The music stopped and the emcee's even smile filled the screen again. "It's lip-synch time!" he yelled. "Our first lip-syncher today is . . ." He consulted a card he held. "Hal Thompkins! Let's go, Hal! Let's hear it for Hal Thompkins!" The rest of the group dutifully applauded. "Here you go, Hal! You sit right here on this stool because you're going to lip-synch a very serious number for us. No cracking up now, because this is a very serious ballad."

Hal climbed onto the stool and settled himself. The lights dimmed; after a guitar introduction, the boy opened his mouth. The cracking voice of the awkward adolescent was heard no more. Instead Manny heard the rumbling baritone of a popular television star, singing the tale of a wild-West hero.

Manny felt embarrassed for the boy. If only you could

know what an ass you're making of yourself, thought Manny, but Hal was oblivious. For all it mattered, the voice he mouthed was his own for the moment. Hal was someone else for the moment, and glad about it.

When the record had played its course and the performance ended, the emcee said, "That was very, very good, Hal! Very good!"

"Good for who?" said Manny.

Next, a young girl, Hal's competition, was called center stage. After another introduction by the emcee and a round of applause, the giggling gum-chewer moved her lips and lo, the honey tones of a popular sex symbol creamed out of her mouth. The girl moved her body and her hands to another's voice. The exhibition seemed somehow obscene to Manny, and he wanted to turn his head away but could not.

This rendition, too, according to the emcee, was very good and better than Hal's by virtue of the greater applause, and so the girl was awarded two record albums. Then came the finishing touch to the fantasy: the emcee himself took the stage and the situation became reversed. When the emcee opened his mouth, Manny heard not the voice of a grown man, but the almost girlish sound of some famous adolescent.

Manny wondered how much the emcee earned a year, and, considering the high sums paid to entertainers, assumed it to be at least forty or fifty thousand dollars. It was not enough, Manny decided, to move your mouth like a ventriloquist's wooden dummy.

His mother came in through the back door, struggling with her packages.

"Mom? Do you need any help?"

She put her packages on the dining room table and went into the living room.

"No, *thank* you, you just sit there and watch your *television* and drink your *beer*. I certainly don't want to inconvenience."

Manny's voice dropped to a whisper. "Mom, I hope you're not going to start up again."

"Have you even looked for anything today?"

"Sure."

"Well?"

"There's nothing for me."

"Of course there's nothing for you. You're the original choosy beggar. Take something, anything. A start. Take a job with your father, just to be employed, so you can say you're working. You know he had to fire Ed today. With a little training you could handle that job."

"Why'd you call me a beggar, Mom? I'm no beggar, and please don't tell me how the old boy started with a bag on his back and now has his own business."

"Is that a crime? Is it something to be ashamed of to work hard so your family is taken care of? It's a pretty cold cookie can look at a father cross-eyed because he made something of himself against the odds with no help from anyone."

"I could do it."

"Then why the hell don't you? Your father pleads with you."

"It isn't me."

"Isn't *you?* What's *you?* Sitting here watching those kids on TV? Is that *you?* You should have a family of your own by now. Then you'd know what *you* are. *You!*"

"It makes me feel good to watch them," he said, sliding

away from the confrontation. "They're so dumb they make me feel intelligent. You should have seen them, Mom. They were lip-synching, you know, just mouthing it while the record plays. Would you like me to do that?" Manny laughed. "This guy makes a fortune doing it on TV."

"If it's an honest living, go on TV and stand on your head."

He turned the TV set off. Manny thought that it was not unreasonable to hope that one man could escape life's necessity, that one man could simply be himself with all his fingers and nothing beyond that.

He went to his room to await his father, the paperboy, and supper. All three were late.

When his father did arrive, he did so with the weight of executive leadership still heavy on his shoulders.

They sat down to eat, and his first words were, "I had to fire Ed today."

Could he believe we'd forgotten? thought Manny.

"It was one of the toughest things I ever had to do." He said it as though he were looking back on a long and difficult career finally concluded. "His wife is pregnant."

"He'll get another job," said Manny's mother. "He's a college graduate."

"Just because you're a college graduate don't mean the roads are paved with gold. You still have to have a lot on the ball. Especially in the business world. Listen, most people who make it in business never even had college degrees. Like me, for instance. You, Manny, just because you don't have a degree doesn't mean anything. If you're ambitious."

"I ain't," said Manny.

"It helps to speak the proper English, too," said his father. "I'll give that to Ed, he spoke beautiful English. There's a danger there too, though, if you're dealing with a lotta yonkos, because they don't trust you if your English is too good, so every once in a while you have to hit 'em with a *woyaku* and say, 'I's be back next week here, ain't?' In Ed's case it was his wife, though. He's a nice kid and ambitious enough, but that brand-new wife was his downfall. He was running home early to her when he should have been taking inventories and filling orders. He was running home for dinner even if he was thirty-five, fifty miles away. What are you gonna do? I had to let him go. I'll tell you, he was crying when I told him. Jesus. I guess he's worrying about going home and telling the wife. It was a good job, but I'm in business, hell, you can't be everybody's nice guy or you'll be broke before tax time."

"It's a shame, that's what it is, with jobs so hard to find," said his mother.

"I warned him often enough. Hell, I knew what was going on. He always promised to knock it off, but deep down he was too much of a newlywed. I blame her. She shoulda realized that a man has to work and can't come running home lovey-dovey three times a day. I wish him well. It broke my heart to do it. He was crying when I told him."

Then began what Manny called his father's circular reflex. He would first repeat himself to emphasize it, to prove it, or to get it all clear in his head. Then he would begin a series of repetitions for their own sake, for their sound alone, and the sound of it would be stimulus enough to repeat it. His mother had also developed the reflex. Manny found it maddening.

His father did not change the subject until the meal was over and coffee was served.

"Where's the paper?"

"He's late today," said Manny's mother.

"Damn paperboy."

Manny went to the door to watch for the paperboy.

"Well, Manny," said his father to his back, "I'm gonna need a good man now. Any idea where I can get one? Good pay."

"Take an ad in the *Call*," said Manny.

"I often wondered how anyone could be such a wiseass without a dime in his pockets. You're a beauty. Where were you when they were handing out pride?"

"Counting my fingers."

"Wiseass."

"Mom and I already talked it over. I'm gonna get a job on TV."

"Huh?"

"Yeah, I'm gonna be a lip-syncher on TV, make a bundle."

"Lip sinker?"

"Get with it, Pops. It's the latest thing. Everybody's a dummy but the guy who makes the record, and we're not too sure about *him*. I'd be a lip-syncher if I went to work for you. I might as well do it in front of millions of other lip-synchers and make a fortune."

"You're a beauty," repeated his father, because he did not know what else to say to him. "I'm glad you weren't twins."

↰ 116

"He thinks he's still a tax deduction," said his mother. "You aren't saving us any money, buddy."

"I ain't costing you any either," said Manny. "I don't eat much, my room is here, I get beer and ciggie money shooting pool and darts. What's wrong with me taking my time?"

"Because you won't have any left when you finally do find out what you want. I'm coming to the end of my patience with you, *pal,* and I don't mean maybe. You need a haircut too," said his mother.

Manny ran his fingers through his unkempt hair.

"I got one last week. All I can do is sit in the chair and take what I get."

"That's your whole trouble!" His father was shouting. "You just take what you get. You sit with your mouth shut, nobody will know what you're worth or what you want. Speak up! Get on the other end of the push, will you?"

"You're my parents, and I guess I love you, but if you keep on nagging me like this, one day I'm going to blow up and there'll be a whole lot of bad feelings."

"Good! I wish you would. Do something. How can you sit in this house night after night after night, listening to your father and me nag you, never going anywhere, no friends or girls . . ."

He leaned against the door frame and inhaled deeply. His mother let loose with the familiar onslaught. "You're twenty-eight years old, you're not a dumbbell, though you've got a hell of a time getting along with people, and . . ."

"I would like to get along with people," he interrupted.

". . . it's high time you give a thought to tomorrow. We're not the kind of people who think the world owes us a living. We have always worked hard, so don't think for a minute you're going to sit on your *dupa* while . . ."

Hurrying because he was late, the paperboy had the *Call* rolled up and was prepared to throw it, until he saw that Manny was on the porch waiting for him. He thought it would be a polite gesture to walk up and hand it to Manny. The paperboy was at first startled to see Manny speak in the scolding voice of Mrs. Pratt, but then winked at him and let himself in on the joke. "Lip-synch, huh?"

Manny turned away but could not stop mouthing his mother's words.

Dear Son,

We knew Manny Pratt's mother and father through business, not socially. They sold the business and retired a few years ago, but still live in town. They have a camper now and during the summers they go up to New England and Canada. It's a real shame that Manny did not go into the business. There's nothing worse than a father who works like a dog to build a business for his kid and then the kid turns out to hate the business and the father has to sell it and buy a camper. This was what happened with Manny Pratt. We will probably also buy a camper except I will not go two feet in it because when you're old you should stay at home. There's nothing worse than someone too old to stand on his feet wanting to run all over the country. Your brother found this out recently when he got two tickets for the Grand Prix races at Watkins Glen and talked Pop into going with him. They didn't have reservations so I insisted they take blankets with them and of course I was right, they had to sleep in the car at the race track. They said it looked like a Rock Festival, sleeping on top of hoods and in tents all over the place. When they got back, I thought they were drunk, but they were so punchy from the effort and the heat they could hardly stand up. Your brother was laughing so hard, and every time he looked at Pop he would double up with laughter. He kept laughing all weekend. They were burned purple. They didn't even change and Pop said the only thing he took out of his bag was his shoe horn. He said every time he groaned your brother would laugh. Well, it is terrible when the spirit is willing but the body isn't. That is getting old and you can't do a damn thing about it.

All I can tell you about Manny Pratt you probably know already. He was a quiet kid, some thought shiftless. Was offered a golden opportunity on a silver platter and wasn't interested. The others you could understand, because they were working around collieries all their lives, and their fathers before them, but when Manny's picture was in the *Call* in a line with the others, it came as a big shock to everyone, because no one even knew he was working at the breaker, and of course he had no need to be. A wasted life if you ask me.

Love,
Mom & Pop

Chapter Thirteen

Columbus Street by St. Casimir's

From four o'clock to midnight Shakey the Cop was the sole uniformed keeper of the peace in Andoshen, Pa. He preferred his shift. The other two cops were married. One of them preferred the eight-to-four shift and the other liked the midnight shift because he did not get along with his wife and preferred to sleep all day.

The parking meters were the responsibility of the officer on duty and every hour on the half-hour they had to be checked and tickets issued to violators. The day man obviously was stuck with that extra duty; Shakey had to make only two rounds, one at four thirty and the last of the day at five thirty.

He would leave the squad car unattended at its Center and Main parking space and carry his citation book up one side of Main Street and down the other and back to the car, then do the same on both sides of Center Street, for those were the only two streets in town with metered parking.

It was a part of his job that Shakey did not enjoy, because the residents of Andoshen had an absolute mania against receiving parking tickets. No one of them could ever imagine a situation in which he was the recipient of a just parking ticket, and although the fine was only fifty cents there was always a matter of pride or principle involved that had at least once, to every cop who ever checked the meters, led to a fistfight on the sidewalk between a law enforcement officer and a citizen who had just torn up his parking ticket and had thrown the pieces into the face of the officer. Shakey knew that whenever he issued a parking ticket he was apt to lose a friend for a year at least.

That is why he did not mind Gyp the Blood running a block ahead of him, and Shakey missed him the rare times when he was not there.

Gyp the Blood had the exclusive patent on this particular enterprise and no one ever tried to cut himself in, mainly because the enterprise was considered slightly less than dignified and was not very rewarding economically.

It worked this way: whenever Shakey began his meter rounds, Gyp the Blood would hurry half-a-block to a block ahead of him, checking the meters himself. If one were in violation and he knew whose car it was, he could usually know in a second where the owner might be and he would hustle into one or another bar or store or barber shop and tell the man that Shakey was on his way. The man would give Gyp the Blood two nickels, one for the meter and one for himself, and Gyp the Blood would beat Shakey to the meter and save everyone a lot of trouble and unpleasantness.

Sometimes he did not recognize a particular car and would have to run into stores at random, telling the patrons that Shakey was on the way. They would give him nickels, two apiece, and say, " '50 Ford, white," or " '55 Chevy, two-tone," or whatever, and he would run out and scurry up and down the street, covering all the violations. If a person had just one nickel for the meter, he would have to give a dime or even a quarter to Gyp the Blood, but many would say instead, "I'll catch you next time," and usually they did or Gyp the Blood would never tip them off again.

Officially, Chief Red Sweeney did not appreciate Gyp the Blood's endeavor. At monthly borough council meetings it embarrassed Chief Red to hear the mayor read to the council members as part of his regular financial report: "For the month past, parking tickets issued, three. Parking tickets paid, two. Parking tickets on out-of-state cars, one. Monthly revenue from parking tickets, one dollar."

It invariably caused a titter and one of the council members would say, "We got a law-abidin' borough here," and another would say, "We got to develop a system for catching those out-of-state offenders." But, of course, everyone realized that Gyp the Blood had to live, too.

One day while Shakey was making the last round of the day of the meters on Center Street, Gyp the Blood racing ahead of him, a call from headquarters was made to the squad car. On the corner, near the squad car, Pietro Bissiri ran a stand. Now, in most places one could say what kind of stand: a newspaper stand, a hot-dog stand, a tobacco stand. But Pietro ran just a stand, a splintery wooden structure that jutted out onto the sidewalk on Center Street and from which he sold terribly bitter Italian stogies, banana peppers, Lifesavers,

Cracker Jacks, cigarettes, the *Evening Call*, prophylactics, True Blue (smoke or chew), clip-on neckties, and a variety of mysterious items that sat in disarray on his slanted counter in open and stained brown paper bags.

As a courtesy, he answered calls to the squad car when it was unattended and he was not busy with a customer.

" 'Allo, I am Pietro Bissiri speaking to you."

"Hyuh, Pete. This is Chief Red. Shakey around? Over."

"Over. He's down on Center somewhere, readin' on the meters. Not long now, he'll be back."

"Look, Pete, when he comes back tell him we got a call there's a dead dog on the road at Columbus Street by the St. Casimir's Church. Tell him to pick it up. Over."

"Over. I will tell him this."

"Thanks, Pete."

"Prego."

When Pietro told him, Shakey said, "Ah, the poor little poochie, to be dead and lyin' on the road and the guy who hit him ran away wit out even lookin'. It's no fun to be a dog and get hit by a car."

Shakey drove the car to the scene of the misfortune and parked behind the body. It was not a small dog, forty to forty-five pounds, Shakey estimated. A mongrel, like all the dogs in town. No collar, probably a stray. Shakey felt a deep sorrow. The sight of a dead dog always depressed him for a full day.

"Poor doggie," he said, "one minute you run around and play nice and try to beg a meal, and the next, here you are, with nobody to do nuttin' for you but call old Shakey the Cop."

From the glove compartment he took out a special form and began to fill it.

"Lemme see, one dog. Time, six fifteen in the P.M. Take care of the date here and the officer on duty. Address, Columbus Street near St. Casimir's."

His pen could not go on. He looked around him to see if anyone were there to notice the anguish and isolation he was revealing. He could not spell Columbus. Nor could he spell St. Casimir's.

He bit the inside of his cheek in shame, and looked around him again. Everyone must be inside having supper. He put the form on the front seat, and opened the back door. He bent down, picked up the dead dog and put it on the back seat.

He drove away to Oak Street, stopped and looked around again, seeing no one. He got out of the car, unloaded the dog and placed him gently on the road, in as nearly as possible the position in which he had found him.

"Now, lemme see," he said, taking up the form, "Address: Oak Street near St. Mary's."

It was then he looked up to see the last thing he wanted to see, Thunder Przewalski leaning against a telephone pole and saying to him, "Ain't that nice, the yonko flatfoot be's takin' his mother for a ride."

Chapter Fourteen

Z-Z-Z-Z-Z-Z

The loneliness did not become intolerable until R. K. Bistricky had had a year in Los Angeles to think about nothing but what he had done with his life, the crazy road it veered onto as the result of someone's chance remark about a Hollywood film star. In all that time no one had called him familiarly by name. He had gone to the same bar every night for three weeks before the bartender said, "Evenin'" in a way that might indicate he recognized him.

He often wanted to call Rita again, to make excuses and set another date, to reach his goal and go home where he belonged. But the fire had gone out of him and all that remained were the ashes. And the shame.

He had to sell his car to eat, and then it was discovered that he was using the garage for living quarters, and he was evicted. Without an income, he found himself skidding farther and farther east, away from Hollywood and Rita, and closer to Main Street and the missions, from which he was afraid he would never emerge, once landed; he could easily become one of the numberless young men who walk the streets of Los Angeles with their shirttails hanging out, engaged in animated self-conversation.

In the mornings he would have coffee at the taco stand (he amused the regulars when he first said *take*-o) at Pico and LaBrea. There he would mill about with the others, waiting for someone to drive by in a truck and yell for two men to help move him out of his apartment, for someone to drive by in a car and yell for one man to hoe a hillside yard, to clean a swimming pool, to plaster a wall, to stain a fence.

The Negroes, a race of men he had never met before, mustered on the Pico side; the Mexicans, a group even more unfamiliar to him, on the LaBrea side, and the few whites like R.K. put their hands into their pockets and paced the L of the intersection alone. Some of the men wore hardhats to indicate that they were once part of something better and would be again. Others had work gloves sticking out of their hip pockets or paint spots on their boots. Some were rumpled and unshaven to show their pressing need, others were clean in fresh T-shirts and khakis, to show their conscientious reliability. All were out of work.

R.K., one of the youngest, looked at them standing impatiently with their toes over the curb, flagging to any rent-a-truck that passed them, and he said to himself, "These men should be put to work."

Still, he slid closer and closer to Main Street himself, like a man sliding down a mud hill on his belly, clutching and grappling, until finally he landed in a downtown apartment-hotel ($1 a day, $6 a week), where he helped both the day and night clerk in exchange for a room, and when the night clerk became more wine than reason, R.K. got his job and the clerk slid into Main Street.

The loneliness of a night clerk who had never met Rita Hayworth. At its worst point R.K. was purely desperate to talk to someone. He sat at the desk, staring into his coffee cup like a three-o'clock drunk, looking for his future or his past and seeing only his present self, the loneliest night clerk in the city. He picked up the telephone directory, determined to converse with the last person listed in it. *Z-Z-Z-Z-Z-Z, 10507 Dunlr Dr. . . . . 837-5566.* He dialed the number.

The phone rang once, and he braced himself to hear someone say, "Hello." But when the ring was broken, he heard a voice, startling in its enthusiasm so early in the morning, sing out, "Hi, there, boys and girls of all ages . . ." He spoke so fast that R.K. could hardly keep up with him. "This is your old friend Uncle Fink, with not one, but two new exciting dolls from Super Toys called Mumsy and Dadsy dolls. Gee, don't they look super? . . . angora T-shirt and simulated mother-of . . . earrings and lots of luscious raspberry lipstick smeared all over her lips and everything. Isn't Mumsy keen? Look at Dadsy doll with razor nicks on his face and his imitation dirty sweat socks and his . . . T-shirt just like . . . Aren't they terrific? Just like real Mumsy and Dadsy people are. And listen carefully while I pull the little cord behind Mumsy's T-shirt. See? She whispers, 'Get me another drink, stupid,' just like real Mumsies really do. And watch while I pull the cord on the Dadsy doll. He says, 'Make your own drink, fat and ugly,' just like the real item. Wowee! Aren't they just too much? And, boys and girls . . . Super Toys have really done it this time. After I give them each a stiff drink, watch what happens. Look at Mumsy doll reeling around and staggering and falling down just like a real, live Mumsy does . . . Look at Dadsy doll, look! He's lunging for the bathroom with his hand over his mouth. How about Dadsy doll's face? Look! It's turning green. Jiminy, aren't Mumsy and Dadsy dolls just too realistic for words, boys and girls? You bet they are. Mumsy and Dadsy dolls from Super Toys. Educational and fun for the whole family!"

Another voice, this one soft and female, said, "This message has been brought to you by zzzzzz, z-z, z-z, z-z."

R.K. listened for a moment to the dial tone before hanging up. He worried that he would not now survive to see the dawn, but the more he worried about it the funnier his situation became, until he began to laugh out loud, and once he began he could not stop. Tears came to his eyes. He reached for the directory, now wanting to tell his life's story to the first person listed. *A.* Same address, same number. R.K. roared and let the tears flow.

Chapter Fifteen

Kayo Mackey, the Boy Who Hurt Gene Tunney

Kayo Mackey opened the door to Brolly's Bar at two P.M., not the best time, but not the worst either. Besides, he would be back again that night when the guys who had jobs would be there. Now there were only four at the bar, and Brolly himself behind it. The four were laid off and drinking afternoon beer on their unemployment checks, sitting one stool apart, one of them tapping the bar with his fingertips. Tonight they would stay at home or play cards at one of the firehouses, and Brolly's would be filled with working men, calm in their minds and with money to spend.

Kayo knew them. Their wives, three of them, worked in the dress factory, and the other wife rolled cigars. Or maybe she sold shoes. No, she was rolling cigars, Marie Piencowski. Kayo himself was not eligible for unemployment checks. Anyhow, he had a job. He was running the pools.

He took a stool and carefully centered his weight on the left buttock. The right one was acting up again, high, where they give you a needle, and it felt like there was a

130

needle there now, a long one, a corkscrew one. He put the pool sheets, backed by a square of softened cardboard and held together at the top by a Hunt Clip No. 3, on the bar, and said to Brolly, "Glassa water."

It was beginning to get cold outside. Whatever happened to summers and springs and falls, thought Kayo, remembering those endless luxurious seasons of his boyhood, swimming early at the Sulphur Creek in icy, startling water that was clear to the pebble-covered bottom fifteen feet below, because it was fed by mine water, full of sulphur, which killed all living things except young boys, whose only worry was the smarting of the eyes the sulphur caused.

It was only slightly warmer inside than out. Kayo knew for a fact that Brolly had been delivered two tons of bootleg pea coal, for he had watched it run down the chute from the truck to the coal bin in the cellar as he talked to the driver about the unseasonable cold, shouting to be heard over the loud *zhizzz* of the coal racing down the chute. But Brolly was unwilling to burn any of it too soon. At night Brolly trusted to body heat to warm the tiny barroom. Kayo suspected that Brolly had an electric heater upstairs where he lived with his wife and daughter, but anyone who heated part of his house with electricity, gas, or oil kept it a guarded secret in Andoshen, especially if he were in business.

Kayo made a mental note to get his wheelbarrow and hustle over to the train yard to pick up the fallen pieces of coal for his own dragon of a furnace and for his "bucket-a-day" that provided them with hot water before the coal was all and he would have to go out to the stripping roads and on his hands and knees separate the few pieces of coal from the many pieces of slag.

He worried about his mother in their little house in the Glover's Hill patch. Old people are always so cold. He should know, he was becoming an old person himself.

He took off his baseball cap and put it on the bar, on top of the pool sheets. Rather, he put what was left of the baseball cap on the bar, because the misshapen, droopy peak had been removed and he wore what remained, so greasy and dirty that one could hardly notice the stylized "A" for Philadelphia Athletics. Wearing it he looked like the mechanics and body men who favored wearing similar half-caps, and he wanted to look like them, to think of himself as one of them, though he knew it was not his line of work; he just hung around the gassies and garages, running the pools, occasionally entrusted to clean a windshield or pump up a tire. There was not much else he could do.

Even those who loved him most admitted that Kayo Mackey was punchy. Not punchy enough to start swinging when he heard a bell, or to mumble incoherently about past victories, as we are told so many ex-fighters do. He was punchy only to the extent of being unable to hold any paying job that required him to be at a certain place at a certain time to perform a certain function, because he was not able to keep his mind on those things. The one steady job he tried had lasted two days. It was a job in the lumber yard and on the second day his mind wandered and he cut off his right forefinger on a circular saw.

Sometimes he would appear to be drifting, and his normal speech was difficult to understand, but that was because of some unfortunate dental work, scar tissue, and a swollen tongue. And as for drifting, that's permitted anyone with a glorious past.

He drank the glass of water Brolly gave him.

"Give 'im a beer," said one of the four.

Brolly drew the beer, skimmed away some of the overdeep head, and drew again. He placed it on a cardboard coaster in front of Kayo and withdrew a dime from the shallow puddle of change in front of the other customer.

Kayo lifted the glass and said, "Here's to you."

The other lifted his glass in return and they both drank.

"To the only man ever hurt Gene Tunney," said the one who had bought him the beer.

Kayo smiled, lowered his head, and moved his shoulders self-consciously, remembering the night.

"What's that?" asked one of the others, who, oddly, had never heard about it. He was probably too young.

Brolly and the other two wanted to tell him, but the one who had mentioned it first insisted on his rights.

"Kayo here once fought Tunney and Tunney said in the papers some time later, 'The only fighter who ever really hurt me was a boy named Kayo Mackey from Andoshen, Pennsylvania.' "

He said it with a good deal of pride. Not everyone can know the only man who ever hurt Gene Tunney.

"I didn't know that," said the other.

"Yeah, I hurt him," said Kayo. "I hurt him all right."

"Where was this? When?"

"I hurt him," said Kayo and lowered his head. He couldn't exactly remember where and when, but he remembered it was smoky and noisy and everything was slippery like sweat and everything smelled like sweat and leather and canvas, and he remembered that he was not afraid of Tunney. His own head was harder than anthracite and the kids used to line up to hit him in his stomach with all their might, big kids in high school. He was not afraid of Tunney, because Tunney could not hurt him, but my God, he was *smart* and he was fast and what he didn't mention when he told the press that Kayo Mackey was the only boy who ever really hurt him was what punch had done it. Kayo could not remember a plan of attack against Tunney, he remembered only going after him and feeling the shock of the punches he landed on him go clear up to his ears until he thought they would burst. He hurt Gene Tunney all right, and Tunney did not hurt him, even though Tunney knocked him out in the tenth and went on to become champion while Kayo, who hurt him, went in the other direction. If only he could remember working for an opening and going into it with speed and grace, and putting one over on Gene Tunney, but all he could remember was striking out with all his force, like a bad pool shooter who fires into a cluster with all he's got, shooting for shit, and sometimes making a ball or two, but always losing the game.

A heavy wave of mixed aromas floated into the bar from the kitchen. Kayo had enough of the olfactory sense left in his battered and flattened nose to smell the blind pigeons, kishkie, and pig's feet jelly.

"Smellin' good," he said to Brolly.

"Come back late tonight. Stand by the kitchen door."

"Would you take a ball of cheese from my mother's goat?" asked Kayo.

"Ahhhh, goat cheese," said Brolly appreciatively.

"I'll take care of it," said Kayo and slipped off his boot to scratch the bottom of his foot. It was called a campus boot and was popular with young men in the late '40s and early '50s. Its sides were quilted and the rims were wide, stylish then, but a trap for every stray pebble on the block. Kayo shook out a pebble onto the floor. He could not remember where, when, or how he got the boots.

The social amenities over, he got down to business. He took his cap away from the pool sheets and said to all of them, "Would youse wanna play the pools today?"

The pools, as a local institution, were a method of gambling, no denying it, and operated in the following way: a benevolent organization rented a store front and painted on the window its name, "American Legion Pool" or "Amvets Pool" or "Nicholas P. Russo Post Pool" or "V.F.W. Pool." There was one pool called, God knows why, "The Hatchet," but the only people benefiting from this benevolent organization were the five men who were its only members.

Inside each pool there was a row of windows, very like the windows at a race track, and behind each window was a teen-age girl who worked for thirty-five cents an hour. You would walk up to the window, give the girl a dime, and tell her your name and address. She would write it on one line of lined paper, next to a printed number, and give you a poker chip with that number printed on it. Above the number on the poker chip was a tiny hole. If you gave the girl a dollar, she would write your name on the top line and scribble over the rest of the paper, to indicate you bought the sheet, and she would give you ten poker chips. These chips you would throw into a glass barrel near the exit.

On Wednesday and Saturday nights, several contingents of old ladies and young children would gather at the various pools at eleven o'clock, sometimes hurrying from one pool to another, trying to cover as many of the drawings as possible. They would press close to the glass barrel. The manager of the pool would turn a crank and make the barrel spin around and around, turning over repeatedly the mass of poker chips that filled it. He would open the small door in the barrel and call on someone in the crowd to dig in and choose a chip. The whole purpose of being in the crowd was to be the one who was chosen to draw a number.

The chip having been selected, the manager would read aloud the number and put the end of a straightened clothes hanger through the hole in the chip and hold the chip out over the heads of the crowd for all to see, to prove that no hanky-panky was going on. One of the teen-age girls whose duty it was to stay late that night would riffle through the sheets of paper to determine who held the lucky number. She would announce the name and address of the winner, and several small boys would run out of the pool and race to his home.

Traditionally, the one who first tells a pool winner of his good fortune rates a small reward. The trick was to be fast, yes, but also to know your way around town, and especially to know all the short cuts. Best of all was to have a bicycle.

The first three chips drawn were for $50 prizes, the next two were for $100 prizes, and the final one was for $500 on Wednesday night and $800 on Saturday night. The bigger boys would not run until the last number was drawn.

On a $50 or $100 prize, the winner was expected to give the boy who informed him one dollar. He was also obliged to give the old lady who drew his number five dollars, and the girl who sold him the number another five dollars, and the names of these old ladies and young girls were always duly recorded at the time of drawing. Sometimes a winner did not come across with the rewards. His greediness—"ignorance" they called it— would become a topic of conversation forever and everyone would agree that he was a poor winner and should never win again if there is any justice in the world. The rewards for a $500 or $800 prize went up to five dollars for the boy and twenty dollars each for the old lady and the young girl.

"Running the pools" was a job without pay for the disabled of the community. It meant that a runner would be given several sheets of numbers on Saturday for the Wednesday pool and on Wednesday for the Saturday pool, and he would try to sell these numbers to the Main Street merchants, and the boys in the bars, the coffee counters, the Majestic, thereby saving the gambler the walking time. The runner's only hope of financial gain would be in selling a winning number and receiving the reward. A runner could literally spend his life in such an occupation and never receive a cent, but usually he would quit and take up a new enterprise after a long stretch without a winner.

For years this was the only county in Pennsylvania that operated what could be called a numbers racket in full public view. The practice had always been ignored by the state government and conceivably not known to exist by the federal government. But then one election year it appeared that, like all good things, the pools might come to an end.

A new candidate for the state congress (no one mentions his name now) accepted the endorsement of the local churches, which did not have the temerity to establish their own pools yet resented the existing pools cutting into their bingo revenue, and stood on a platform of crushing the evil face of vice.

Surprising everyone, he was elected, and although, like most skillful politicians, he tried to draw the attention of the electorate away from his campaign promises, he was finally forced to action. His two targets were the open prostitution in the county seat, Gibbsville, one block from the court house, and the pools in Andoshen. The first went underground and stayed there, much to the disappointment of a generation of Northeastern Pennsylvania college boys; the pools, however, hired Attorney Michael Patrick Watson Quigley, an Irishman, to defend their interests. His job was not to fight the congressman in court; there was no case. His job was to keep the pools open.

They were forced to close for a week while Quigley conceived his brain child, and it was like a dark season on Broadway. The culture had collapsed. People became sullen and uncommunicative. The congressman was cursed in the streets and Quigley was urged to prod the miracle of his mind.

One night he sat alone listening to old Dorsey records, and the stroke of genius came upon him of its own accord. He had been thinking about Tommy and Jimmy Dorsey, born on the same block as he. They had been schoolboys together. He thought of how far they had gone, and of the other talent that had surfaced from the coal regions. The regions had produced several musicians of distinction, numerous professional athletes, a writer or two of some notoriety, and Jack Palance.

He thought of all the talent yet untapped, and when he did, the plan was there, fully blown.

The pools would become talent agencies. The teen-age girls behind the windows would become talent scouts. The public would come in, slap down their dimes or dollars, and register their talent or talents: singer, dancer, musician, actor, writer, athlete, artist. Their names would be written next to a number, they would be given poker chips to drop into the barrel at the door, and they would wait until Wednesday or Saturday night to see if a boy would run to their doors to tell them that they had been selected in a talent search to go to Philly or New York for a talent test. They could either let the Talent Agency arrange for their transportation and hotel, or they could take the cash and make their own arrangements.

Thus came into being the VFW Talent Agency, the Nicholas P. Russo Post Talent Agency, the Hatchet Talent Agency, etc., and they all agreed that there was no business like show business.

Michael Patrick Watson Quigley was paid a substantial fee and the congratulations of an appreciative community; the congressman nestled comfortably into obscurity; Kayo Mackey, the boy who hurt Gene Tunney, became a talent scout, though he and everyone else still referred to his job as "running the pools."

Brolly and the four at the bar went partners for forty cents apiece and bought two sheets of numbers in the name of "The Five of Us, Brolly's Bar, Town."

Brolly gave him two bills, which Kayo wrapped in a torn sheet of newspaper. He wound a rubber band around the newspaper and put it into a pocket of his baggy slate gray pants. He finished his beer and went outside without a word, still trying to remember the night.

"There's a guy coulda had a future in puckin' in the ring," said one of them.

"What happened?" asked the one who hadn't known about Kayo. "Booze?"

"Kayo never drank much. I think he just got the crap knocked outa him."

"But a guy who hurt Gene Tunney . . ."

"He hurt Gene Tunney all right, but the others hurt *him*," said Brolly, settling on his stool to read the afternoon *Call*.

Dear Son,

K. O. Mackey (his fight name)—born 1895, died 1956, miner by occupation—was a Coal and Iron Policeman for a while before becoming a fighter. He fought Gene Tunney during WW I in the service and knocked him down, but not for the full count. Gene won the fight. Tunney was reputed to have made that statement years ago. After the War, K.O. turned professional and fought Gene again in Jersey and lost again, but K.O. said he was a victim of a fast count. He used to come into the store with the pool sheets. He fought the well-known Battling Kershutsky, and about 1919 he lost this fight also. One nite in the O'Hara Theatre in Andoshen, where the Lyric used to be located, in about 1916, he fought two men, and this nite he knocked them both out. One of the fighters was known as Rocky. A fighter by the name of Jock James from the coal regions fought Tunney, and this fight ended in a draw. Later, K.O. fought this same Jock James and knocked him out in the first round with a shot to the head. I got all this from his trainer who is still in town and says he will tell you anything he can remember but unfortunately he kept no records in those days, like they do today. K.O. was a fine man that everyone liked very much and when he had a heart attack he borrowed Bongo Belly's truck and drove himself up to Peddler's Hill Hospital where he died at the front door.

Love,
Mom & Pop

Chapter Sixteen

Partnership

The two Bistricky families were still living together when the furrier next to Ella's Lunch went out of business. The vacancy caused Ella some anxiety; she imagined another restaurant moving in.

"It'd be just my luck," she told the others late at night, sitting around the kitchen table, "for somebody, after all these years of working my ears off, to move a hash house in next door and undercut me. It'd be just my luck. A Howard Johnson's'll move in."

"There's a way you wouldn't have to worry about it," said R.K.

There was almost always sarcasm in her voice whenever she spoke to R.K. "Pray tell," she said.

"Expand. Take the joint next door, knock down a wall and expand. Double your business."

She dismissed this idea as she dismissed all his ideas, as she tried to dismiss his very presence.

"I don't have enough headaches, working like a slave to keep up with the business I got."

"It's better to double your business than have it cut in half."

"You know, R.K. might have something there," said Bill. "You could set up more tables in the extra space and have it more like a real restaurant."

"It costs money to remodel," said Ella. "Knockin' down a wall ain't just a matter of knockin' down a wall. Besides, once I did it I would need more help, and try to find somebody who won't steal from you."

"I could do the remodeling, free of charge," said R.K. "You just pay for the materials and we can borrow or rent the tools and equipment."

"Since when are you such a good Samaritan?"

"I'll do a beautiful job. I know about these things. Then once it's finished Dianne and I will work for the place without a salary so that we can become partners. It'll be a real family business."

Dianne was upset by this swift bargaining of her husband, using her labor as part of the bargain.

"It's always *been* a real family business," said Ella.

R.K. slid his hand under his tiki charm and scratched his chest.

"I think it's a good idea," said Bill. "If we can more than double our floor space without too much expense and if we all pitch in and work, as partners, we can all make more money than we are right now."

In bed, Ella and Bill continued the discussion. She agreed the plan sounded beneficial to all, but confessed that she just did not trust R.K. Bill was hurt and said, "He's as honest as I am," but there was no way of assuring this, beyond accepting that if Bill said it, it must be true. "There's something about working with relatives," said Ella. "Would you rather work with strangers?" asked Bill. "Relatives can steal from you just as easy," said Ella. "No one ever stole from a fair employer or partner," said Bill. "Cripes, Bill," said Ella.

They took over the furrier's. R.K. quit his job with the sheeny and took up the carpentry work, the sanding, the painting. He went about it with the enthusiasm of a boy on his first paying job, bare-chested, a belt of tools around his waist, wearing jeans and engineer boots. Even Ella admired his industry, though she trusted him no more for it, and she wished that he would wear a shirt once in a while.

Ella stayed open until it was time to break through the wall, and then she closed for the operation. R.K. suggested that instead of knocking down the whole wall, they make an archway. The jukebox could stay in the lunchroom proper and all the tables could be arranged in the other area, which they could call the dining room. Coffee and sandwich people could sit at the counter, those ordering a meal could enjoy the comfort of a dining room. A beaded curtain or swinging doors could separate the two areas. You could put bullfight posters on the walls to give the place some atmosphere. Maybe hang a fishnet or something. You could put curtains on the front window which could be drawn for privacy or opened if you wanted to watch the people walk by while you ate. A sign could be placed on the front door: "Dining Room. For counter service use other door."

It was done, and business was not bad.

The routine of work they established put Bill behind the counter, Ella in the kitchen, and R.K. in the dining room, while Dianne was to float from area to area, spelling the others so that each could go home to take a quick nap. Everyone worked hard.

R.K. had a free and easy way about him that customers found pleasant, and working people who previously ate lunch at Ella's only twice a week began to eat there three and four times a week. During the slack hours R.K.'s friends from the Majestic provided them with a good coffee trade, and they had the sense to leave when the eating customers began to arrive. Ella also noticed a dramatic upswing in the after-school Coke trade, especially among the girls, who liked to fill the dining room and try to get the better of R.K. when he teased them. Ella warned him that he should not become too familiar with young girls and he answered, "What are you talkin' about?"

When it came time to make R.K. and Dianne legal partners, Ella balked.

"What's right is right," said Bill. "Maybe they never put any money into the place, but they've worked as hard as us, sometimes harder, to make a go of it. R.K. did all the remodeling at next to nothing for us. You remember, it was his idea in the first place, and you gotta admit he personally did an awful lot for business."

"I know, I know," said Ella, "but partners are like a marriage. I'd rather pay them off for all their work and put them on a salary."

"You still don't trust him, do you?"

"He's not like you, Bill, I don't care if you are brothers, and as for that California cactus, 'nuff said."

"But what's right is right."

"I think sometimes people can get too close to people. It seems like forever they've been living right on top of us. I know I would feel better if they'd just move the hell out."

"How can they? If we made them partners, like we agreed, and gave them their fair cut of the profits, they'd be out right away."

And they were. When they left the house Ella felt a net of nerves fall away from her. To celebrate, that night after the kids were in bed, Ella closed the blinds, took off her clothes, and walked nude throughout the entire house.

Chapter Seventeen

Not Goin' Anywhere

Estelle Wowak, like so many people whose lives were once lonely, rehearsed conversations. When she was a little girl and saw something on the street, she would tell it over and over again in her mind, on her way home to tell her mother. *There was this dog . . . I saw this dog . . . there was a man with a stick . . . a dog and a man with a stick . . . I was across the street . . . I was with Wanda . . . I was on my way . . .*

In her anxiety to tell the story quickly and effectively she could never complete it in her own mind. Sometimes she tried to construct the other side of the conversation, what would be said to her, but people never said what she thought they should. She discontinued that practice and tried to concentrate on her own story.

As she sat stripping the tough veins off the broad wrapper leaves, pretending to listen to the reader do a novel by a young girl from France, she rehearsed what she would say to him after work. *Reader, we're not goin' anywhere . . . we're not goin' anywhere . . . goin' anywhere. . . .* The phrase was lodged in her mind. If it was mysterious to her, could it mean anything to him? Where did she expect to be going? *I don't want to be like the other dames . . . the other broads . . . the other girls . . . who can think of nothing but getting married . . . you taught me about love, Reader . . . and I agree with you a hundred per cent and nobody can take away what we've had . . . and I'm not sorry for a minute of it . . . but we're not goin' anywhere, Reader . . . not goin' anywhere . . . goin' anywhere . . . what's the point of kidding around, let's go get married . . . it's easier . . . if you want to, let's, but don't you dare tell our kids I asked you . . . if you don't want to, I'm not goin' to cry . . . but I'm afraid we're not goin' to be goin' anywhere . . . goin' anywhere . . .*

The reader finished the novel and said, "Just about quitting time."

"Time for one short poem," said Joe Yuschock.

"Right."

"Make it Dylan Thomas," said Mrs. Griffiths.

"e. e. cummings," said the reader. "Small letters."

"Oh, him," said Raymond Przytulski.

"You remember, no titles on his poetry. Here goes:

> *"in spite of everything*
> *which breathes and moves, since Doom*
> *(with white longest hands*
> *neatening each crease)*
> *will smooth entirely our minds*
> *—before leaving my room*
> *i turn, and (stooping*
> *through the morning) kiss*
> *this pillow, dear*
> *where our heads lived and were"*

"I don't get it," said Rae Bernicky.

↳ 148

"Well, you don't have to get everything to feel what it means," said Estelle.

"Listen to her, will you."

"Anyone can tell it's a love poem," said Estelle. "That's all the more you got to know. You either feel it or you don't."

"Well, Estelle's the one to feel it, all right, all right," said Betty Demalis with a lewd laugh.

"Moonin' around here like little Ophelia outa Shakespeare the Bard," said Marie Piencowski.

Estelle lowered her head and straightened out her day's work.

"I ain't felt it in years," said Anna Maglusky, with even a lewder laugh.

"Okay, scholars, that does it for today," said the reader, emptying his jar of coins and putting his books back into the shopping bag.

They were out before the others and as they walked along Main Street, Estelle said to him, "You see the way they make fun of me?"

"You're the baby of the bunch. Pay no attention."

"If it wasn't for you, I could sure get sick of that cigar factory."

"My mother's playing bingo tonight. We could use my place, as long as we're out by ten, ten thirty."

She went to her memory for the conversation, her half of it, that she had rehearsed.

"What time should I be there?" she asked.

"About seven."

"Is that about seven, or five after, or ten after?"

"Well, after she's gone, five after to be safe."

"Right, and should I sneak in the back door? Will you have a towel over the bed?"

"What's wrong, Estelle?"

"Can I concentrate on you, or will I have to listen, in case she comes back early?"

"Why all of a sudden are you . . ."

"Reader, it ain't working out the way it should."

"Everything seemed all right yesterday."

"Well, it only seemed that way."

"Estelle."

"We're not goin' anywhere, Reader. We can keep on like this till we get old, but this is as far as we'll get, waitin' for your mom to go play bingo, tryin' to pretend to everyone that we're not doing it, but, hell, everybody knows. It's goin' nowhere, if you know what I mean."

"I didn't know that's the way you felt."

"Look, my eyes are wide open, nobody's twisting my arm. I told you once that I'd do anything you wanted me to. That still stands, but, hell, Reader, look at how it is. You and me, we're not goin' anywhere, and it bothers me. C'mon, give me a ring and let's say the words in front of people who know us, and cut the crap and start bein' an honest-to-God couple."

"Do you think I don't want to marry you?"

"I don't know what to think. I never knew why you would bother with me in the first place."

"I love you."

"Gee, Reader, do you?"

"Who wouldn't?"

"Then?"

"Estelle, we couldn't live on what I make. On what both of us take home."

"Couldn't we?"

"The only thing is to go to the city and try to get decent jobs in some kind of factory."

"I'm willing."

"But if I don't take care of my mother, she's had it. Besides, you and I aren't the types that can leave Andoshen and live somewhere else. Some can and some can't. We can't. That leaves us in the cigar factory."

"It's a dirty job, but somebody's got to do it," she said sarcastically. "Where would the country be without cigars?"

"C'mon, Estelle."

"We could live on what we make."

"Don't you want kids?"

The question made her pause. "I didn't think about that." She paused again. "I never thought before about how damn poor we are. We're poverty-stricken, you know that? My God, why didn't I ever know it?"

"Because we're home."

"Suddenly I look at us and know there's nowhere we *can* be goin'."

"There is one answer, if you really want to get married."

"I really do, Reader. It'll be nicer."

"I do too. Don't think I don't want to. I want to, terribly much. It will make me proud."

"So all you have to do is drop down on one knee. Hell, you don't even have to do that."

"There's one way, as I see it."

"What?"

"I can go into the mines. It's more money."

Estelle stopped walking. She turned to him and said, "You would do that? To marry me?"

"Yes."

"Is that our only out?"

"I guess so."

"Then forget it. My father's a miner."

"So was mine."

"*Was,* is right. See what I mean? I'd rather have you like I do for the couple hours your mom plays bingo than have you all the time broken, coughing and wheezing at night, and with parts missing. Or not have you at all. Forget it, Reader. Cripes, I never *realized* how stinkin' poor we are."

The plateau above the natural pit was within easy access of the main road. One day someone, since forgotten, drove his wagon off the highway, backed up to the pit, and shoveled off his cargo of refuse.

Others followed, until there was no denying what the place had become, and the council designated it as the municipal dump.

Marksmen would take their rifles with them and get in a few shots at the rats.

Then the Depression came to Andoshen and with it the homeless looking for a flat piece of ground and something with which to build a shack. They settled above the dump and helped themselves to its bounty, building a community they despised and naming it to dishonor the man they held responsible for its existence.

They shared equally in the treasures of the dump. The dump was haberdasher, shoe store (often they resoled their shoes with old brake lining or pieces of discarded tires), furniture mart, grocer. During the bitter cold winters they burned wood, which they stockpiled all year long, in salvaged washtubs, and they slept under quilts that they had made themselves using rags sewn together and stuffed with strips of old newspapers.

The most bitter among them was elected Mayor.

Chapter Eighteen

The Mayor of Hooversville

There is a saying in Andoshen: If you have a truck, you have a job. Like most sayings, it is true often enough to be self-perpetuating, but it is not always true. The real trick, of course, is to get the truck in the first place and then see if you have a job. If you cannot get a truck, then you get next to someone who has a truck, and if he gets a job, maybe there will be a lesser job in it for you—trucker's helper.

Thunder Przewalski was a trucker's helper. Actually, it was one of the last of the things he was, and he practiced it only when nothing else was available, and he practiced it only with Bongo Belly, a man with a truck whom he disliked less than the other men with trucks. And, owing to the condition of Bongo Belly's ancient International, most jobs with him were not long ones.

They called him Bongo Belly because he liked to drum on his stomach, a huge beer belly that spilled over his belt in every direction. (It was said that he had not seen his sexual organ in years.) His belly was naturally suited to drumming because it produced a variety of tones, depending not only upon *how* it was struck but also *where* it was struck, like the steel drums of Trinidad.

His other distinction was that he shot pool with an old mop handle, the metal hardware and a strand or two of rag still attached to the useless end of it. To a stranger, he was an unnerving sight, calmly chalking the end of a mop handle as he surveyed the table before shooting. It was hard for him to get a game at the Majestic because he won fifty per cent of his matches, and no one wanted to shoot him for fear of what it might do to the ego to lose to a shooter with an old mop handle.

When he worked, Bongo Belly would line up cleaning and hauling jobs, contact Thunder, and together they would clean out a yard, basement, or attic and haul the trash to Hooversville. Many of the businesses in town had a standing appointment with Bongo to clean out their cellars and storerooms, and if anything of value were in the vicinity the proprietors kept an inconspicuous but wary eye on the clean-up team.

One day, late in the afternoon, they were shoveling their last load of the long day into the pit of the open dump, christened Hooversville by the four derelicts who lived on its summit in frail and leaning shacks built of the materials they salvaged by helping people unload their trash and sifting through it before it rolled down the hill to the bottom of the pit. They took all the tin cans and flattened them and if they did not need them for the roofs or walls of their tiny one-room shacks, they saved them and sold them to the sheeny, along with stacks of newspapers and bundles of rags. This is the way they survived, the four of them, in a pure communistic society, four men of indeterminate age and backgrounds, three of them reflections of each other, the fourth a midget, the only one in town, who was called by the people of Andoshen the Mayor of Hooversville.

As Thunder and Bongo unloaded this last truckful, the wastes of Mary McGraw's Long Bar, the entire population of Hooversville was stationed at the end of the truck, helping them.

Thunder tried to shoo them away.

"Okay, youse, this is the last load. Nothing worth nothing here. Just junk. Dirt and broken glasses in cardboard boxes. Nothing you can use here. Be seein' youse . . ."

"Aw, let 'em go through it, Thunder," said Bongo Belly.

"I'm savin' 'em some time is all," said Thunder, and then he spoke to the other four again. "Don't waste your time. *Ićdo domu spać*. Just broken glass here. If youse cut off your fingers, you'll tank me for tellin' you to go scram."

They were down to the last few cartons, and it was clear that the four were not going to leave until the truck was empty. Thunder finally was forced to look into one of the cardboard boxes, and there, nestled in broken glass, crumpled cigarette packs, and used-up bar rags, were two quarts of rye whiskey and a gallon of muscatel.

"What's goin' on here?" said Thunder, looking into the box. "Is Mary McGraw gone nuts?"

"Whaddaya talkin'?" said Bongo.

"Well, she usen't to throw out full bottles of whiskey and wine."

Bongo tucked in his belly, leaned forward, and looked

into the box. Hooversville's population ran to the side of the truck so that they too might see full bottles of whiskey and wine.

"Goddammit, Thunder, you thiefed from a steady customer."

"Thiefed? Me? This is not my mistake. Maybe Mary McGraw wanted to throw it out. Maybe it went bad."

"Maybe they hid in there, all by themselves, trying to escape to Hooversville."

"Now you're being silly," said Thunder.

"Thunder, I been knowin' you for a long, long time, and I wish there was one decent thing I could say about you."

"I mind me own business," said Thunder, suggesting one for him.

"A thief on me truck," said Bongo Belly.

"I'm innocent. You don't believe me, take 'em back and tell Mary she trun 'em out by accident."

The residents of Hooversville loudly cleared their throats in unison, prompting Bongo Belly to think about it carefully.

Bongo Belly thought about it for a moment, but Thunder knew that it was impossible for him to return such a windfall.

"If we took them back," he said finally, "Mary would tink we stole them dishonestly and would never hire us again. I guess we're just stuck with 'em."

"Now you're using the old noodle. Okay, let's shovel out the rest of this crap and be on our way somewheres for a snort."

Thunder began furiously to kick loose refuse over the end of the truck.

The midget Mayor of Hooversville spoke up. "Bongo Belly and Thunder Przewalski. There is a tradition in Andoshen, an unwritten law, as they say, that what passes into Hooversville is forever and ever the sole property of them that lives in Hooversville."

"I'll unwritten law you, you little snot," said Thunder, who raised his fist and added, *"Bęnda bida!"*

"Look, buddy," said Bongo to the midget, "you're welcome to anything we throw over the end. God bless you. But there ain't nothin' entitles you to this booze. What's fair is fair."

"I agree," said the midget. "We wouldn't want it all. That's what put this country where it is today, people wanting it all. We would expect that you share it even-Steven with us, like we would do likewise to youse, if the situations was reversed."

"Well, you put on a very nice song and dance, and I give you a big hand," said Bongo, "but you still ain't getting any of this booze."

"We have been associates with you for a long time, but you have never held out on us before."

"We never had booze before."

"We occupy a position of some respect in Andoshen. We stay to ourselves here. We're always polite to people and we help them unload their trash. We never get in trouble and we always tell the truth."

"Uh-oh," said Thunder, sensing the drift of his presentation.

"Certainly Mary McGraw . . ." began the midget.

"Okay, you sawed-off politician," said Bongo, "you got any clean glasses in them shacks? We don't drink from no bottles, you know."

He took the two bottles of whiskey and Thunder grabbed the gallon of muscatel.

They sat between and to the front of the two shacks farthest from the edge of the dump and its concomitant odors, sitting in a circle on the ground like Indians in conference. Jelly glasses, more of Hooversville's bounty, were provided, and Bongo Belly wiped his with his sweaty T-shirt.

One of the three normal scavengers said, "When do the festiviries begin?" This was the first and last time either Thunder or Bongo had ever heard him speak.

Bongo twisted the cap off one of the whiskey bottles. The sound of the breaking seal gave them all a sense of wealth and well-being, and the act felt good against Bongo's dirty hand. They held their jelly glasses together and he carefully poured, conscientiously giving everyone an even cut.

Bongo Belly held his glass high, proposing a toast.

"Here's to the county jail at Gibbsville. Thank God we never been there and pray God we never have to go again."

They threw back their heads and drained their glasses. There was a good deal of *oh*-ing and *ah*-ing and snorting and belching and kicking the ground with the heel and the execution of one perfect fart, for which everyone tried to take credit, until the rights were not clear even to the one who had actually performed the deed.

The glasses were filled again and drunk again and filled and drunk and filled once more, and they began, one by one, to go back on an elbow and look up at the sky and comment upon the beauty of the waning afternoon. The wind was in their favor and they did not get

the sulphur smell of the Kimberly Run Fire, though they could see the steady flow of smoke drifting skyward. Periodically they would hear the sound of a car or truck on the road some fifty yards behind them begin its short descent through the blue smoke and into the town. From far in front of them came the rumble of the trucks and shovels working the strippings, from day into night into day again.

Bongo began to sing, accompanying himself on his belly:

> *"Whistle while you work,*
> *Hitler is a jerk,*
> *Mussolini pulled his weenie,*
> *Just to see it squirt . . ."*

The midget went into his shack and returned with an old cigar box. He flipped it open and with a grand sweeping gesture asked, "Smoke?"

Inside the box were trimmed and clean cigar and cigarette butts, previously used but still to be entirely consumed. Thunder and Bongo, as guests, were given first choice. They fingered the butts and selected the neatest, longest cigars. Thunder dropped his on the ground, but picked it up, kissed it up to God, and put it between his teeth. The other four helped themselves and they all lit up and went back on both elbows, inhaling and releasing the smoke of stale tobacco to the sky.

Thunder began to warm up and hum as though he might sing his Song, but instead sang softly, "Shanty in Old Shanty Town."

They felt content and good when he finished the song,

and the population of Hooversville built a small fire in the middle of their circle, not so much for heat but for light and for the comfort of a fire among friends.

"You're still living in your shanty in the patch, ain't?" asked Bongo of Thunder.

"Where else would I be?" said Thunder. "I'll be committin' murder one of these days in that patch if them ladies don't stay outa my hair."

"Aw, you love it."

"I know what I love and I know what I hate."

"What do you love?" asked Bongo.

Thunder was silent for a moment, then said, "Well, this whiskey ain't bad."

They looked at the fire, and they began to sing,

> *"When the lights go on again,*
> *All over the world . . ."*

Bongo said to Thunder, "Jesus, I thought my voice was rusty nails, but you're worse than I am."

"Shit, I never been that worse in me life."

Bongo did a solo on his belly. *Tico Tico.* And then it was time to open the wine because the two quarts of whiskey had been drunk. One of the Hooversville four, the one who was anxious for the "festiviries" to begin, was dead asleep, his head cradled in his arms. The others looked at him as their wine glasses were being filled, and laughed like drunken men lying in a circle in the dirt.

Since they were drunk and words were harder for them to mouth, they made up for clarity with volume. Each of them raised his voice to speak, even the diplomatic midget.

"What *is* your name?" Bongo shouted to the midget. "I don't know any of youse guys' names."

"We lost our names when we lost everything else," the midget shouted back to him. "Why should we keep our names when they don't mean anything? Cash in hand has captured all meaning in this country."

"Whaddaya talkin'?"

"Just what I said."

"Well, you mean you don't have no names?"

"That's right," shouted the midget.

"Whaddaya call each other, then?"

"Comrade."

"Now you're talkin' irradical. That's Red talk, that comrade stuff. You a Red?"

"Sure I'm a Red. If you was as poor as me and had to join a circus and let people laugh at you so's you could eat, you'd be a Red too. You'd be anything."

"Hey, Thunder, this squirt's a Red," said Bongo Belly.

"Imma Green," said Thunder, pulled his little finger and belched, "Bow wow!"

"It's not that I have anything against you, little fella, that's fine with me, don't get mad at me, it's just that I ain't never talked to a real Red irradical before."

"I ain't no radical. I live in Hooversville and stay to myself and here I'll die on one of these mornings and they can roll me into the dump with the rest of the refuse."

"Yeah, but you're a Red still, you said."

"You ever meet a poet?"

"A poet? A poet? Where the hell would I ever meet a poet? Whaddaya talkin'?"

"So, you never met a Red either."

"I don't get it. Whaddaya sayin', that poets and Reds are alike?"

"On one basis."

"Sissies, huh?"

"I never knew a guy to talk more about nuttin' than you," shouted Thunder. "You got a bliffy for a brain."

A bliffy is ten pounds of shit packed into a five-pound bag.

Bongo turned to him slowly and lowered his voice for emphasis.

"Thunder Przewalski, I wish I had one decent ting to say about you, to save for when you die."

"That's the second time today you said that. One more time and you get a puck in the puss."

"I ain't afraida you, you goddam gorilla, you."

The population of Hooversville who were still awake began to push themselves backward through the dirt, away from the circle.

"You tink you own a truck you own anybody takes a ride on the ugly ting," said Thunder.

"I own more'n a truck. I work and pay plenty taxes and a family support. *You!* You ain't got chickie or child, truck or job. I do you a big favor to let your gorilla skin on the back of my truck."

"Big trucker! Big trucker! You run the ugly ting on piss from the sewer creek."

"Which reminds me you never chipped in for gas, not a penny, for all the times *my* truck took you from here to there."

"Oh yeah? Whose wine you drinkin'? Whose booze you drunk on?"

"Not yours."

"It always comes down to ownership," said the midget. "Whose booze, whose truck? That's all there is to fight about. All the arg'in' in the world is whose *booze,* whose *truck.*"

"You keep outa this, you goddam midget," said Thunder.

"Oh, sure," said the midget, "that's the next thing. You can always count on it."

"Pick on your own size, you grummy old gorilla," said Bongo Belly, meaning to say "crummy." And then he irretrievably said, "I don't have a decent thing to say about you, all the years I known you."

"Okay, that's three."

Thunder crossed what had been the circle on his knees and hooked Bongo in the mouth. Bongo, who was on his elbows, did not have far to fall. A cloud of dust rose around his head when it bounced. Bongo brought back his leg and kicked Thunder in the face with the bottom of his boot. Thunder went back to the ground and they both lay there for some time, motionless, their feet almost touching.

"Two men of our time," said the midget, "casualties of the money war."

"See if you ever work on my truck again," said Bongo without lifting his head or moving any part of his huge body.

"Your *truck!* Your *truck!* I'm ready to york up from listening about your truck."

"It's always a truck," said the midget.

"You'll see what you have to york up when you have an empty belly. You'll be dreamin' about my truck, I can tell you that."

"That's enough of that happy horseshit about any yonko truck that makes me sick in me stomach."

Thunder stood up. Bongo also struggled to his feet and then bent over, looking for a rock. Thunder slammed him twice in the side of his immense belly. The sound of the blows seemed to create echoes from other parts of the stomach. *Thump-ump-ump! Thump-ump-ump!*

Bongo fell down and rolled over once and tried to catch his breath.

Thunder staggered the full diameter of Hooversville, released the hand brake on the International, put his back against the battered grill, and pushed it over the edge of the dump. It slid over the mounds of refuse like a dead sea lion and came to rest on its rear end at the bottom of the pit, looking not entirely out of place there.

Bongo Belly, from his horizontal viewpoint, thought that his eyes must be tricking him. The sound he heard, that too must be a trick. But he looked along the earth line and saw only Thunder where Thunder and his truck had been. He brought himself to his hands and knees, and on all fours he crawled across the ground to the edge of the pit. He looked over the side and saw his beloved truck looking up at him. He brought back his head and howled like some lost creature baying at the implacability of the moon.

Then he picked up the shovel that had not gone down with the truck and swing it full circle at Thunder. His aim was bad, and the flat of the shovel caught Thunder on the elbow with a resounding *ponnnnng*. Thunder screamed in agony and bent over and tucked the injured elbow into his crotch and began to cry, "My funny bone! You smashed my goddam funny bone!"

At that instant Bongo was lifting the shovel again, preparing to smash Thunder's head as well. Thunder saw it coming and ran away with his elbow pressed against his stomach. The citizens of Hooversville, with the exception of the one still asleep, scattered in all directions. The midget, in cries of panic, fairly assessed the prevailing situation: "Man berserk with a shovel! Man berserk with a shovel!"

He was.

He ran after everyone, wildly swinging his weapon. When no one was within range, he swung it at the night, all the while howling like a mortal brother to the damned. He stood above the sleeping man and slammed his shovel down an inch from his face. The man awoke, saw the shovel and Bongo's face in the eerie light of the campfire, and seemed to shoot away like a Roman candle, knowing immediately that a number of horrible things had transpired while he had slept.

Out of frustration and a need to hit something more personal than the ground, Bongo took a swing at one of the shacks. With one blow he knocked down a whole wall, giving the shack the cutaway appearance of one of those bombed-out buildings in Europe after World War II, with furniture and personal possessions still intact but walls completely demolished.

The midget ran up to Bongo and tried to kick him, but Bongo threatened him with the shovel.

"My house!" he cried. "You spoiled my house, you overgrown crazy man, dumb yonko, you!"

"You got insurance?" Bongo asked, becoming calmer now by virtue of his guilt.

Suddenly Hooversville was alight. The six of them

drifted together again around their fire and looked into the set of headlights, knowing that no one would be bringing trash at this time of night. A door slammed shut and in front of the headlights appeared the large uniformed figure of Shakey the Cop.

"Youse be's havin' some company?" he said to the four he knew lived there.

No one answered. Once they saw who it was, they turned their backs on him.

"Who you got here to be makin' such noises and disturbance of the peace that family people passin' on the road have to tell Shakey the Cop that there's bloody murder and walkin' divils takin' over Hooversville?"

Still no one answered, but Bongo Belly squatted on the ground and began to keen for his truck.

"Who's that waterin' the fields?" asked Shakey the Cop, walking over to him. "Why, it's Bongo Belly. What for you're in Hooversville at night insteada wit your family and why are you cryin' for?"

"You'd cry too if your truck was at the bottom of the dump," sobbed Bongo.

"Dis is true," said Shakey, as both a question and an agreement with the statement. He walked to the edge of the dump and looked down at the truck. He giggled and then apologized to Bongo, saying, "Excuse me. When somebody sees somethin' they ain't seen before sometimes they laugh maybe. Don't mean nuttin'. I would like to ask how your truck got where it got."

"You should hafta ask?" said Bongo, who sat down and pointed at Thunder's back with his toe.

"Who is this holdin' his arm like it's busted? I shoulda knew. Never once did I ever get called to Hooversville, the most peaceable patch in Andoshen. But Thunder Przewalski goes to Hooversville onct and soon Shakey the Cop is close behind."

"Go piss up a drain pipe," said Thunder, and threw a bottle cap at him, missing by several feet.

"I'm guessin' Thunder Przewalski drove your truck into the dump. Does dis be correct, Bongo Belly?"

"He *pushed* it," said Bongo and began to weep again.

"For dis we can prefer charges," said Shakey.

"Ain't you gonna ask who busted me funny bone, Dick Tracy?"

"I wouldn'ta busted it, if he'd leave me truck alone."

"Ah, I see, I see," said Shakey judiciously. "Well, there's room in the jug for both youse."

"My comrades and I, of course, Officer Shakey, are blameless," said the midget.

"Dis I can believe," said Shakey.

"Aw, c'mon, Bongo, I'll getcha damn truck outa the hole," said Thunder. "It ain't broken so bad. If anything's wrong wit it I'll fix it meself. I worked on it before for you."

Bongo considered it and saw jail for both of them as the only other choice.

"All right," he said, "and then you'n me are quits."

"You're breakin' me goddam heart."

"Is it no charges that's gonna be preferred then?" asked Shakey.

No one answered.

"Well, then, I'm gettin' back in the squad car. It's almost the end of my shift and I better won't be causin' any more trouble if I was youse."

They sat in silence until they could no longer hear the motor of the squad car, and then Bongo picked up his shovel and held it on his lap, waiting for the return of the urge to brain Thunder Przewalski. It was sure to come.

Dear Son,

At that time, everyone who was out of work blamed President Hoover, even tho he had nothing to do with the Depression. The men who squatted there, built shacks, were homeless men and all alone in the world. After the Depression went, four of them stayed. They managed to survive by separating saleable junk, and selling it. Also, collected and stored wood for the winter months to keep them warm. The old clothes people threw away were also picked up, they even were able to salvage food such as stale bread, cakes, etc. that the grocers took to the dump. They always waited for our truck, because they could always depend on a good supply of one-half-smoked cigars. In those days Pop bought about ten cigars a day (El Productos) and usually smoked them halfway and put them on the edge of the counter and when they went out he threw the other half into the trash barrels. They were so hot for those cigars that they would unload the truck. They were not too happy when Pop quit smoking. They didn't say so, but you could tell they thought he was being pretty inconsiderate. Hooversville is all bulldozed now.

Love,
Mom & Pop

Chapter Nineteen

Christian Charity

Shakey the Cop drove away from Hooversville with Thunder on his mind. There was a boy could make a liar out of Father Flanagan. And Will Rogers, for that matter. They were children together and had sometimes worked the same jobs before Shakey got his good job with the borough, but Shakey could not remember a time when Thunder was not exactly the way he was tonight. Shakey had no illusions about the nobility of the human spirit, yet still he looked for excuses for Thunder. If only he had had a decent home, a mom and daddy to give him a good clout when he needed it, if only he were not so ugly, if only he had a steady job, or a good woman, or someone who cared about him, someone who would walk through a puddle for him. But Thunder was the kind of person you just naturally hated. He encouraged you to hate him. Once in a blue moon, however, you could see the shadow of a good man in him. Would a bum risk his life to save an old woman he had no use for anyway? Would a bum offer to help get Bongo's truck out of the dump and fix it for him? (Shakey would have liked to continue these extenuations but ran out of material.)

If Shakey were a soul-saver, he decided, he would go for the long shot and try to redeem old Thunder Przewalski, but since he was a cop he would probably wind up cracking his skull or plugging him. Still, wouldn't it be nice to have the Lord meet you at the stoop to heaven and call the angels to the door and say to them, "Shake hands with the yonko who made Thunder Przewalski a decent human being."

Shakey picked up his mike and put in a call to headquarters. "Chief Red, Chief Red, dis here's Shakey the Cop callin'. Over."

"Roger, Shakey, the chief went home to bed. This is Bobby. What's cookin'? Over."

Bobby was the chief's eldest boy.

"Roger. Hyuh, Bobby, how's it in school? Over."

"Roger. I'm bustin' me knuckles on the typewriter for Miss Atikian. I got the hots for her. Over."

"Roger. Who don't? Listen, Bobby, did your daddy tell you I was goin' up to Hooversville?"

"Yeah, what's up?"

"Roger. Old Thunder Przewalski and old Bongo Belly are up there visitin' and they got in a beef 'cause Thunder pushed Bongo's truck over the side. Bongo busted up Thunder's arm, but they settled down all right, so I think everything's Roger. Over."

Bobby laughed and said, "I hafta go up tomorrow and take a look at that. Did you chase 'em outa there?"

"Naw, they buried the hatchet, so I went. Over."

"Roger. I don't know, Shakey, they're both piss 'n vinegar if they had a few. You shoulda pulled one of 'em outa there at least or somebody might get kilt. Over."

"Okay, I'll be doin' a U-turning and tell 'em to move

their asses to another ward. Roger Wilco, over and out."

By this time he had almost reached his post at Main and Center. The streets were deserted. It was eleven thirty.

When Shakey pulled into Hooversville a second time, his door was opened by a jumping midget in a state of panic. His three comrades were crouched against the openings to their shacks, and next to the fire was the unmoving form of Thunder Przewalski.

"Mr. Shakey! Someone has killed Thunder! My comrades and I were nowhere near the scene of the crime. We were all down in the dump looking for cans and when we came up, there was Thunder on the ground."

Shakey went to Thunder and put his hand on his heart. He opened Thunder's shirt and put his ear to his chest.

"He's alive," said Shakey.

"How can that be?" asked the midget. "Bongo gave him a shot with a shovel enough to finish a horse and rider."

The back of Thunder's head was well caked with blood and dirt, but it was no longer bleeding.

"I would like to know where Bongo Belly went to."

"This I do not know," said the midget. "We was looking for cans in the dump."

"Wit candles? And if you was in the dump how come you could see Bongo give 'im a shot wit the shovel?"

"Please, Mr. Shakey, we had nothing to do with it. We mind our own business here. We don't get involved."

"Don't get your bowels in an uproar. Who's sayin' youse do?"

"After you left, Mr. Bongo was sitting still and probably wouldn't have took the shovel to Thunder, but for Thunder provoking him to do so."

"Provokin' how?"

"First Thunder said that Bongo Belly thinks he shits ice cream but that his farts tell on him."

"Grown-up men talkin' like dis," said Shakey.

"Then Thunder became very insulting and right before he got it with the shovel he said to Bongo Belly that he, Thunder, was intimate with Bongo's grandmother, mother, and daughter, and then he had uncomplimentary things to say about the three of them. Bongo waited till he turned the other way and then he gave him such a crack with the shovel you could hear it on Peddler's Hill. Which reminds me, should an ambulance be called for Thunder?"

Shakey put his hand on the back of Thunder's head and diagnosed, "It ain't fractured."

Thunder began to regain a fuzzy consciousness. He moaned, opened his eyes and saw Shakey, and said, "Jesus, Joseph . . ."

The midget withdrew and like the others crouched in front of his shack, three-quarters intact.

Shakey lifted Thunder, cradling him like a baby, and put him into the front seat, the first time Thunder had ever been afforded that honor.

"Listen here, Przewalski," he told him, "you lean forward and keep your bloody bean off of the borough's upholstery."

All the while telling himself that he was doing the wrong thing, that he was risking job and reputation, that he was courting disaster, Shakey took Thunder home. He was unconscious again when they got there and Shakey had to carry him from the car up the steep outside steps to his apartment above a garage, struggling to maintain his balance with the considerable dead weight of Thunder in his arms.

He placed him on his own bed and put a pillow beneath his head, unmindful of the blood. He left him there and drove to headquarters and gave the squad car to his relief, who gave him a lift back to his apartment. Thunder was still unconscious. Shakey filled a bowl with warm water and added a few drops of detergent and agitated the water with his fingers to stir up suds. He turned Thunder over onto his stomach and bathed his head clean. The gash was not too serious. Shakey thought it could probably stand a number of stitches but would let Thunder decide for himself. In the meantime he made three butterfly bandages out of adhesive tape and closed the gash in this way. He could see a huge lump swelling. He looked at the elbow and saw that it too was swollen and turning purple.

After he washed Thunder, he took off his shoes and covered him with a blanket. He brewed some coffee and poured himself a cup and sat at Thunder's bedside throughout the night. At one point Thunder awoke and lifted his head and saw Shakey. He said again, "Jesus, Joseph . . ." and fell back to the pillow and slept until late in the morning.

When he did wake up, Shakey gave him three aspirin and three glassfuls of ice water. Then he gave him a shot of rye and followed it with a mug of hot black coffee. Thunder was halfway through the coffee before he looked around him and ascertained that he was not in jail or in the hospital. He touched his elbow with one finger and groaned. He put his hand on the back of his head and groaned louder.

"Where the hell am I and where the hell is Bongo Belly so I can kill him?"

"This is where I live," said Shakey.

"Huh?"

"You're in my place. I did somethin' for you I never done for you. I didn't throw you in the jug."

"This is the inside of your place?" asked Thunder.

"Well, goddammit, you know, I don't *live* in that squad car. I go home like anybody else and put away me gun and sit in me chair. I got a kitchen here I cook in, a crapper in the corner, and that's me bed you're in right now."

Thunder looked at that part of the bed that his body was touching and said, "This is *your* bed?"

"Well, god*dam!*"

Thunder said, "I'm goin' home. Point me to Rattlin' Run," but he could not muster the strength to get out of bed.

"You stay where you are, you got any brains left. You're lucky you ain't a dead man now lyin' in Harry's funeral parlor."

"No thanks to Bongo Belly. The madman tried to mudder me, with a shovel, you."

"What didcha expect the man to do? You tell him you was . . . *in*timate . . . wit his grandmother, his mother, and his daughter even yet."

"I lied about his daughter," said Thunder, finished his coffee and asked for more.

Shakey poured it and poured one for himself.

"Whaddaya brew this wit, pistol oil?" asked Thunder.

"You're very welcome, I be sure."

Thunder looked around him again. "So this is the inside of your place, huh?"

"I gotta live, just like anybody else."

"I didn't tink it would be dis clean."

"I *keep* it clean," said Shakey with some pride.

"How comes you don't get a wife to keep it clean?"

"How comes *you* don't?"

" 'Cause you're too ugly and mean, that's why."

"You too, only more," said Shakey.

Thunder put down the coffee cup and pressed his fingers against his temples. "How comes you brought me here?"

"I felt sorry for you."

"*You?* How comes you wasn't sorry for me all the times you bashed in me head and trun me in jail and blamed me for tings I never even done? How comes there was never no sorry then?"

"You can use it now more 'n then."

"What're you up to, Shakey, you old bastard? A dog don't change his stripes overnight."

"I ain't up to nuttin'. Once in a while a guy likes to play Christian. It's good for the soul."

"For the *soul?* For your moth-eaten, baggy, old, scabby old *soul?* When you go they're gonna give you an old coal oil lantern and put you on the dusty road to hell, directin' traffic."

"And I'll be givin' you a ticket for drunken drivin' and runnin' over dogs."

Thunder laughed in spite of himself, hurting his head.

"Quit tryin' to split me noodle, screw."

"An egg I can give you, wit some toast, and I got a potato cake in the ice box," said Shakey.

Thunder shrugged his shoulders as though it were im-
material to him, but when the food was prepared, the
good smells filling the tiny apartment, and placed on the
kitchen table, Thunder planted an arm (favoring the
bruised one) on each side of his plate, lowered his face to
within a few inches of the plate and dug in, making the
sounds of a man who has seldom eaten in the company of
another.

"Where'd you get this potato cake?" he asked.

"Whaddaya mean, get? I *made* dis potato cake."

"You cooked it?"

"You bake it, that's what you do to it."

"Good!" Thunder said and shoveled some more into his
mouth.

When they finished breakfast, Shakey provided cigarettes. Thunder smoked his with coffee, and Shakey
smoked his as he cleaned up the breakfast dishes. Thunder looked on in disbelief, finding it hard to accept that
he was actually sitting at Shakey the Cop's table, being
waited on by none other.

Thunder smoked the cigarette down to his fingers and
dropped the smoldering end into the ashtray.

"I suppose you're waitin' for me to say thanks," he
said.

"Whaddaya, wanna gimme a heart attack?"

"Well, you coulda done worse by me, I'll admit that."

"You should have a sawbones look at that head and
that elbow."

"Aw, I guess they'll hold up as long as the rest of me."

Thunder wanted to leave but was having difficulty
making the move. He was comfortable now.

"You got a nice place here," he said.

"It ain't bad, but it's awful small and the rent is sky high."

"Whaddaya puttin' out for it?"

"Thirty-five. Whaddaya pay at Rattlin' Run?"

"Twenty, but my place don't even come close to this."

"Thing about Rattlin' Run is it's too far to walk to town."

"Lotsa times I get a ride."

"You got furniture any?"

"Junk," said Thunder.

"This stuff comes wit the apartment. Junk also. What I need is more room. For me hobby."

From the mouth of Shakey it sounded like a foreign word.

"Hobby?"

Shakey pulled a cardboard box from under the sink and opened it.

"I like to walk in Wadden Park and around," he said, "and look for pebbles, all different kinds. Then I get a good piece of bark or a dead branch or somethin' and then I glue the pebbles to the wood."

He showed Thunder an example. Thunder held it and ran a finger over the pebbles and turned it around. "Whaddaya do wit it?" he asked.

"Well, you don't hafta do anything wit it. If I had some bric-a-brac shelves or somethin', I'd put them on the shelves and have a good look at them whenever I wanted to. Probably a dumb old hobby, but I get a kick out of it. I don't know why. Then I like to listen to the baseball games on the radio and drink a quarta beer."

"You could probably use 'em to weight down a stacka papers if you had a stack sittin' somewhere, or put one in the bottom of a goldfish bowl, if it would stay on the bottom."

"That's a damn good idea, Thunder. I tink I'm gonna do that, just like you said. Boy, you come up wit a damn good idea."

Thunder was strangely pleased with himself and said, "I don't get a hobby. Nuttin'."

"That's 'cause you don't got no steady job. If you got a job steady, you would want a hobby to relax wit when your work was over."

"I'd ruther not have no hobby."

"To each his own, as the song says."

"Besides, there ain't no jobs here except the coal holes and I had me fill of coal holes."

"There's some topside jobs. You keep your eye open on the strippin's or in the breakers. Sometimes I hear about a slot in a breaker. I'll keep me ear open and put in a good word for you."

"I don't need no coppers puttin' in their two-centses for me."

"Don't be bitin' off me head, I'm only tryin' to do a good turn."

"Do a good turn for yourownself."

Thunder was still not able to push himself away from the breakfast table.

"Do you like your place there at Rattlin' Run?" asked Shakey.

"I'd like it a lot better if me goddam neighbors would leave me alone."

"Why don'tcha move out on 'em?"

"And where would I move?"

"I got the inside dope on a place last week. You know old man Pfeiffenberger's place?"

"Yeah, that's like a regular house."

"Sure is. A nice one. Good location, huh?"

"Old man Pfeiffenberger lives there."

"He told me himself since his wife died he don't need no house and he wants to go live somewheres in an Elks home or someplace and rent out the house so wit social security and the rent and everythin' he'd be sittin' pretty. Wanted me to rent it from him."

"How much does he want?"

"Sixty a month. A good deal."

"*Sixty*? He'd kick me out the first month."

"Whaddaya payin' now?"

"Twenty, like I told you."

"Couldcha swing thirty?"

"Some months yes and some months no."

"Well, I been lookin' for a nicer place wit more room, but I can't afford no sixty a month neither."

"Wait a goddam minute. . . ."

"It's complete furnished and got two big bedrooms and a dinin' room separate and a hallway and a kitchen . . ."

"One goddam little minute . . ."

". . . and in the cellar a concrete floor. A big cellar, nice and cool you could use it for anythin' . . ."

"If you tink . . ."

". . . and the kitchen, oh, boy, nuttin' like I got here. You tink that potato cake was good, you should taste onct what I could make in a kitchen like in old man Pfeiffenberger's place. . . ."

"I'll be goddammed if . . ."

"What an opportunity! Good deals like dis don't grow on trees, to have a real house, as good as nearly anybody's, with a . . . *woi yesus,* I forgot to tell you about the yard . . ."

"I'll go to hell on roller skates before . . ."

"Big enough to plant big fat onions 'n beefsteak tomatoes 'n all the spuds you can eat 'n cukes 'n rhubard 'n kolarabi 'n carrots . . ."

"Beefsteak tomatoes?"

"As big as your fist, and there's a grapevine in the back and old man Pfeiffenberger and his wife used to sit under it when she was alive in the summers, and dem grapes are just about ready."

"Grapes?"

"You can eat 'em till your belly aches and wit the rest you can make a *barrel* of wine."

"A barrel of wine?"

So Thunder Przewalski and Shakey the Cop became roommates. Old man Pfeiffenberger was at first reluctant, having known Thunder all his life, but Shakey prevailed. Bongo Belly helped them move with his International truck, laughing continuously, and the boys at the Majestic and the boys at Brolly's Bar could talk about nothing else, each predicting how and when such a misalliance must end.

Chapter Twenty

The Hollywood Diner

The dining room of Ella's Lunch, which used to be the furrier's, had a large back room, just as Ella's Lunch had a back room, which was the kitchen. R.K. suggested to his partners that they install a steam table in this back room, along with plates and beverage dispensers. This would save steps and time and streamline the whole operation.

"I'm against it," said Ella. "All I ever wanted was to work for myself. This place is as streamlined as it should be. The money we're making has wings on it."

"It ain't gonna cost that much," said R.K. "The expense is tax-deductible and it would probably pay for itself in no time."

Bill agreed with R.K., and it was done.

A short time after the steam table and beverage dispensers were installed, Dianne began to miss a lot of work. First, she was not feeling well. Then, little Bridget was not feeling well and Dianne had to stay home and take care of her because she was a very sensitive little girl. Finally, Dianne did not come to work and gave no reason at all for not coming.

"I see Her Royal Highness is not with us today," Ella would say.

"Yeah, well, she'll be in tomorrow," R.K. would answer.

But she stayed away and Ella was furious.

"We got *two* kids, you know, and somehow they manage to survive with both us working. Your little princess won't wither and die if the Queen Mother gets out and works for a living like the rest of us."

"Oh, knock it off, Ella," said R.K. "You ain't losing any money."

"Maybe not, but we're all working a hell of a lot harder to support an anemic little blonde from California."

"Knock it off, Ella. You don't have to sling personal stuff around."

What Ella didn't know then but eventually found out was that Dianne had been slyly studying typing and shorthand at home, using correspondence courses, in order to develop a negotiable skill that would free her from the hot greasy confines of Ella's Lunch.

"That's it! I'll be goddammed if I'm gonna send the little lady through college. That is definitely that. I've *had* it."

There were many hard words between Ella and R.K. Bill tried to act as arbiter, but soon had to give it up and stand by, embarrassed, while his wife and his brother called each other indelicate names. At one point Ella told R.K. where he could stick his tiki charm, his remodeling job, his wife and child. R.K. replied that only hers could hold such volume. They did not restrict their animosity to after working hours, and as a result their customers were pulled into the controversy. Soon half the town was choosing up sides.

The partnership was dissolved.

R.K. sealed up the archway and ordered the equipment necessary to run a restaurant in his half, where the furrier had been. The Coca-Cola company supplied him with a sign almost identical to Ella's except that his eating establishment was to be called "The Hollywood Diner." R.K. sent away for autographed pictures of movie stars and hung them on the walls and had a grand opening during which Stanley Prizbilik won the door prize of dinner for two and two tickets to the Capital Theatre.

After the dust of the differences between Ella and R.K. settled, the people of Andoshen found themselves in a very awkward position. It was easy for those who had been close to one and did not care for the other, but for the majority who liked both, it was quite trying. Here were two restaurants, side by side, the proprietor of each a decent enough sort. The two proprietors, however, would gladly cut each other's throat. For the customer it was not as simple as patronizing one on one day, the other the next, because if you came out of R.K.'s picking your teeth or letting out a notch on your belt, there was Ella looking out of her window, pretending not to see you. The next day you might eat at Ella's and she would be a bit cool, and of course upon paying your bill and walking outside you would bump into R.K., who could not conceal his disappointment in you.

Many decided, reluctantly and regretfully, that the only way to peace of mind in this situation was to refrain from eating at either establishment.

Both Ella and R.K. were soon within sight of bankruptcy.

Bill went to work at the Blue Mountain Coal Breaker, and Dianne became secretary to Attorney Michael Watson Patrick Quigley, and each of them supported the dying businesses of their respective spouses.

Chapter Twenty-One

Rum-Dummery

Beginning with the first Tuesday after Memorial Day and ending with the first Tuesday after Labor Day, the weekly meetings of the Rum-Dums were held in the Columbia Grove, more usually called the grove, the bush, or (by Doc Rice the dentist) the forest primeval.

From September to May, due to inclement weather, there were no meetings except for the annual indoor winter extravaganza, the only gathering to which women (and men who might not normally be) were invited. The extravaganza followed a sit-down dinner for three hundred and was always written and directed by the editor of the *Call* and always involved a number of the men in drag doing an off-color parody of a current Broadway musical, such as "Annie Get Your Gunnysack" or "The Pajama Frame" or "Carouse-a-Sol."

The Columbia Grove (named for the local brew) was a clearing at the end of a long dirt road that started at the blacktop. It was surrounded by wooded hillocks and featured two great stone fireplaces, a number of picnic tables, and a huge roof supported by wooden stanchions. Planks had been affixed along all of the stanchions so that the result was a rustic open-air rectangular bar with a roof above in case of unexpected rain. In the center of the rectangle three or four kegs of beer would be tapped and connected to coil boxes. Members would serve as bartenders as their names came up on a rotating list.

Likewise, each week a team of four members would assume the responsibility of preparing and serving the food. There were no dues for the Rum-Dums, but every member who planned to attend the Tuesday meeting would have to find one of the four on the serving committee and pay him the required two dollars for the dinner and beer.

A typical menu, cooked on and served from the stone fireplaces, consisted of: two dozen steamed clams, bean soup, green salad, corned beef and cabbage and boiled potatoes, corn on the cob, Italian bread and butter. There was no dessert.

After the meal the members would toss their paper plates into garbage cans and their silverware into immense pots of hot water on the fireplaces. They would then gather at the bar.

The Vice-Grand Guzzler would call for silence, which would not be completely rendered, and then he would lead them in song:

> *Hurrah, hurrah, for the Rum-Dums,*
> *Hurrah for the Knights of the Bar,*
> *We drink our beer with all good cheer,*
> *And we are mighty glad that we are here.*

After the first verse they would pause and drink heartily and sigh as though they had finished a long shift before taking up the second verse:

We're the Rum-Dums, Jolly Rum-Dums,
Drinkers to the core,
From a barroom to another,
Looking for some more.
Oh, G.G., nights are too short
For our barroom sport,
Morning comes too soon.
If the G.G. puts up with us,
We'll all stay till noon.

They would all lift their glasses and now total silence would occur, and the Vice-G.G. would count from one to ten, on each number the glasses would rise a bit higher, and the Grand Guzzler himself would speak:

" 'Tis ten o'clock, that mystic hour, when the great elbow of Rum-Dummery creaks and bends, and goblets of amber fluid are raised on high to drink a solemn toast to those against whom the pledge of temperance has reared its ugly head, but also to those whose wives and sweethearts keep aloof.

"Drunk or sober, a Rum-Dum is never forgotten, never forsaken, as long as his convivial brothers get together. To our absent brothers."

His toast would be repeated by all in unison, "To our absent brothers," and all would drink.

Then they would sing again:

We're true Rum-Dums of a sort,
Good fellowship we seek,
Good beer drinking is our sport,
Meetings are every week.
We go roaming here and there
In pursuit of beer,

So raise your glasses up and drink
To all the Rum-Dums that's here.

"To all the Rum-Dums that's here!"

Only one other formality remained. Each guest was to be introduced and each guest was to display his talent for the entertainment of the members.

Doc Rice was the first to rise. "Gentlemen, my guest this evening is Stump Bonomo. Some of you may know him as the reigning champion of the Tri-County Finger League. His digital expertise does not end, however, with that famous contribution of the Italians to our culture. Mr. Bonomo has also mastered the ancient art of playing the spoons, and he has equipped himself with two of our best."

Amid applause, Stump ducked under the plank and sat in the center. He played "Roll Out the Barrel," alternating between his wooden knee and his one of flesh. It was a stirring performance.

(The composer of the piece was known to all of them and most had known him personally. His name was Jolly Jack Robel, and during the Depression he reputedly sold all rights to his song for one thousand dollars and considered himself one of the most successful of contemporary artists. The song later went on to sell in the millions, was sung in an Academy-Award-winning movie, and has since become a part of the American heritage of folk music, long after the thousand dollars were gone. But he had achieved Andoshen immortality: he was "The Boy Who Wrote 'Roll Out the Barrel.' ")

Next Lawyer Michael Patrick Watson Quigley stood up and introduced Wing Wingrodski. "This young man," he said, "has a way with a word, and if he fulfills his promise may some day become a writer, or a lawyer . . . or a thief."

Wing himself said, taking stage center and stilling the laughter, "Telling horror stories is my specialty, but I think this ain't the time or the place, so I'll just tell you what happened to Sadie Schmidt when she went to work the other morning. Every morning was the same. She would pass by a line of men on each side of her, doing their jobs, and as she passed them she'd call them by name, 'Hello, Harry. Hello, Sammy. Hi, Jerk.' "

Naturally, Wing imitated her voice and minced along as she might.

"Well, one day, this particular morning I'm talkin' about, the manager of the plant caught her and he took her aside and said, 'Look, Miss Schmidt, I don't mind you walking through calling all those fellows by their first names, that's all right I guess, but why did you have to call that one poor guy *Jerk?*' Sadie said, 'Look, mister, that guy is my brother and if I want to call him jerk, I'll *call* him jerk. Whaddaya think of that?' The plant manager said, 'Now, wait a minute, we have a company policy here that says no two members of the same family can work in this plant. Now I don't know whether to lay you or jerk off.' "

Those who got it immediately spit out their mouthfuls of beer in order not to choke. As the slower ones caught on, they beat their mugs on the planks. A few fell off their benches. Wing Wingrodski almost guaranteed that when his name came up on the waiting list he would be admitted to membership. It might take several years, but once up he would be in.

Mr. Wowak, Estelle's father, then rose to introduce his guest. "My guest is Tony Taylor from the cigar factory. Maybe some of you know him. Readin' is what he does best, and he's gonna read a couple things for us tonight."

The reader had racked his brain for something they might appreciate. He knew that the hour and the food and the beer would make them sentimental, but there was always resistance to poetry, and of course he hadn't known he would be following Wing Wingrodski.

"Gentlemen, I thought I'd read you a poem by a minor poet from right around here in Pennsylvania, from the Dutch country. I know that several of you speak the language. Hope you like it. Here goes.

"*Ain't*, by William J. Meter:

> "*When the maple gets its red leaves onc't,*
> *And the* gicklyfees *ain't sweet no more;*
> *When the sneaky cold kills all the fields,*
> *You'll be my sweetheart, ain't, just like before?*
>
> "*Remember when we blowed the dandelions*
> *In Adams' field, to see the kids we'd get?*
> *Ain't the field was gray with dandelions*
> *And you kissed me and said my mouth was wet?*
>
> "*I love you so . . . and we can get a house*
> *And you can fix it nice with paint.*
> *And when the stars is out we'll feel so fine;*
> *But when the stars is all, you'll love me, ain't?*"

Their applause and cheers of appreciation were better than he had expected. He heard someone say, "Ah, there's nothing like a read of poetry to warm up old, cold hearts."

"Now, that's what I call poetry."

"That's *people* poetry."

"Stuff you can understand."

After an Irish tenor, a harmonica player, another dirty-joke teller, and a Lithuanian juggler, the group sang one more traditional song before settling down to serious beer drinking.

"Little Sir Echo, how do you do, hello?"

From off in the woods came the answer from someone who had slipped away earlier.

"Hell—o!"

"Little Sir Echo, how do you do, hello."

"Hell—o!" from the woods.

"Hello."

"Hell—o!"

"Hello."

"Hell—o!"

"Little Sir Echo, how do you do, hello."

"Hell—o! Now go the fuck to bed!"

The conclusion of this song signaled the departure for the early quitters, some of whom even at this early hour could not leave under their own power.

"Crazy, huh?" said Mr. Wowak to the reader.

"Unusual, let's say."

"Bet there ain't another bunch like this in the United States."

"Not even in Russia."

"How's it goin' at the cigar factory?"

"It's an easy job, doing what I like to do anyway, but I'm practically starving."

"In America no one starves," said Mr. Wowak.

"That's not exactly true," said the reader.

"Well, you won't, and you're doin' what you like. Fairly clean, ain't it?"

"Yeah, once you get used to the smell."

"Safe?"

"Completely."

"That counts for a lot."

"Thing is," said the reader, "I want to get married."

"Anybody I know?"

The reader returned the miner's smile.

"I raised Estelle as good as I could," said Mr. Wowak. "I had years of tellin' her what to do, but she's a woman now, and that's all over. She does what she wants now."

"She wants to get married."

"I know," said Mr. Wowak.

"We can't afford it."

"That's always a problem."

"The two of us together, we could probably squeak along, but what if we have a kid?"

"It happens."

"You're telling me."

"Look, Tony, get out of this town. It's a dead town, a depressed area . . ."

"Also home."

". . . it's different for us in the mines. We never knew anything else. Now we got houses and families and if we keep up our union dues, *maybe* there'll be a little pension, some social security, probably some Black-Lung benefits, God save us. You're young enough to get a job somewhere, maybe in the car plants, and make good money."

"You're right, but I waited too long. One time maybe I could have, but now the place is next to me. I get the heebie-jeebies when I'm away from it. And Estelle's the same way. The strangle hold of home."

"A smart guy like you should know better."

"Has nothing to do with brains. It's guts."

"So whaddaya gonna do?"

"I want a job in the mines."

"And you're talking about guts. That's *all* you'll need. You're crazy, that's what you are. You ever been down in a mine?"

"No."

"Your daddy was a miner."

"I know," said the reader.

"And that's what you want for yourself?"

"I want to get married."

"There's no poetry down there, Tony. Don't let anybody tell you different. The work is too hard for a mule to do, and you're scared from one end of the shift to the other, poopin' your pants when you hear a creak you ain't heard before and you stop to think how far underground you are. Below all the worms and bugs, where there's no living thing but you and the other miners and a few rats that'll have dinner with you. You'll feed 'em too, 'cause of the other stuff they eat. And when you finally go up and get home, there's no way to wash it away, outside or in, and when you sleep at night you dream about it."

"I still want to get married."

"I can't stop you."

"Get me a job."

"No."

The reader said nothing more, just drank his beer. Mr.

Wowak too was silent for a long time. Finally he said, "I'll do this, Tony, I'll see if there's anything in the Blue Mountain Breaker. It ain't much easier but at least it's safer. You'll come home as black as if you was diggin' the stuff, but chances are better you'll come home with all your fingers."

The reader got the job at the breaker and he and Estelle got married. They moved in with his mother, who was happy to have them. A young man who had flunked out after one year at Albright became the new reader at the cigar factory.

Dear Son,

Rum-Dums started 30 years ago, with a few men from the Mackerel Wrapper, Bell Telephone, and Penna. Power & Lite Co. At first, there were only about a dozen men, later, they set up some by-laws, and one was limiting the number of members to 45. They have a board of Governors, Secretary, Treasurer, and the head man, who is called a Grand Guzzler, G.G., for short. In order to be a G.G. you must first be voted in by the board of Governors. To join the RD's you must be invited to their Tuesday nite parties and when there is an opening, which happens when an RD dies or moves out of state, the board of Governors votes on your membership. There is always a waiting list. They do not allow any liquor, or women (women can't even enter the grounds for any reason), cards or any form of gambling at these affairs. Beer is the only beverage allowed. If you misbehave by violating any of their by-laws, you are automatically out, but this has happened only a couple times. Thru the years, lawyers, Doctors, business men, brewmasters, and other professional men were members, still are.

Love,
Mom & Pop

P.S. Pop was on the board and was a G.G. six years ago.

Chapter Twenty-Two

Eggshell

The day after Eggshell Oechsle had done the "dastardly deed," a term reporters and Doc Rice favored, the Andoshen *Evening Call* devoted its first page to the many details. The next day, reflectively, they ran a three-column picture of him, under the heading: THE STORY OF A BAD BOY. A stranger in town might look at the picture, shake his head grimly, and say, "That's a bad boy, all right."

His wild bushy hair and vacuous eyes made him look disoriented and confused and probably annoyed at having been made the integral element of a process he did not understand or value. Below his picture was the story of his eighteen years. The boys at the Majestic gathered around one paper and listened as the story was read aloud, and they chuckled over Eggshell's early escapades, which brought back memories for all because they had participated in these escapades, either actively or vicariously. They read the story and chuckled and wondered how old Eggshell had lasted as long as he had.

When he was twelve, the story said, he had a job watching Matt's Garage and Body Shop while everyone took off for a long dinner. One day it was very cold in the garage and Eggshell got into a car and started it, turning on the heater to keep warm. He fell asleep, and by the time Matt and his two helpers returned, Eggshell had turned blue, the hue of which made the hairs on Matt's neck stand on end. The doctor and the Rescue, Hook, and Ladder truck arrived at the same time. The doctor gave him the once-over and said, "Goner."

Since they were there anyway and had the new equipment (which they had never used, and wanted to), the team from R, H, and L gave Eggshell the full treatment. The crowd that gathers to witness any human drama watched with admiration and awe as the R, H, and L team efficiently performed their duties. Suddenly Eggshell's arm twitched and his chest heaved. Cries of *"Woyaku!"* were heard and the inevitable order, "Give 'im some air! Move back!" was issued.

Eggshell survived, which insured the good reputation of R, H, and L, but damaged irreparably the already shaky reputation of the attending physician. Eggshell survived, but it was said that he was never quite right afterward. His friends chose this event as the mystical bad break in life which causes everything that follows to be spoiled up, ending finally in tragedy.

The paper also described the time Eggshell was lost in the woods. He was missing for three days and nights, and everyone from Troop 21 of the B.S.A. to the First Catholic Slovak Ladies Association in America and Canada organized a search party, which in some cases, notably the Rum-Dums, actually became a party in the usual connotation of that word. The next Sunday, hard words from the pulpit were leveled at that element of the community which could revel in the teeth of a young boy's ordeal.

Eggshell finally walked out of the woods on a highway halfway to Harrisburg. He walked to a roadside stand and spent his only dime on a birch beer, and after he drank it he sat musing over the events of the past three days, one of the most memorable of which was an afternoon spent sitting and masturbating in an icy forest stream.

The man who owned the stand recognized him from the picture he had seen in the paper and asked him, "Ain't you the kid's been lost in the woods?"

"Guess so, unless there's another. *I'm* sure lost."

"Well, hell, kid, everyone's figuring you're one dead duck."

"Well, hell," he said, imitating the man, "I ain't, though."

The man called the police and everyone rejoiced. Eggshell was asked why, since he had a dime, he hadn't called someone as soon as he found his way out of the woods and saw a phone.

"I was thirsty," he answered.

When he was fifteen Eggshell discovered a cyst high on his back, near his neck. Every three minutes Eggshell would touch it to see if it had gone away.

"Well, I got cancer," he said to the boys at the Majestic, because he knew, like everyone else, that a lump on the body that wouldn't go away was the forerunner of cancer, and cancer killed you. Knowing those facts, and having had previous experience with the medical profession, he saw no reason to consult a doctor.

Someone told him that raw yams were good for cancer, so he began to eat them exclusively. He found they were easier to digest grated. The first two days were like trying to quit smoking, something he attempted once when he was twelve. By the end of the first week, however, he had become used to raw grated yams and had no desire for anything else.

The cyst did not go away, but by the fourth week of his yam fast something incredible happened to his pool game. He could not be beaten. He found himself deciding on impossible shots and then simply *telling* the ball to go into the specified pocket when the cue ball hit it. He won Moxie after Moxie, instructing the counterman to put them in the well for him until after he was cured of cancer and could drink them.

By the sixth week on raw grated yams his game had unfortunately gone to pot, but who could expect otherwise? After all, the cue stick was growing leafy branches, the pool balls had grown little legs and were running away from him, and the cue ball began to sass him, saying, "Hit me, go ahead, hit me as hard as you can, you punk."

When the balls became yams and crumpled into grated piles whenever they hit together and Eggshell would hover over the table trying to brush them into his hands and then into his mouth, the boys at the Majestic thought it was no longer funny and hauled him off to Doc Rice, who, though his license extended only to dental work, knew a sebaceous cyst when he saw one and lanced Eggshell's for him.

One other side effect of the forty-seven-day raw yam fast was that Eggshell became the world's leading connoisseur of yams. Only the very finest made any difference to him.

When he was sixteen, the newspaper account went on, he was working under an old Ford supported by one of the flimsy bumper jacks they include with the original purchase of an automobile. The jack slipped, as they often do, and the car came down on him, breaking several ribs and pinning him to the floor. He lay there for nearly an hour, waiting for death, and was finally discovered by his father, who called the Rescue, Hook, and Ladder, same team.

Several months later, fully recuperated and shooting pool at the Majestic, Eggshell was reminded once again by the others of his basic stupidity, clearly illustrated by the fact that he would slide under a car supported only by a cheap bumper jack. And what about the yams? And what about the time he came out of the woods? And the time he jumped off the roof with an umbrella? And the time he took a leak on an electric fence and damn near electrocuted his peter? And the time he ran the car in a garage with all the doors shut? And the time with the Indian?

"I wish the time wit the Ford on me woulda finished me off," said Eggshell.

"You don't mean that," said Jake the Fake. "In this world it's one shot and gone, and even if there is a heaven there wouldn't be no pool tables up there, so what good would it be?"

Jake the Fake had been run over by a train, and any man who has been run over by a train has earned the right to become a philosopher.

"The church says there's a heaven."

"Church is like cowboy movies," said Jake the Fake. "You seen one, you seen them all."

The time with the Indian could be mentioned in passing but to discuss it was forbidden by Eggshell, and, uncharacteristically, the boys at the Majestic never used it as a weapon against him. The newspaper account, however, freely rehashed the incident, though the best part, of course, was unknown to the paper.

Eggshell had caught motorcycle fever, a malady that strikes most sixteen-year-old boys, is seemingly purged by their parents, but actually lies dormant for another sixteen years, at which time it flares up again, to be purged this time by their wives. Sixteen years later it strikes yet a third time, but by now their wives have lost interest, and the only ones who *could* purge the raging fever, their children, are more apt to feed it, so that at forty-eight these men finally succumb to the disease and don their helmets, boots, and gloves to scream down the highway on two wheels after the sun. The lucky ones break only their collar bones and pamper the ache lovingly for the remainder of their lives.

In Eggshell's case there was no one to say no. His mother had run off years ago with two sailors, local boys home on leave, who convinced her that there was nothing like a war to free the spirit and to insure an atmosphere of good fun for twenty-four hours a day. They told her she'd better get with it because there was no way to know how much longer the war might last, though for their own part they hoped it would go on forever. Both Eggshell and his father believed the reports that she was presently behind the bar in one of the innumerable Norfolk sailor joints, but neither had any sort of curiosity about her. His father would not deny him the Indian bike as long as it was understood that it would not cost the father a dime.

So Eggshell set out to buy the Indian, which had been sitting in Moe's garage for months, covered with canvas, while Moe lay on his porch nursing his broken back, the result of a lack of proper respect for gravel. Moe had resigned his presidency of the African Violets Motorcycle and Garden Club and put the Indian up for sale.

It was not very difficult to raise the money because Eggshell was an excellent thief when he wanted to be, though it gave him no real pleasure and he practiced thievery only when he needed something badly, like the Indian. He also hired out as muscle, though this too, more pleasant than stealing, gave him no genuine satisfaction. Moreover, the risks were greater, commensurate with the rewards. It was in pursuit of this occupation that he almost became involved in big trouble: murder.

He was helping out at the Vets and was told to keep his eye on a certain Dutchman in the front wing of the upstairs facilities. This was the room of the nickel slot machines, and the Dutchman was suspected of using slugs. If Eggshell could catch him at it, he was to break a few fingers in the interest of punitive justice.

He loafed around, having a beer, dropping a few nickels into a machine, and listening to the Dutchman, an all-day victim of the charm of a particular Bally machine, talk to his one-arm bandit as he might a mean dog, saying, "Oh, mister, you, if I had some bad sauerkraut, would I ever feed it to you full and make you sick to throw up all them nickels."

At one point Eggshell left him alone in the room for thirty or forty seconds and then ran quickly back inside.

The Dutchman saw him coming and began frantically stuffing a nickel into the machine, but Eggshell held the metal arm fast and inspected the rectangular window on the front of the machine that revealed the last five coins put into it. Three of them were not coin of the realm.

"Whatcha pullin', Dutchy?"

"What? What? I'm here playin' all day, so now what?"

"You're puttin' slugs in the damn machine, Dutchy," said Eggshell, tapping the glass window with his fingertip.

"What slugs? What do I know from slugs, I'm an old man."

He squinted and looked where Eggshell was tapping and said, "Oh, a mistake has been made. Them are trolley car tokens from Scranton. I had 'em in the pocket same as the nickels, ain't?"

Eggshell grabbed his hand and began to break his fingers. The Dutchman twisted out of his grip and ran in terror to the window, going through it and down two stories to his death.

The Vets claimed the old man was alone at the time and must have been despondent over losing his money and therefore committed suicide. No one but the law believed this. There was some fuss concerning a minor on the premises at the time, and many, including the widow, were inclined to put the finger on him, but it was explained that he was employed for janitorial duties and was nowhere near the scene of the misfortune at the time of the tragic suicide.

Eggshell kept his mouth shut and received enough money to buy Moe's Indian. The incident was reported and soon forgotten, in a manner familiar to the county. Eggshell tried to remember, for his own benefit, whether he had reached out to grab the man or to push him through the window. He had the tactile memory of both his hands touching the Dutchy's back, which led him to conclude that he probably gave him a little shove.

Certainly, getting the Indian was an event. From his porch, Moe explained to Eggshell, who had never driven a motorcycle, that although it was basically the same principle as a car, in practice there was a world of difference because both hands and feet are busy and one must feel absolutely physically attuned to the machine in order to handle it around corners and at high speeds. Eggshell listened to him with only half an ear because once he had learned the gears and where clutch, gas, and brakes were located, he was eager to present himself to the town in his new role. He had already acquired the studded boots and gloves and motorcycle cap (no phony helmet for him), which could not cover all his hair and made him look as though he had hairy wings on his head, ready to fly him through space. He had put out thirty bucks for a Harley-Davidson jacket, and it was a beauty of black leather and six zippered pockets and studs. As Moe spoke, Eggshell impatiently worked a wrist zipper.

Instruction over, he put his foot on the starter crank, and like initial intercourse put his full weight to the plunge that can never again be duplicated, the first. The Injun engine caught and roared and Eggshell showed all his teeth to the road and moved down it smoothly, on two wheels at last!

For the first three blocks he paid his dues to caution, then screwed on the gas. He rounded his first corner at high speed, leaning incredibly far, as if he had never walked a day in his life. He was so pleased with the corner that he wanted to stop on that frame of the movie of his life and study himself in the third person.

He forgot that he was still underway, and he hit a curb. The Indian flipped once and came to rest on a porch. Eggshell flew higher and farther, Mercury with the misplaced wings, and crashed through the living-room window of Mr. and Mrs. Peter Panimo. He lay unconscious on a bed of twisted Venetian blinds and broken glass at the feet of Nancy Panimo, their teen-age daughter, who had been sitting at a card table against the wall with her younger sister Carol, working a jigsaw puzzle.

While Carol screamed and covered her face and huddled against the wall, Nancy bent over Eggshell and lightly slapped his cheeks, as she had seen them do in the movies.

He came to and felt the cool touch of her hand against his cheek and looked into her lovely dark Italian eyes with only one of his own because some blood had run into the other and clouded it.

"I love you," he said. "Marry me, I don't care if we are different religions."

He hadn't even noticed that his left ear had been torn away.

Nancy was a private rebel, and although she tacitly agreed with her father that no girl should take seriously any boy who flies through her window on a motorcycle, causing damage to someone else's property and mutilating himself in the bargain, she still thought it awfully romantic to meet under such conditions, since most girls meet their dates at parties, dances, things like that. She found Eggshell amusing and liked to go out with him, and decided she would continue to do so, at least until he removed the bandage.

Eggshell, however, fell viciously in love. So much so that he would not even allow the boys at the Majestic to utter her name, as though she were a goddess too holy for her name to be spoken aloud. He asked her to marry him every time he saw her, until eventually she tired of it and told him her life would be happier if he would withdraw from it.

He cried, for the only time in his memory.

His recovery was slow. Just when everyone thought he was over it, he publicly threatened to kill the young man who was said to be dating Nancy, and in fact began to stalk him, appearing in doorways whenever the new young man got out of his car. The young man finally complained to Chief Red Sweeney about it and Red told Shakey the Cop to lean on Eggshell, mentioning several unsolved crimes for which the proper criminal had not yet been found.

And so the seasons changed and winter came, and one Saturday night Eggshell took his bath and shaved and dressed and thought he would probably walk uptown and shoot some pool. His uncle, who lived with his father and Eggshell, was asleep in his room, having just concluded a forty-eight-hour bender. His father was at the kitchen table, finishing his supper.

Eggshell cut off a good chunk of baloney and gnawed it lethargically, leaning against the refrigerator.

"Big shot," said his father.

Eggshell said nothing.

"It's too cold to parade up and down Main Street."

Eggshell still did not speak.

"And you're dressed too nice to be thieving. Where're you headed? Turn your head and listen with your ear you got left and answer your old man when he talks to you."

"To hell with you," said Eggshell and continued to gnaw the baloney.

"You going to see your guinea? *Any*body's guinea! The skinny little guinea with the meatball nose!"

"Whaddaya mean, meatball nose?"

It was not a challenge, but a simple question.

His father began to sing it, "The skinny little guinea with the meatball nose, the skinny little guinea with the meatball nose, not to mention the pizza ass."

His father left the table singing it and lay down on the living-room sofa singing it and acutally fell asleep singing it, "The skinny little guinea with the meatball nose, the skinny little guinea with the meatball . . ."

Eggshell wiped his hands on the dishrag and went to the hall closet. He took out the single-barrel shotgun and reached into the small square box on the shelf for two shells. He put one into the shotgun and the other into his mouth. He pulled back the hammer, aimed at his sleeping father's head, and fired. He broke the barrel, flipped out the spent shell, and inserted the one he carried in his mouth. He pulled back the hammer and pointed the shotgun at the top of the stairs, waiting for his uncle to appear. When he did, staggering and shading his eyes, Eggshell said, "You're just as bad," and shot him. The uncle rolled down the stairs, his feet clattering against the railings of the bannister. It reminded Eggshell of a cowboy movie.

Eggshell went back to the closet and put on his jacket. He took the shotgun and the box of shells with him and walked out of the house.

He was shooting eight-ball with Billy Buddusky when Chief Red Sweeney came into the Majestic with both Shakey the Cop and Dumshock the Cop, and everyone knew immediately that somebody was in the most serious kind of trouble. Shakey had his hand on his club and Dumshock had his hand on his revolver.

Chief Red went directly to Eggshell, who was bending forward to make a shot, and said calmly, "Eggshell, put down your cue."

Eggshell took the shot, made the ball, and put down his cue without disturbing any of the other balls on the table. Billy Buddusky backed away from the table and sat on the bench next to Duncan, who dangled the rack between his knees.

"Let's take a ride to the station," said Chief Red.

"You givin' me a choice?"

"Nope. Putcha hands on the edge of the table, legs back and spread apart."

Eggshell did as he was told and Chief Red frisked him.

They put him in handcuffs and sat him in the back seat of the squad car with Shakey and drove the four blocks back to the station.

"This ain't a surprise to you," said Chief Red, with no hint of a question in it.

"They got what they deserved. It's the only favor for the world I ever done."

"You were always a mean kid."

"So now everybody can get even with me."

"What did you do with the shotgun, Eggshell?"

"Threw it in the culvert at Juneberry Alley. With the shells. Was gonna take it to Main and Center and start blastin'. That's what I was gonna do."

"What made you change your mind?"

"Didn't have no gloves."

"Huh?"

"My hands got cold," said Eggshell. "Carryin' the shotgun and shells."

In the county prison, awaiting trial, Eggshell Oechsle refused to stand to salute the flag. He said he was too tired. His fellow prisoners, with a little help from their friends, painted him in the national colors.

Dear Son,

Eggshell Oechsle.

Just writing his name gives me the shivers. Brrrrrr! What a spooky kid. You can imagine how the Panimos felt, knowing their daughter once was mixed up with him. She was always a bratty little thing.

What a grisly sight he was, with one ear and his puffed-up eyes and his mouth always hanging open. Should have been put away after he killed that poor man in the Vets that time, but as Walter Winchell once said, "If you want to kill your whole family and get away with it, take them to Lantenengo County, Pennsylvania." He really did say that once. I think it was after a man from Gibbsville stabbed his brother 42 times on a busy street downtown and was found innocent.

As far as I know, Eggshell was put in the State Hospital and is still there.

Love,
Mom & Pop

Chapter Twenty-Three

Angels of Destruction

It was ten o'clock at night and Ella was weary to the most hidden of her bones. It would have been a good weariness if it had been the result of heavy business, but it was the result instead of waiting and watching the door, hoping for customers, different customers who would order more than coffee and peanut butter pie.

She wiped her forehead with a dish towel and threw the towel into the sink. This lunchroom was to be a good life, she thought, and now it will be the death of me. What poor Mother would say if she could see what's happened.

She poured herself half a cup of coffee and sipped it black as she filled the bucket and got the mop. If she had it to do over again, she would still marry Bill, though to be honest remaining single seemed to be the better way. Bill was a good man, kind and gentle and generous, but a husband should be more: wise, hard, and ahead of things. Why didn't Bill see it would happen like this? Of course, there were the children and marriage is necessary for that. No one had better kids. But she could not say she enjoyed them, and when she did have a chance to be with them she was too tired to be anything but irritated by their noise and impossible demands on her energy.

She began to swing the mop along the floor in wide arcs, left to right, right to left.

If only R.K. had not come back to town. That man is the angel of destruction. In his heart he is a pool-room bum and will never be anything but, no matter how much he talks about the hotel business and now about the restaurant business. A pool-room bum, no matter how good he thinks he is at remodeling and attracting people to the place. Where are those people now? They've left him. Attracting people. That's how the angels of destruction work. They look good, they talk good, some of them even smell good. They tell lies with the deepest of sincerity until finally they believe in their own lies, and anyone who gives them five minutes of their time deserves all the trouble they get in return. Oh, they look good, though, in a tarnished forty-nine-cent way, with tiki charms against their bare chests, with straps around their wrists, with huge pinky rings that they must move from one pinky to the other, keeping ahead of the green caused by cheapness.

She finished mopping the floor, emptied the dirty water into the sink and put away the bucket and mop. She carried the metal rack of clean coffee cups back into the lunchroom and began to stack them under the counter.

What is this thing about brothers? Why do they feel they have any claim on each other after they've both become men? After they become men and take wives, why do they feel any responsibility toward each other and each other's wife? If Bill had been a good husband, a smart husband, he would have given them a cup of coffee that night and wished them well instead of taking them into his home as permanent guests where they could parade around in their underwear and cheap tiki charms. If Bill had been a good husband then, he could be *a* husband now, and she could be a wife, and they would not be two still and exhausted lumps side-by-side on a double bed.

She took the empty metal cup tray back into the kitchen. She heard the bell in the lunchroom that signified a customer had entered. "Damn!" she swore through her teeth. "They wait until I'm closing before they come in."

She left the kitchen and saw R.K. sitting at the counter. She looked at her sweaty hands and brushed the hair away from her forehead. Though there was a counter between them, she was conscious of her old stockings rolled below her knees, the way the fat old Polack women who work at the dress factory wear them.

"What the hell do *you* want?"

"Well, let's see," he said, picking up a menu between two fingers, as though it carried dangerous bacteria. "I want a hamburger. With fried onions."

"The grill is off. Go next door . . . if you got the stomach for it."

"They closed long ago. They don't need the business."

"We're closed too. As of now. We don't need the business any more than they don't. Ha, ha."

"You're the original, ain't you?" said R.K. "Cut off your nose to spite your face."

"Oh, sure, I'm Mrs. Meanie. *I* was the one wanted to enlarge and remodel. *I* was the one wanted to be partners with deadbeats. *I* was the one wanted to install a second steam table. *I* was the one had it all worked out. It was *my* lazy wife decided she was too good to work in a restaurant. *I* came home from California with nothing in my pockets but my hands and with me a knocked-up wife and no place to live. *I* was . . ."

"You're beginning to bore me," said R.K.

"How you 'n Bill could come out of the same womb is the eighth wonder of the world."

"Look, Ella, don't you think this has gone on as long as it should go on? How much longer you think either of us can last?"

"Go home and take care of your stupid wife. She might have to lift a little finger to wipe her skinny butt. After a hard day on Lawyer Quigley's lap."

Ella leaned her stomach against the counter. She felt childish and vindictive, but she could not help herself.

"That's not what's eatin' you," said R.K.

"I don't blame her. If you can get away with it, I say get away with it."

"Is that what's eatin' you?"

"Why don't you go back to California?"

"I was born here."

"You're miserable and you're ignorant. You make me sick," she said.

"I can see how sick I make you."

"You're ignorant, as ignorant as they come."

"Me?"

"Ignoramus."

"You think so. I've been around."

"Like a doughnut."

"Ugh."

"Mr. Hollywood. Running across the country to suck around movie stars and then comin' home with your tail between your legs. Who're you kidding, you chronic liar."

"Cut it out," he said.

"Hotel business, my ass! You were probably pimping . . . or worse."

"Okay, just knock it off."

"Rita Hayworth wouldn't *spit* on you!"

R.K. got up and snapped his first two fingers against her belly, just above where it touched the counter. She fell back, eyes wide and gasping for her breath. R.K. jumped over the counter and twisted her arm behind her back and pushed her ahead of him into the kitchen. He spun her around, pushed her back against the sink and forced his lips against hers. He pressed his hand between her legs.

"That's what was eatin' you all along, queenie. Says the ignoramus."

"God, how I hate you," she said, kissed him, and parted her legs.

Chapter Twenty-Four

Gunner Walsh

Gunner Walsh came into Brolly's just after the noon whistle blew at the brewery. Doc Rice was drinking his lunch; his next appointment was at twelve forty-five. "My God, I've spent all morning with my fingers in the rotting mouth of an old man," he said. "What is Truth? What is Beauty?" Thunder Przewalski was not working and sat in his corner drinking beer, from time to time sprinkling some salt on it to work up a new head. Wing Wingrodski and Bull McCoy were discussing the virtues of one of the parish priests and several of his young female parishioners. Brolly himself was still reading yesterday's *Call*.

It was clear to all that the Gunner was in pain. His mouth curved downward and his teeth were clamped together and he limped. He tried to settle one buttock onto the stool, like Kayo Mackey on a cold, damp day, but gave it up in favor of standing.

"Let's have a shot of Kessler's and a beer, Brolly," he said. "I just come from the doctor's."

"Excuse my temerity," said Doc Rice. "I am a professional man and self-employed and it appears to me that you are distraught."

"Doc, don't talk to me about this rot, I got the scars to prove it," said Gunner, throwing down the shot and chasing it with beer.

With the insight of a tavern keeper of many years Brolly said, "What do you expect? I told you a dozen times to go home. I told your wife on the phone a dozen times that you just left. You make a liar outa me, a drunk outa yourself, and a frustrated woman outa your old lady. What do you expect?"

"You remember me from the old days, Brolly. In the old days if I was on a guy I'd beat him unmercifully half to death till you couldn't hardly even recognize who he used to be. Now when I get in a fight I might still beat the badness outa him, but then I feel like sorry for the poor punk. I even help him up and brush him off and ask him if he's hurt bad. I buy the punk a beer. I'm getting old and soft, what I let that tiny woman get away with with me."

"*A desirable calamity,*" said Doc Rice, "*desirable calamity,* and, Brolly, we are friends and I'm sorry to have to tell you this, but since vodka can't go bad it must be your orange juice."

"Your rotten insides, prob'ly," said Thunder Przewalski.

"My goodness, I've been singled out," said Doc Rice, putting his hand to his heart. "The Ruin of Rattlin' Run, local hero and scallywag has deigned to speak to me."

Thunder pulled his little finger as though it were a trigger, and he belched aloud, forming the belch into, "Bow-wow."

"The sum total of his education," said Doc Rice. "As my monthly contribution to charity and the less fortunate, Thunder, permit me the pleasure of working on your teeth. Gratis, of course."

"I work on me own choppers."

"*God,* how did I ever land in this place, where men put greasy pliers into their own mouths?"

"You were born here, Doc," said Brolly. "All of us were born here."

Doc Rice shuddered.

Wing Wingrodski, who liked to pick up gossip, embellish it, and pass it on, urged them back to the matter of Gunner Walsh's wife.

"Marriage," said Gunner. "Who can figure it out?"

"*A dull meal with dessert at the beginning,*" quoted Doc Rice.

"C'mon, Doc, can it, will you?" said Wing.

"Couples are splitting every day," said Gunner. "And you know why?" He paused before offering the revelation. "I think more couples split up because of something the two of them don't have in common. Yessir." He ordered a third boilermaker. "You take me now, I like my baseball, I like my football, I like my dis, I like my dat."

"Irrefutably," said Doc Rice.

"I think I'm entitled to watch my games in the afternoon, listen to 'em at night if I want to. She got no use for it. So yesterday in the afternoon the Russo Post softball team is playing the Good Friends and Neighbors Firehouse, and I catch for Good Friends and have no use for the guineas from Russo Post, and she knows dat. So she says, 'You have to come home early because Annette and Harry are comin' over and I'm gonna pan broil some steaks.' Annette and Harry are her side of the family that for years were out in Oklahoma standin' in mud up to their asses with the wind blowin' sand in their faces. Then all of a sudden they come back again and I have to interrupt my softball game to eat steaks wit 'em. So I told her okay but I was gonna stop at Brolly's after the game and have a couple coolers. You know how we always come in here, Brolly, stinkin' hot."

"But, Gunner, the rest of the team went home for supper and you were still here drinking beers with your wife on the phone every two minutes."

When the happy softball player, three for four with one of them a home run, and three R.B.I.'s, did get home, drunk with victory and Columbia beer, it was eleven thirty. His wife was in the kitchen washing the supper dishes. Her guests had been gone for an hour. She put some soap and water into the frying pan and put it back on the flame, and made sure to direct only her back to the sound of her husband's voice.

Gunner said, "Kicked the spaghettis outa them tonight, eight to one. I had a homer. I'm so tired I don't think I want supper. I'm just gonna hit the old rack. Taps, taps, all hands turn into your own bunks, taps. The smoking lamp is out, taps."

His wife said nothing and would not turn around.

He shucked off his softball uniform and fell face down on the bed and was soon asleep, the room swirling around him. He snored like a man who had hit a homer and drunk too much beer.

His wife used a pot holder to pick up the hot frying pan, and she emptied the churning sudsy water into the sink. As casually as she did that, she walked into the bedroom and pressed the bottom of the frying pan against her husband's right buttock.

The white searing pain carried to his fingertips, his toes, the tip of his tongue, and the tip of his penis, and his brain exploded in fluorescent stars.

"Mother of God, girl, I can smell my own flesh cooking!" he screamed.

Wordless, she let him suffer for some minutes before spreading soft butter on his burn to quiet his whining and whimpering. But the butter did not help much.

The doctor said that although he had never before seen a pan-burned ass, he did not expect ever to see one again as bad as Gunner's.

"I never had anything to hurt like that," said Gunner to the boys at Brolly's, tears in his eyes, hungry for their sympathy.

"Lucky you wasn't sleepin' on your back," they said to him.

Chapter Twenty-Five

Settling

The reader came home limping from his first day at the breaker. Estelle thought that he had been hurt already, in just one day, and wished that all men could make good money in safe, clean occupations.

"No, I'm not hurt," he said. "I'm just stiff and bone tired. I sit with half my rear end on a plank and lean over the conveyor belt."

"What's your job?"

"Picking slate. I'm a slate picker."

"Dear God," said Estelle.

"It's not that bad. I can stand if I want to, but it's easier sitting on one haunch, though you're stiff at the end of the day."

"I wonder how long I'll be worth this."

"C'mon, Estelle, I'm just not used to it yet."

"It'll drive you crazy," she said.

"No, it's not that bad. It's interesting how quick you're able to pick out the boulders that have coal from the ones that are slate. You just look for that glint of black, sometimes only a thin line. Those you let go onto another conveyor belt that takes them to the main breaker for processing."

"I know," she said.

"It's not that bad. The waste I pull off the belt. It goes down a chute and into a truck below. They take it to one of the culm banks nearby."

She said nothing.

"They give you a huge leather glove for your left hand so you won't cut yourself on the rocks. Another guy works with me, on the other side of the belt. He's got the right glove. We have this little building just for us two, right next to the breaker. One truck from the mines drops a load above us, another truck picks up the waste below us."

"What do you talk about, you and this other guy?"

"Well, we just sort of said hello. When the work starts you can't talk. There's too much noise. The building shakes a lot. The girders are wood. We can talk when we eat, though."

"What did you talk about, then?"

"Oh, I don't remember. Different things."

"I'll run your bath. Rub you down."

"That'll be nice."

"You can quit any time you want to," said Estelle. "It was your idea."

"Right. That's the way I look at it too."

To pass the long monotonous hours of separating slate from coal, the reader silently recited poetry. Since not even shouting could be heard above the noise of the operation, he soon began to recite aloud, all the poems he knew. Sometimes he would sing. His partner never noticed.

Estelle and the reader settled into a kind of slate-picker's happiness. They made good use of every clear Sunday.

One night, sitting together on the sofa, he broke wind, and she said, "I guess that means we're getting used to each other."

The reader's mother died and the slanting shanty became theirs. Like the other women, Estelle cursed the coal dust that blew through openings that water could not penetrate and coated their furniture and got into their linens and into their throats. She cursed the strippings on days when they were blasting, when the windows would rattle and the house would jump and some glasses would fall and break.

The reader became a bit hard of hearing and consequently raised his voice when he didn't have to.

They cheated on the rules and used prophylactics for a time but found they could not easily afford to buy them at three for a quarter and instead practiced rhythm, which seemed to work, until one night they felt too great a need for each other's body and lost their restraint. Estelle became pregnant and in that condition could not stomach the close, humid smell of tobacco and had to quit her job.

They loved each other very much and found great comfort in the home they made together, but often Estelle would fear what marriage made necessary, and often the reader, as he picked slate, would think about the time he wanted to be a poet and move the world.

Chapter Twenty-Six

Looking for Thunder

When two days had passed and the third arrived without Thunder, Shakey thought at first, "The hell with 'im."

But then he worried for fear Thunder was lying somewhere dead, or worse, had killed someone and was on the lam. "*Woi Yesus,* how come I gotta be the one to watch out for him? I ain't the only cop down by Lantenengo County." Shakey thought there must be an end to doing things for those who get only what they deserve. On the other hand, he missed the brute.

When he took over the squad car at four o'clock he asked Swat, who had the previous shift, if he'd happened to run across Thunder during the past eight hours.

"Maybe that was the bounce I felt on the junkyard road. I thought it was a bag of rags, fell off of the sheeny's truck."

"C'mon, Swat. Didcha or dintcha?"

"Wuz he late for din-din, sweetie?"

"Swat, another minute and I be's workin' you over."

"You keep your mitts to home, you goddam bulldog."

"You ain't worth' of that uniform you're wearin'."

"Oh, crap, Shakey, you're such a damn Boy Scout you give me a sore stomach."

"Well, I'm terrible sorry for that. Maybe I should tell you what you give me, maybe. All I asked was if you seen 'im."

"No, I didn't see 'im, somabitch."

"That's all you hadda say and some air coulda been saved between us."

He took possession of the squad car and called head-quarters.

"Chief Red, dis be Shakey the Cop at Main and Center. I got it."

"Roger," said the chief, the want of a nap in his voice.

He made the trip around town and looked into Ella's from the car. Later, he parked and poked his head into Brolly's.

"Thunder been around?"

"Not for a couple days," said Brolly.

"And don't think we don't appreciate it," said Doc Rice, and then added, smelling his hands, "Jesus God, I've been all day with my fingers in the mouth of a whore. And to think some day I'm going to die."

On a long shot Shakey tried Hooversville. The inhabitants huddled in front of their shacks and the mayor said, "Mr. Shakey the Cop, we have broken no laws here in Hooversville, or elsewhere, might I add, save the law of survival."

"Don't getcha bowels in an uproar," said Shakey. "I'm only looking for Thunder Przewalski."

"This man is not welcomed in Hooversville. What's he done now?"

"Nuttin', I was only looking for him."

"Is it true that I understand you 'n this person are sharin' a common house?"

"If it's any of your business, yeah. You share the cost, you share the house."

"But now here you are lookin' for him."

"How'd you like to keep your snotty little beak in your own business?"

He went by Bongo Belly's house and saw him in his undershirt at the curb, tending to his old truck, which had its hood raised. Shakey pulled the squad car to the curb and got out.

"Say there, Bongo Belly, you seen your friend Thunder lately?"

"*My* friend?"

"Well, ain't he?"

"He should be stranded on the desert without toothpaste or toilet paper."

Bongo looked at the motor of his truck. He was sweating and dirty with grease. "I would like to have the man what invented dis truck, and wit me at the time I would like also to have a nice two-pound ball peen hammer."

After he said it, he bent over (with no small difficulty) and picked up his hammer from the sidewalk, as though in preparation for receiving the wish.

"I been lookin' to hell and yonder for two days and ain't seen a trace of 'im," said Shakey.

"Everybody's got troubles. If that's yours, you got the least of them."

"Well, I wouldn't mind findin' the walkin' divil, 'cause I'm bein' afraid he mighta got hurt or something."

"This is always a good possibility," said Bongo Belly.

"I'm gonna keep lookin' for him in the squad car, but ting is, I'm gettin' a little worried 'cause I'm not findin' him."

"Hmmmmm," said Bongo Belly.

"Ting is," said Shakey, "how 'bout gettin' in your truck and helpin' me look?"

"Me truck is broke," said Bongo Belly.

"Either say you will or say you won't, so we know what kinda man you are."

"I told you it's broke, and it *is* broke."

"I seen you dis mornin' ridin' around town in it just like it wasn't even broke."

"Dat was dis mornin'. Dis mornin' don't mean nuttin' to dis rotten truck."

"Seems to me a man oughta say what he tinks is right."

"I told you it's broke! Whaddaya want, a note from me goddam mudder?"

"How come it's only broke when I ask for a favor from it?" asked Shakey.

Bongo Belly lunged into the hood cavity of the truck with ball peen hammer flying. He gave it six or seven vigorous clouts, saying, "Huh? Huh? Huh? Huh? Huh? Huh?" Then he turned to Shakey, crying, and said, "There, *now* it's broke!"

Shakey got back into his squad car and drove away, thinking that Bongo Belly was becoming a man hard to talk to.

He decided to try Dumshock's house. Dumshock had had the midnight shift, but it was late enough in the day for him to be up and about. He parked the car and knocked on the door. Dumshock himself answered, holding a bottle of beer in one hand.

"Christ, Shakey, what the hell's up?"

"Oh, nuttin', nuttin' at all. Don't get shook. Just passin' by and thought I'd say hello."

"Is that right? Well, that's okay. That's all right by me. C'mon in." He called back through the long narrow house to his wife. "Christine! Old Shakey the Cop dropped in for a social call. Bring 'im out a bottle of the famous beer from England. You know the stuff."

The houses in Andoshen are built narrow and long and tight together so that the only natural light available comes through the front and the rear windows. The rest of the house must be illuminated by electric lights, whatever the time of day.

Shakey took a seat on the living-room sofa. Dumshock's fourteen-month-old daughter was on the floor, playing with his service revolver. Whenever the barrel of the gun pointed in his direction, Shakey winced.

Dumshock laughed and was delighted with her.

"Chip offa the old block, ain't she?"

"Little rascal," said Shakey.

Dumshock's listless wife served the beer. It was a dark bottle with a fancy label which read:

SUSSEX PILSNER
BY ORDER OF HER MAJESTY THE QUEEN
REGISTERED NUMBER 725–8332

Shakey took a swig of it and said, "Ahhhhh."

"Good stuff, huh?" asked Dumshock.

"Yeah," said Shakey. "English, huh?"

"Look at the label."

"Yeah, by order of the queen, with a number 'n every-thing."

"Pretty fancy, huh?"

"Yeah. Must be dear to buy."

"Look at the number. Look funny to you?"

"Whaddaya mean?"

Dumshock slapped his knee, laughed, and said, "That's the phone number of the brewery right here in little old Andoshen! They're bringin' out a foreign beer to run competition wit themselfs. Same beer, different bottles!"

It seemed the biggest joke in the world to Dumshock, and Shakey tried to appreciate it, but the baby girl kept waving the gun in his direction.

Shakey pointed to her and asked, "Loaded, Dumshock?"

"Safety's on," he said. "Ain't she a chip offa the old block, though? Look at her. Twirl it on your finger, little darlin'. Plug old Shakey a couple times. Aim for the guts, little darlin', aim for the guts."

Shakey chugged the beer and was stepping into the squad car when he remembered to call back, "Dumshock, on your shift last night didja happen to see Thunder Przewalski roamin' around?"

He had the baby girl, still with the service revolver, in his arms.

"Lemme stink. No, can't say that I did, Shakey."

Shakey the Cop got into the patrol car and drove away, unwounded.

Thunder did not come home for two more days. When he did return, he was wearing a porkpie hat and a purple lump above his right eye. He had two dollars in one pocket and a pint of Old Overholt in the other.

Shakey looked up from the bark to which he was affixing pebbles and said, "Fine ting."

Thunder grinned proudly.

"A very fine ting indeed," said Shakey the Cop.

Chapter Twenty-Seven

Tyra

There was only one Negro family in Andoshen, though they were not the first of their race to spend time there. At the turn of the century there was one William "Billy the Kid" Plummer, who made his living appearing at fire house, church, and ethnic picnics in the numerous groves, standing behind a stretched canvas with his head protruding through a hole so that the picnickers could throw baseballs at it, three balls for a nickel.

One hot August afternoon a group of young boys had been provoking him by throwing stones instead of baseballs, without paying for the pleasure. Plummer said he only meant to frighten them when he picked up the hatchet, but he threw it and killed Mickey Ryan, thirteen. He was given a trial at the County Courthouse in Gibbsville and subsequently hanged in the adjoining prison yard. Old man Pfeiffenberger, who was just a lad then, had been taken to the hanging by his father, who pointed out to him that Plummer was dying like any other man, clasping and unclasping his hands.

Sometime after, in the thirties, the area saw its first

Negro anthracite miner. He was named Poke or Pike or Peck. Because of his color he was an object of curiosity and stood out in a crowd, except for those minutes at the end of the shift when the miners walked home in a group from the colliery, all of them coal black. He had no family, and was lonely, and soon left town.

So the first Negro *family* to settle in town with any sense of permanence was the Bernard family. The father was in charge of the stables of Mr. Gowen, who owned the Blue Mountain Colliery and the coal breaker that was part of it. He was recruited for the job in Kentucky when Mr. Gowen decided that, in his own way, he was a king and should now enjoy the Sport of Kings.

At his place in the Valley he constructed corrals, stables, and a small house behind the stables for the Bernards: mother, father, and daughter Tyra.

Though the mother and father seldom left Mr. Gowen's property, Tyra integrated the local school and got along well with the other children and the teachers. She was a social girl and soon became one of the most popular students at school.

As the years passed and she entered high school, minor problems developed, especially when she grew to be a beauty.

The boys would not deny that they found Tyra attractive (though they kept their fantasies private) and this created great concern on the parts of their mothers and fathers, who did not want to be the first in-laws of Negroes in Andoshen, Pa.

The older boys and men who leaned against the Majestic let Tyra know what they were thinking whenever she walked by. When she heard them hoot and whistle she would increase the sex in her wiggle, both in scorn and gratitude.

For her own part, Tyra was interested in two or three boys, who would have cut their own throats for her, but she, as they, squelched her desire, for the sake of her parents. It was a lonely life for her. She had gone through three years of high school without a single date.

"Mom, I want to go out with boys. To the drive-in movie and neck, like everyone else."

"You keep your wants to yourself, girl."

Except for summer vacations with relatives in Newark or Philadelphia, encounters too brief to be a threat to her heart, Tyra Bernard did not have dates and missed the magic of falling in love and being loved in return and walking down the street with her hand in the hand of a boy.

She grew to hate Andoshen and urged her parents to move back to Kentucky or to Philly or to Newark, but they had never had a better life, and if it was lonely, at least it was secure.

The night of the Junior Prom drew near, as it must for anyone who goes to high school, as it has for generations. Everyone was pairing off, months before the event. Tyra knew she would not be asked, and if she should be asked, she knew she would not be able to accept.

It looked as though she would be the only one in her class who would not attend the social function of the year, but her mother suggested that they import her cousin from Philadelphia to escort her to the prom. The idea was odious to Tyra, but less so than the thought of staying home on that night.

Cousin Ralph was imported from Philly and provided

with a white dinner jacket and accessories. He made small effort to disguise his reluctance to drag his *cousin* through her prom.

As they were leaving the house and her parents were urging them to have a good time, Tyra turned to her escort and said, "I'm going to introduce you as Ralph from Philly, and if you tell anyone that you're my cousin, I'm going to kill you."

Tyra did not attend the Senior Prom the following year.

After graduation she went to Philadelphia and got a job with the P.P.D. She married one of the policemen on the force. Two years after their wedding they drove upstate, intending to stay for five days at the little house behind the stables and have a nice visit with her mother and father. She and her husband took a stroll through town that evening and later slept in the double bed she had slept in most of the nights of her life, but they both felt isolated and vulnerable and isolated there. She cried that night and the next morning they returned home to their apartment in Philadelphia. Her mother cried when they said good-bye; her father couldn't understand.

Dear Son,

After the Blue Mountain Breaker came down, Gowen put a bullet through his head, about three days after, and you can be sure there wasn't a whole lot of sympathy for him in this town. About the only thing could be said is at least he lived in the town, a lot better than the rest, but still in town. Not like the others who make the only money here but spend it somewhere else. No one even knows who owns most of the collieries.

Oh, well, when you come right down to it the coal regions were born with a black eye and will always have a black eye. And yet we stay here, and when you get right down to it, we love it here. It's enough to break your heart.

The Gowen place was bought cheap as beans by Irv Childs, the contractor. Irv didn't want any horses so the estate sold them off somewhere. The Bernards left town, who knows where, and had to find another job. Good luck to them, because they weren't young anymore. The daughter went to work in Philly before all of that, and unless I miss my guess someone I know was a little bit in love with her.

Love,
Mom & Pop

Andoshen, Pa., is one square mile exactly, the only town with those dimensions in the continental United States, so say the residents. There were, at peak, 119 licensed bars within its limits, and numerous other establishments where one could have a ten-ounce glass of beer for a dime.

Little compliance with legal drinking age exists, and one starts downing the amber brew around the age of 17, taking up the challenge that has never been achieved: to have a beer in every bar in town one Saturday.

Of the 119 bars, Brolly's is the best.

Listen, everybody felt bad
When Joe was knifed at Brolly's,
But that was no reason to cancel
The fish barbecue for Sunday,
Trout that Stashu caught.

When Joe fell to his knees,
Holdin' in his goodies,
He said, 'He fucked me up!'
What? 'He fucked me up!'
Which nobody could say otherwise.

There was enough fish for everybody twice,
And we danced around the chalk outline of Joe
That Chief Red made on the floor for the pictures.
Even Joe's closest friends had to laugh
To see him drawed so crude on Brolly's floor.

Chapter Twenty-Eight

The Boys at Brolly's

Wing Wingrodski was on his way to Brolly's for a few coolers after the long hot pumping practice for all members of the Polish American Fire Company. In Strawberry Alley he encoúntered a group of ten-year-olds playing Bloody Bones, and he entered the game, promising that he would throw with his left hand and keep his left eye closed at all times.

Bloody Bones is a street game played with a football, not actually a football but what passes for a football in mining patches where no one can afford the real item. It is made by taking an issue of the Andoshen *Evening Call* and folding it lengthwise into halves, then quarters, and then rolling it very tightly from one end to the other and tying it with three short lengths of twine. Spiral passes are a breeze, but kicking it is not very satisfactory because it is so hard, and becoming "It" in a game of Bloody Bones can be downright painful. Eventually, of course, this football becomes ragged, falls apart, and is discarded. It is the one thing that every child can have, and have as many of as he pleases, though no one needs more than one at a time.

The object of Bloody Bones is for "It" to throw the football, the harder the better, at another participant, hitting him and thus making him "It." One throws it hard so that there is never any dispute about a hit or a miss; everyone can hear a hit, and hear the agonized cry of the one who has been hit.

Because of his size and distinctive T-shirt ("Sig Edmundson Cams") Wing was the favorite target, in spite of the fact that even with his left hand his return blow was twice as hard as a ten-year-old's.

He played for about twenty minutes, until his thirst refused him any further delay. He yelled uncle to the boys, but before leaving reached out and flicked his hand across little Herman's fly, opening two buttons with the jerk.

"Double," said Wing. "Man on second, no outs, top of the first."

"Shit!" said little Herman.

"Don't ever use bad words," admonished Wing Wingrodski. "You know why?"

The boys gathered around him, sensing a tale.

"Why?" they asked.

He looked around him at the gathering darkness and crouched and said, " 'Cause there's a monster who's named Boris Karloff . . ."

"I heard of 'im," said one boy and several others agreed that they had too.

". . . and he talks like this: 'So you're the little boy who uses bad words. Welcome to Murky Mansion.' "

"What does he do then?"

"Whaddaya think?" said Wing. "He eats their Adam's apples, right offa the neck."

"Jesus Christ!" said little Herman.

Wing wrapped his hands around the boy's neck and imitated Boris Karloff, "Welcome to Murky Mansion."

Little Herman pretended to hit him in the stomach but pulled his punch. When Wing flinched, he sacrificed two punches to Herman, who delivered them forthwith on the arm, making sure to wipe them off afterward or else he would sacrifice a knuckle twist on the head, which can hurt more than the two punches on the arm.

Doc Rice had gone to Brolly's directly from his office, as he usually did, close on the heels of his last appointment of the day.

"How're you doin'?" asked Brolly, puting down a cardboard coaster.

"Just barely, just damn barely," answered Doc Rice. "What's for you?"

"A shot of your famous Old Undershirt with water on the side, please. Two, three. Sometimes I wonder at five o'clock when I lay down my drill if ever I'll be able to pick it up again."

He looked at his hands and like Lady Macbeth imagined blood on them. He rubbed them together.

"Relax, Doc," said Brolly.

"Personally, I never saw why all the fuss over the discovery of electricity."

"Relax, Doc, have a good time."

"Night baseball. That's about it."

Doc Rice took the shot and a half, Brolly's liberal measurement, and washed it down with water. "They say that your stomach is the size of your hands folded together," he said. He folded his hands and held them in front of him. They were gnarled and shaking. "God bless it," he said.

"Relax, Doc," said Brolly.

"Good advice, as always."

Stump Bonomo was led into the bar by Gunner Walsh and Boss Mahoney, who cupped their hands over their mouths and imitated the trumpets of the king announcing His Majesty's arrival. In Stump's hands was a trophy, the statuette of an athlete in a track suit giving the sign of the extended middle finger.

"Hear ye, hear ye, all persons that's present," announced Gunner Walsh. "Before you is not the second runner-up, not the runner-up, but the absolute high champ-*eeen* of the Tri County Finger League! Ta-da-da-*da*-da-DA!"

Gunner Walsh and Boss Mahoney danced around him, and Stump Bonomo executed a modest bow.

"Speech! Speech!"

Stump held up his hands for silence and said, "Fellow citizens of Andoshen, with a great deal of pride I bring home this honor to our little community. May I say there were guineas there from every town and patch in the three counties, and I sat on my stool, a little afraid, a little humble, and the odds scared me. I thought, who am I, a little one-legged wop from a shanty next to the Stink Creek. How can I beat this whole crowd from all over the regions? But then I thought, why not? Somebody has to win. I thought, by God, maybe I won't win, but they're gonna know they was in a *La Morra* match.

"For the first round I drew a kid without a hair on his ass, tryin' to make his name. Outa ten points, I give 'im two. It was embarrassin'. But for the second round I drew Neilly Costello, an Italian Protestant from McAdoo who's never had to buy a beer in his life. If he ain't drinkin' offa the dart board, he's drinkin' offa his fingers. But I suspicion he was nippin' before he come because I beat 'im ten to seven and I wasn't even tired, you. I had three more rounds and no one got more 'n seven points on me and then I drew some old farmer with meadow muffin on his boots. Stink! But that old son of a bitch could finger. My shirt was stickin' to me back by the time it was over. I squeaked by him by one lousy point, and who do you think is in the semi-finals?"

"I was poopin' my pants," said Gunner Walsh, who had seen it all. "He was against some cocky bastard in a Mafia suit who kept smilin' like there wasn't no doubt in his mind. He kept lookin' between points to his pals and winkin'. I hated that cocky bastard. I said to meself, if Stump gotta lose, let him beat this cocky bastard first. That's all I ask."

"And I *did!*" said Stump.

"Beat the cocky bastard," Gunner clarified.

"So there I was, Stump from down by Stink Creek, in the finals, one round for nineteen points, after throwin' out all those fingers and compoundin' the minds of the opposition. And now I'm up against Rollo, last year's champ, lookin' fresh as a daisy and me wit me ass draggin'. Hell, I know guys who are mentally unable to even *play* Rollo. They can't even look at his forehead."

"You shoulda seen it," said Gunner.

La Morra is more than a match of minds, it is a match of psyches, and experts of it have no patience with elementary mental pursuits like chess or bridge. In structure it is simplicity itself. Two players face each other, each with his throwing hand in a clenched fist, the other hand covering it protectively like a precision instrument. The players raise and lower both hands three times, in an almost pleading manner, and then the fist is uncovered and the player throws it forward, popping out from one to five fingers, simultaneously shouting out in Italian any number from two to ten, the first time loud and clear, the repeats like so many echoes: *"CINQUE! Cinque, cinque, cinque, cinque, cinque, cinque . . . cinque . . . cinque . . ."* The last one or two become almost inaudible. The player who has called out the total number of extended fingers wins the point and immediately they play for the second point.

It is a finger game, but every part of the body is used and exhausted by the playing of it. The eyes especially can mean victory or defeat, depending upon the quality of the soul that controls them. The player usually focuses his eyes on his opponent's forehead, attempting to bore through it and know the other's mind the instant before the opponent decides how many fingers to throw out. It is not a practice meant for everyone.

La Morra is more than a game; it is an art born and nurtured in romance, and it is impossible to play it in English, though many Anglos have tried to become Italians to master it. A few achieve some moderate success, but most are unable to acquire as adults what the Italians were bequeathed at birth.

The first point, as in other competitions, gives one a distinct psychological advantage. Getting the second and third points as well, however, can give this advantage back, because the killer overconfidence can destroy the

best of players in spite of their skill. This may have occurred in Stump Bonomo's contest since Rollo got the
first three points and Rollo had gone the distance before
and might have failed this time to balance his confidence.
By the time they reached seventeen points they were tied.
The crowd around them pushed closer and since there is
no referee in *La Morra* the players themselves had to ask
for room, breaking momentarily their band of concentra-
tion. The crowd moved back, ashamed to have caused
discomfort. The players' seconds stood close by with ice
water.

"On the eighteenth point," said Stump, "I'm practically inside him, not all the way, but practically. I see on
his forehead *sètte* chiseled there. Maybe for two seconds
but it was like two days. *Sètte.* Clear as a bell. But my mistake was throwin' three instead of four, 'cause he threw
three. But he called *cinque* so I was still alive. Then I
think, he's gonna stay with the three. He's gonna stay
with the three figurin' I will too and he's gonna call *sèi,*
figurin' I got him figured to drop one and I'll call *cinque.*
See, he was droppin' one all through the game, just
waitin' till it counted and then he would hold pat and
there I'd be expectin' 'im to drop one. 'Course I knew he
was smart enough to know that I would figure him to re-
verse the pattern and hold when we reached seventeen
and was still tied, so maybe he would take the unpredict-
able road and throw out five. And then I thought, why's
that sucker expect me to hold pat? Since I called *sètte* why
don't he figure I'll stick to that and just whip out an extra
finger?"

All of this deliberation took place in the three seconds
prior to the throwing of the fingers, but at the unmeasur-

able instant before the throw Stump be*came* his opponent and knew that Rollo would hold with the three. Stump threw out one finger and shouted, *"QUATTRO! Quattro, quattro, quattro, quattro, quattro . . . quattro . . . quattro . . ."*

His opponent had thrown three again and called out *Sèi* and lost the point, and though there was another point to be played Stump knew then that Rollo, at least on this night, would not be able to win no matter how many points they played.

"I been to New York City and twenty-two county fairs," said Gunner Walsh, "and I ain't *never* seen anything like it."

Stump Bonomo raised his hands above his head and spread the fingers and said, "And I did it all with these, the ten magic fingers. Nine and three-quarters."

The tip of his right index finger was missing.

"That's his secret weapon, that shorty," said Gunner. "It was throwin' 'em all offa balance."

The boys at Brolly's felt obliged to discuss the continuing partnership of Shakey the Cop and Thunder Przewalski, because of all the unnatural things occurring in town this was currently the most unnatural. They had been together longer than anyone had predicted, and as the relationship now seemed permanent it took on a rather unwholesome air to the rest of Andoshen. At the very least it seemed a conflict of interest on Shakey's part to be living with a criminal type like Thunder.

"They go together like a cough drop 'n a cuppa coffee," said Boss Mahoney, and the others laughed and screwed up their faces.

⌐ 246

"I think Shakey's a good influence on him. I haven't seen his name in the papers since they been shackin' together."

"He's been a mother to that boy."

"I'd like to know who's paying the rent on the place. Old Thunder ain't worked steady since Hector was a pup."

"I hear Shakey's found a job for him, and he's been hexed to civilize Thunder."

"That's a hex only the divil himself would be mean enough to lay on."

"Maybe Shakey's feelin' guilty about all the times he put the wood to Thunder's bean and trun him in the lockup."

"But, hell, Thunder went of his own free will. That's what I don't understand, 'cause before he wouldn't give the sweat offa his ass for the likes of Shakey."

"Thunder ain't no dummy. He's gettin' a nice clean place, probably for free, old Shakey's been feedin' him all the yonko food he can eat, and he ain't gettin' clouted over the head all the time any more."

"But, damn, it ain't right. It ain't . . . I don't know . . . it ain't . . . *right*."

"He even got 'im a job."

"What doin'?"

"Jesus, you don't think they'll make a cop outa him, do you?"

"Well, hell, they made a cop outa Shakey, didn't they?"

"Yeah, but Shakey is only dumb, he ain't dumb and mean and crooked."

"He's *too* dumb to be mean and crooked. He don't have the smarts to fix a ticket."

"I heard that years ago the Majestic poker players were gonna cut him in on the action, like they did the rest of the department, but then they found out that Shakey didn't even know poker was illegal."

"Well, that's why some people are bums and some people are engineers."

"Gimme a match," said Stump, putting a cigarette into his mouth.

"My ass and your face," said Gunner Walsh.

"My farts and your breath," said Wing Wingrodski.

"I walk all the way from the patch to drink in this bar," said Doc Rice, "because there are so few real people left."

"Hey, Brolly," said Stump, "how come you don't have a dart board in here? There ain't a damn thing to do here but drink and listen to insults and crack pistachios wit your teeth."

Doc Rice shuddered.

"Whaddaya want, an egg in your beer?" said Gunner Walsh.

"People in here don't know how to relax," said Brolly. "They don't know how to behave 'n have a good time. If I had a dart board in here, I'd be pulling darts outa the asses of me customers. People who come in this bar don't know how to have a good time 'n relax."

"How many pleasures have been enjoyed by robbers, patricides, tyrants?" said Doc Rice.

"Well, I don't believe I said anything about that," said Brolly.

"Ah, *ha!*" said Doc Rice conclusively.

"Doc, you're the kinda guy could confuse a vegetarian," said Gunner Walsh.

"I'm not entirely untraveled," said Doc Rice, "yet this is the only town I've ever been in where a man can walk into a store and buy a single cigarette."

"Yeah, I had one too, but the wheel come off," said Gunner.

"Me too. I had one but it shrunk in the wash," said Wing Wingrodski.

This exchange could have continued indefinitely but for Bongo Belly's entrance.

The others greeted him in chorus as men who drink in the same establishment are inclined to do. Normally Bongo Belly would have returned the greeting and perhaps even bought the man next to him a beer, but tonight he was preoccupied, and in addition to having a torn jacket he was obviously physically and emotionally shaken. The others knew the condition and waited for Bongo Belly himself to offer up his story for conversation. When finally he did speak, he said only, "What truck?" and then again, "What truck?"

He drank his beer, signaled for another, and said, looking straight ahead of him at the mirror behind the bar, "What truck? What truck?"

Although the others thought the situation probably called for more weighty comment, Bongo Belly sat, and drank a lot of beer, and repeated the words, "What truck? What truck?"

Even after they got back on the subject of Thunder and Shakey, and someone had wondered aloud how

Chief Red viewed this new alliance, Bongo disrupted the rhythm of the discussion by asking, "What truck? What truck?"

After which the discussion would have become difficult, for Thunder himself came into Brolly's, looking like a premature ejaculator. He sat at the empty side of the bar, the corner of it between him and Bongo Belly.

"Gimme a draft," said Thunder, " 'n one for him."

He nodded toward Bongo Belly.

Oblivious, Bongo reached for his glass and found it full again.

"That's on Thunder," said Brolly.

Now, bar etiquette is very clear and definite on what should have followed. Bongo had only three options: 1. To lift the beer between two fingers, incline his head, say, "Here's to you," and drink. 2. Feeling reticent, to do as above but remain silent. 3. When the one who bought the beer is an object of absolute hatred and scorn, to say, "I can buy me own beer," and refuse to drink with him.

Instead, Bongo Belly looked up at Brolly and said, "What truck? What truck?"

"Oh, Jesus, did you look outside?" said Thunder. "The stars be still shining, the moon be still there frowning."

Bongo Belly spun around like a man alone in the woods hearing the snap of a twig behind him. He saw Thunder sitting at his left and slapped his hands over his eyes and began a series of low, pain-filled sighs: *"Ohhhhh, ohhhhh, ohhhhh . . ."*

The others showed concern.

"What the hell's the matter wit 'im?"

"Did you ever own anything you was so crazy about that you put it up in a silver pedal stall?" asked Thunder.

"A truck? What truck?" said Bongo Belly.

"Jesus, Bongo, we're still above ground, the air is still sweet, our peckers are still in workin' condition."

"I'll give you your ground, I'll give you your sweet goddam air. I'll give you your workin' goddam pecker," said Bongo Belly.

"I'll fix the damn ting."

"Oh, you'll fix the damn ting? That's a good one. This is where I came in. Watch me laugh. Ha, ha, ha, ha, ha, ha! Will you fix also me goddam broken arm?" Bongo Belly pulled at his torn sleeve. "Will you fix the empty guts of me goddam children?"

Even Brolly's interest was piqued.

"You want to know what happened? I'll tell you what happened," said Bongo Belly. "I take ole numbnuts here to Gibbsville to get his rocks off. I'm a respectable married man, I don't need any of that stuff, but I can understand a poor pervert who just stole five bucks from his roommate and wants to go to Gibbsville for the treatment, so I take him and wait for him, all the time sittin' with a pimp who looks like he wouldn't be opposed to havin' a slice of my throat. Numbnuts goes upstairs with a bean pole with a face like a peach pit."

"The closer to the bone, the sweeter the meat," said Thunder.

"On the way home we're singin', two parts,

> *Where do you work-a, John?*
> *On the Delaware Lackawan.*
> *What do you do-a, John?*
> *I push-a, push-a, push.*
> *What do you push-a, John?*

I push, I push-a da truck.
Where do you push-a, John?
On the Delaware Lackawan-a-wan-a-wan-a-wan,
The Delaware Lackawan."

They all applauded, and Wing Wingrodski tossed a penny at him.

Bongo Belly ignored them and continued: "So we're drivin' home 'n old numbnuts here, whose name I can't even pronounce because I hate him so much, says he wants to drive."

"And you *let* him?"

"When he's givin' you an earache and he's tellin' you he'll go slow . . . and when you naturally figure that any man who wants to drive a truck has a license and knows what he's doing and can handle it . . ."

Doc Rice said, "When a man mounts a woman and spends himself thus, he often afterwards feels capable of even greater things."

"We're comin' down the Frankville hill, and the first car that comes up the other lane old numbnuts moves way the hell over and he's makin' a new road where there weren't none until he clips pole number thirty-nine and we go rollin' back to the road. Landin' on the *roof!* On the goddam *roof!* And he's gonna *fix* it!"

Bongo Belly put his head in his arms and sobbed, "What truck? What truck? I don't want to live anymore."

Hearing Bongo tell of it and watching his absurd reaction to it made Thunder believe that it was not as bad as he had originally judged. He burst out laughing and the others joined him.

"Be glad you wasn't killed," he said to Bongo.

"Be glad *you* wasn't," said someone to Thunder.

"There's nothin' that bad can kill me."

"You think so!" yelled Bongo Belly, reaching over the bar for the half-full quart bottle of Coke. "I'm for tryin' it!" he yelled and brought the bottle down over Thunder's head. It made a *klonk,* and the Coke splashed out of the open end and down into Bongo's sleeve, but the bottle did not break and neither, apparently, did Thunder's head.

Bongo looked at the bottle in disbelief.

"There. You happy now?" asked Thunder, a little wobbly. "Even-Steven. You don't owe me nuttin', I don't owe you nuttin'."

"I owe you somethin' all right, and I'm gonna pay in full."

He looked around him for something more lethal than a Coke bottle.

Brolly said, "Either you settle your beef outside or I call a cop."

Bongo Belly selected the bar stool he had been sitting on.

"Okay, that's it," said Brolly, flipping a dime to Doc Rice. "Doc, call the cops."

"Delighted," said Doc and went to the pay phone on the wall behind him.

Thunder blocked the bar stool with his left forearm and connected with a right to the shoulder which spun around Bongo Belly, who then came at him with a lowered head. He butted Thunder against the wall. They both went to the floor in the corner and each tried to establish the most painful wrestling hold he knew. Brolly

looked over the edge of the bar and checked their progress, muttering, "No one around here knows how to
relax, how to have a good time."

Doc Rice held the telephone receiver in front of him
and looked at it with bemused incredulity.

"What about it, Doc?" asked Brolly. "Are they after
gettin' Shakey down here?"

He had to raise his voice to be heard over the grunts
and groans of the combatants on the floor.

"I have Bobby on the line," said Doc Rice. "Chief Red
is under the weather."

"So tell Bobby . . ."

"He says Shakey can't come right now."

"Why the hell not? I been payin' taxes till I can't stand
up straight."

"Well, it seems he's down at the Sulphur Creek washing the squad car."

"Jesus Christ, it's *dark* out!"

Doc Rice put the phone back to his head and said to
Bobby, "Jesus Christ, it's *dark* out."

"He's got a lantern," said Bobby.

Doc passed this information along to Brolly, who
checked the flailing arms and legs on the floor and noticed that someone had kicked a hole through his wall.

"Call the goddam mayor!"

"Who's to guarantee that all of this is really happen-
ing?" asked Doc, but made the call to the mayor's home
anyway.

Mayor Lefty had run for office on the slogan, "It's
Time for New Blood," which could have been a mistake
in an area where language was taken literally and there
was still plenty of old blood to wash away, but Lefty in

his campaign explained that what he meant was it was time to give youth a chance, and at thirty-five Lefty was the youngest man ever to run for the office. Most of the electorate were surprised to be reminded that Lefty was only thirty-five, because so many men of forty-five believed him to be their elder, and most people, unless they paused to think about who else had been in Lefty's graduating class, would have said he was at least fifty. Lefty had at an early age begun to dissipate, a disease indigenous to anthracite coal fields.

Once reminded of Lefty's chronological age, the voters rather fancied him.

The campaign had been great fun. In addition to having the youthful vitality to match the rigors of governing such a borough, Lefty pointed out, he was more qualified than the incumbent because A, he was a high school graduate, and B, since he had always had a good job at the lumber yard, which of course he would keep during his term of office, he was less apt to have a finger in every political pocket in the county, as he justly accused his opponent of doing. His opponent was on relief at the time of his election and was understandably more or less piggish once he sat athwart the open coffers.

The other plank in his platform was his criticism of the police force, the members of which he accused of being overpaid, underworked, undertrained, and lacking in intelligence. None of them had a high school diploma. He singled out Shakey during the campaign and told the story of how Shakey went to Philadelphia to bury a half-brother, and while taking a constitutional late at night encountered two policemen having trouble with a small gang of juvenile delinquents in leather jackets and studded belts, carrying lengths of chain. Shakey jumped into the middle of it, calling, "Andoshen Police Force!" to his two big-city colleagues. The delinquents spun away from the group like victims of centrifugal force, making for the alleys and the rooftops, leaving six of their own on the ground: unconscious on their backs, or on their knees, or holding their stomachs, or spitting out their broken teeth. Shakey, rubbing a split knuckle, stepped toward his horrified police brothers to exchange professional amenities, but they told him to go away somewhere, fast, according to Lefty when he told the story publicly.

Contacted by the *Call* for a rebuttal, Shakey would say only, "When they seen what good work I did they asked me to join the department down there, but I told 'em Philly was too big of a place for old Shakey."

Lefty won by a landslide and afterward apologized to the boys on the police force, explaining that this is what a politician had to do to get elected these days. He often made coffee for them and sat with them watching the fights on TV in the tiny police station and lockup on the second floor of the Good Friends and Neighbors Volunteer Fire Company. But Shakey never forgave him and would not drink a cup of the mayor's coffee even if it was five o'clock in the morning.

Two weeks after Mayor Lefty took office Mr. Buddusky at the high school revealed that the mayor had not received a diploma but a "certificate," certifying that for at least twelve years he had attended the local public schools for at least the minimum number of days required by law.

One month after Mayor Lefty took office he was included in the payoff of several illicit local and county corporations, he received a fifth of his favorite from every after-hours tavern keeper, and he was invited to visit, every Monday he was in the mood for it, the garage apartment of a sturdy Lithuanian lady who lived beyond her means.

But before these rewards and spoils were tendered he made the rash promise in an eleventh-hour address to the voters that he would never be farther than a phone call away from them.

Doc Rice quoted the promise when he called him about the difficulties presently in progress at Brolly's Bar.

To his credit, Mayor Lefty was there in less than ten minutes. He was wearing an *A*'s baseball cap, a pair of Wranglers rolled up at the bottoms, a T-shirt that could have doubled as a menu, and a .38 blue-barreled snub-nose strapped to his hip. He back-cleared his nose.

"Your Honor," said Doc Rice.

The mayor wasted no time with words. He pulled out the .38 and everyone, Brolly included, dropped to the floor. Lefty aimed at the hole already in the wall, just above the area of the disagreement, and squeezed off a shot. He missed the hole, but fortunately also missed the disputants, and the new hole he made in the wall was in size inconsequential.

There is nothing like a live round fired at random or into a neutral corner to foster calm renegotiation. One would have thought by the way Bongo Belly and Thunder arose and drifted away from each other, brushing the dust off their clothes, that they were civilized strangers who had inadvertently collided while preoccupied with things more important than their direction.

Brolly and the others slowly brought themselves to up-right positions.

"And the night shall be filled with music," said Doc Rice.

"You missed 'em," pointed out Wing Wingrodski.

"Goddammit, Lefty, I coulda done *that* meself," said Brolly.

"Shoulda," answered His Honor, holstering his arm.

He turned to Bongo Belly and Thunder, who had re-sumed custodianship of their beers, Bongo patting his pockets like an executive to check the possible loss of his valuables.

"I wuz in the middle of kiskis and fried eggs," said the mayor.

Men in high office enjoy the luxury of terseness.

"I was making a citizen's arrest," said Bongo Belly, using a term he had heard often enough, but had never understood. It had a nice legal ring to it.

Thunder was impressed, doubly so because he thought Bongo was attributing citizenship to him.

"Oh, you wuz," was all the mayor was able to say.

"That's right," said Bongo and the situation seemed to stand still until Doc Rice said, "Perhaps it would help to hear the charge."

"Now you're talkin'," said Thunder. "You'll never get a finger in my mush, Doc, but there's no arg'in' wit an education."

"I'll give you your charge onct," said an indignant Bongo Belly. "Premedicated destruction of another guy's truck. How's that for a charge?"

"Huh?" said His Honor.

"That's some charge," said Wing Wingrodski.

"Let us ask the plaintiff, gentlemen of the jury, to define his terms," said Doc Rice, assuming the role of attorney for the defense, grasping at the opportunity to be someone else.

"You tell 'em, Doc," said Wing Wingrodski, having a great deal of fun. "I stutter."

"You sit down and drink peaceful or it's wit me to the lockup," said the mayor.

"Let me see you sit down and drink peaceful when a guy's rolled over your truck that you use to make a livin' wit," said Bongo Belly.

"He did dat?"

"He's makin' a picanic outa a hambone," said Thunder.

"You did dat?"

"I told 'im I'd fix the damn ting."

"I'm gonna hafta lock you up, Thunder," said the mayor.

"Why me?"

"You're no damn good," said the mayor.

"Do I hear a second?" said Doc Rice.

"I'll second that movement," said Wing Wingrodski.

"I'll turd it," said Stump Bonomo.

"I believe I'll fourth it," said Boss Mahoney.

"I'll take the fifth," said Gunner Walsh.

"Nobody likes you," said the mayor to Thunder.

It did not strike Thunder as news.

"Don't that hurt your feelings?" asked Brolly.

"No," said Thunder.

"Everybody says you're no damn good."

"I ain't."

"You sound proud of it."

"Whoever said everybody's gotta tink you're good?" asked Thunder.

"Don't it bother you nobody gives a damn if they lock you up forever?"

"I'm gonna worry what a bar full of shit-the-pantses tinks?"

"The defense rests, Your Honor," said Doc Rice.

Shakey the Cop walked into the bar. He seemed unsteady on his feet and wild in his eyes, a feature Mayor Lefty was last to notice because as soon as he turned and saw him he chastised him with, "Where the hell wuz *you?*"

"There's trouble down at Brolly's," said Shakey.

"Dis *is* Brolly's, shitferbrains. Trouble's damn near over soon's I bag Thunder."

"You bag Thunder and the trouble's beginnin'."

"Huh?"

"You heard me."

"You tryin' to push around the goddam *may*or of a city?" said the mayor.

"You tryin' to push around a citizen?" countered Shakey the Cop.

Thunder was beginning to feel almost like a contributing member of society, a citizen, being simultaneously railroaded and protected by the forces of government and law.

"You're interferin' wit justice, yonko," said the mayor.

"Thunder don't move till I find out what he done."

"He wrecked me goddam truck is all," said Bongo Belly.

"It was an accident," said Thunder.

"Accidents ain't illegal. That's called *an act of God*," said Shakey the Cop.

"Blasphemy! Sacrilege!" said Doc Rice.

"I'm gonna tell the council to fire your dumb ass," said the mayor.

"And I'm gonna break your dumb jaw," said Shakey.

"Lay off, Shakey," said Thunder. "I'll go wit 'im. They got no charge against me no way."

"The hell," said Shakey. "Whenever there's trouble it's Thunder they gotta pinch."

"What the hell is this?" asked the mayor. "What's Thunder to you, a suckin' cousin?"

"Lefty don't understand the meanin' of friendship," said Wing Wingrodski.

"Keep your Polack nose outa dis."

"As we say in Quaker, fuck *me*," said Wing.

"You get back to your shack and feed your fat-ass face, Your Goddam Honor," said Shakey.

"You're lookin' for it," said Lefty, and they slowly began to square off.

"Your fat-ass wife too," said Shakey.

The mayor let his hand dangle next to his sidearm.

"You got a brother? Feed your fat-ass brother's face too," said Shakey as he unfastened his holster clasp.

"My God," said Doc Rice, "it's Dodge City."

"Look, you summabitch, I'm loaded on sugar," said Shakey, "and I'm ready for bear. Had two Baby Ruths and a giant Hershey's."

"What's he talkin' about?" asked Gunner Walsh.

"He's got the diabetes and he's crazy wit sugar," said Thunder. "C'mon home, Shakey, I'll straighten you out."

Shakey never took his wild eyes from the mayor. Finally he said, "Draw, Lefty, it's me or you."

"A wise man knows the time for departing," said Doc Rice and ran out of the bar. The others followed him, except for Brolly, who fell to the floor and covered his head with his arms, and Thunder, who continued to sit behind his beer.

"You're crazy. You shouldn't be no policeman," said the mayor.

"Draw," said Shakey.

There is a door to the kitchen in Brolly's and from the kitchen there is a door to Elderberry Alley, which leads to Coal Street and to Lefty's oven, wherein was warming his plate of kiskis and eggs, and it was this route that Mayor Lefty covered in remarkable time for such a large man, thinking that the best thing to do, in the long view, was to forget the whole thing had ever happened.

To get it out of his system, Shakey drew and fired a shot into the Bally pinball machine, killing it, judging from the smoke and hissing sound of its death rattle.

He reholstered his gun and Thunder took him by the arm, saying, "C'mon home, yonko, I be givin' you your medicine. You let the cat outa the bag, flatfoot."

"Don't you worry about Lefty, I got his number."

"Yeah."

"That wasn't no taxpayer's bullet. I be replacin' that one from me own pocket."

"Yeah, yeah. Hell, Chief Red woulda let me go. Why dint you go home to bed? Nobody'd miss you."

"There was trouble at Brolly's."

"There's always trouble at Brolly's."

"Whenever you're there."

"Don't you start on it."

"You'll be a good man yet," said Shakey, "if you live long enough."

"I'll be a good man when I'm six feet under, like everyone else."

"If only you'd had a daddy to give you a good clout when you was a kid."

Thunder, still supporting him by one arm, lifted Shakey's arm and gave him a quick punch to the ribs. Shakey groaned and slipped, but Thunder kept him from falling and continued walking him to the squad car.

"That one wuz for free," said Shakey. "The next one you pay for."

The boys went back inside to their unfinished beers. Brolly unplugged the defunct Bally machine and said, "The bar business ain't no good business. If I had a son, I wouldn't want him in this business, in this town."

They rehashed it and discussed it from every conceivable angle until finally they closed the place, standing together with beers in hands, their noserags hanging out of their pockets, their pants cuffs hanging on their boots, singing, *Where do you work-a, John? On the Delaware Lackawan* . . .

In reporting the incident the next day to the pool shooters at the Majestic, Wing Wingrodski got all the mileage he could out of it and concluded with the observation, "I didn't know whether to shit or go blind."

"So what did you do?"

"Shut one eye and farted."

Dear Son,

Life in Andoshen, Pa., is different than other places. That's why it's so hard to leave it if you haven't done so when you were young. You feel like someone from the moon. Pop and I have been talking about leaving for Arizona ever since 1932. We still are. So is everyone else around here. But no one ever will, because when you get right down to it, where can you have so much fun? Remember when you came home for a visit and bought beers for the bar and still got change from a dollar? Remember when our ceiling caved in? I'll never forget the look on your face. There we were, sitting on the floor covered with plaster. And I looked at you and started to laugh. I thought you were going to cry, but then you started to laugh too. Nobody has time around here to worry about their kids having traumas, so the kids know enough not to have them. Only the rich kids have them if their ceilings fall down. Around here you brush off the plaster and have a good laugh. I can't wait to read that scene.

                                        Love,
                                        Mom & Pop

Chapter Twenty-Nine

The Collapse of the Blue Mountain Breaker

It became, along with the repeal of Prohibition and the attack on Pearl Harbor, one of those few events by which everyone in town could always remember two or three minutes of his ordinary routine life that normally would have been forgotten.

Wing Wingrodski was shaking a pebble out of his boot on his way to the first of the day at Brolly's. Brolly himself was in the process of replacing the spent deodorant cake in the urinal. Doc Rice had just pulled a particularly nasty molar and was taking aspirin to recover from it, though he believed that the alcohol in his system made aspirin ineffective.

Estelle Taylor was taking a breather from her housework, wishing that she had become pregnant at the beginning of last summer so that she would not have to suffer through the August heat in her ninth month. Ella Bistricky and R.K., partners once again, were getting ready for the lunch trade. Shakey the Cop was on his way to the station to play some pinochle.

Thunder Przewalski, the reader, Bill Bistricky, Manny

Pratt the lip-syncher, Stump Bonomo the Tri-County Finger Champion, and twenty-two others were at work in the Blue Mountain Coal Breaker.

The pots and pans at Ella's Lunch danced on their hooks for a few seconds and everyone there and outside on the streets knew that the noise they heard was not blasting from the strippings. The sound of it was too low, too organic, too prolonged. At first Ella thought that the town was finally going down and she tried to take the money out of her register, but through the window she could see Center Street full of people running south toward the Blue Mountain operation.

She screamed, *"Bill!"* and ran out of the place with the others. R.K. locked up and followed.

The cigar rollers felt their work tables jump and they left their tobacco to run with the crowd. The boys at Brolly's, at the Majestic, the old people at Wadden Park, Doc Rice and his patient, all ran down Center Street, because in a coal town disaster is a frequent visitor, and there are those who are in it and the rest who run to watch, to wait, to count. There are the women who say to themselves as they run, "If it's him, it's him," and other women who say, "Not him, please, God, not him, not anyone." There is the first wave of rescuers: firemen, police, miner first-aid teams, Knights of Columbus, Knights of Pythias . . . and those who feed them. In this case, a block party was in preparation at the Holy Ghost Polish National Church, and the women who were preparing the food which would be sold at the party threw it all into huge pots and carried it to the site and distributed it to the exhausted rescuers who held the pierogies and bleenies in gloves coated with ashes and coal dust, for the first time eating this kind of food without joy, like coffee and doughnuts.

It had rained continuously for three days, and many believed that this had weakened the foundation, but first the workers and later a mine inspector had recommended that the obsolete timber girders be replaced with steel ones better able to withstand the constant vibration of the machinery. But the girders had never been replaced, and when the first one cracked the others followed and the one-hundred-foot building came down like a house of cards. Only the scraper line chain kept the trestle portion standing.

At the moment of collapse, one old-timer on the ground level, who had developed over the years the seasoned miner's alarm system for danger, said to his partner, just seconds before it went, "*Some*thing! Get out of here!" The old-timer ran the twenty feet of rail track out of the breaker in time. A few seconds of confusion made it impossible for his partner to run with him but he had the presence of mind to dive under a waiting gondola a second before the timbers and machinery rained down upon it. The gondola saved his life.

Stump Bonomo was on the highest catwalk when it happened. In spite of the usual deafening sound of the machinery and the usual vibration of the catwalk, Stump swore he heard a timber give way, heard it *crack*, and felt everything list to the left. He grabbed the hand rail to his left and held tightly and yelled, "I'm goin' on a ride! God meet me at the end!" as he was pitched forward along with the entire catwalk.

When the noise and the motion ceased, Stump shook some planks and sheet metal from his back and found himself alive in the hot August sun atop the immense pile of junk that had a moment before been the Blue Mountain Breaker. He tried to stand but discovered that his wooden leg had been smashed to slivers. He unstrapped it and lay back on the pile of timbers and laughed and threw what remained of it away. A mechanical extension ladder appeared next to him and Bull McCoy was on it, extending his hand.

"Grab aholt, Stump, dis one wasn't yours."

"Look at it!" cried Stump. "It's splinters! Smashed to tiny splintereens. If it wasn't wood, that old leg woulda been a goner, tore away for sure, and here I'd be bleedin' like a turkey and missin' a goddam leg!"

"You're a lucky bastard, there's no ar'gin' that."

"Ha! Just think if that leg wasn't wood, you," said Stump and crawled to the ladder.

There was a natural high rim around the breaker site, and everyone in town was standing on it, staring down at the pile, at the smoke and dust rising from it. They were so close to it they could hear the screams of the men trapped inside and see their faces when they were extricated. As the rescuers uncovered survivors they passed their names up the hill to the rim because each man was so black with coal dust he could not be recognized by his waiting relatives. When a body was found, no one said anything except to summon the doctor to the scene, who would declare, "This man is dead," and go on to the next, the priest and Extreme Unction following him.

Stretchers were used to carry the injured and dead to two Frankville Community ambulances, the Andoshen Community ambulance, the Philadelphia and Reading Coal and Iron Company ambulance, and four hearses owned by local morticians. Some of the injured panicked and went into shock when they saw they were being carried to hearses. One cried, "Not yet! Not yet! I made this one!"

A crane was brought in to lift a large flywheel, under which a man had been killed. The removal of the flywheel also loosened enough timber to free Bill Bistricky, who was alive and not seriously injured. The name was passed up the hill. "Bistricky. Bill Bistricky. Just banged up a little."

R.K. put his arm around Ella to comfort her, in full view of all, unafraid, because two relatives were comforting each other, and that's what it was, and it was enough.

One man was uncovered except for a twelve-by-twelve timber girder across his legs. His head was revealed when they slid away a piece of sheet metal. The man blinked at the sun and said, "Hello, you."

"Hyuh, Ace. Looks like you're stuck."

"Yeah, at the legs."

"Yo! Get a jack in here! No men are gonna be able to budge it," called the rescuer to the others. "We'll have a jack in a minute," he said to the trapped man.

"I'll be here."

"Hurtin' much?"

"I wish I could pass out. I'm always hearin' about guys goin' through hell and the papers sayin' 'He never lost consciousness.' I was always afraid of being a guy who couldn't lose consciousness. Looks like I am one."

His voice weakened.

"We'll get the doc to give you a shot," said the rescuer and yelled over his shoulder, "Doc! Let's have a doc!"

The jack arrived and was put into place. They pumped it and the girder rose.

"There's some daylight, Ace," said the rescuer.

"That's a comfort," said the man who had been trapped, and he lapsed into unconsciousness.

"Doc! Doc!"

The doctor arrived and felt his pulse and put his stethoscope to the man's heart. "This man is dead," he said, and moved on. The priest arrived and dropped to one knee.

When it happened, the force of it moved the slate pickers' station off its moorings and the conveyor belt stopped and the boulders on it bounced to the floor, along with the reader and his partner. The reader got up and jumped through the window before the tiny station toppled, and landed on the bed of a truck full of culm. What had been the breaker was wrapped in a ball of black dust. As the dust was blown away, the cries of the men inside were carried on the air. The reader jumped over the side of the truck and ran to the wreckage, digging at it with his bare hands and muttering, "This is not for me. I am a reader, I am a poet."

The throaty buzz of chain saws cutting through the mass of timbers made the watchers on the rim grit their teeth. Only when the saws stopped for repositioning or for a few seconds' rest could word be passed up the hill.

Acetylene torches were used to cut through the twisted metal.

Estelle had not seen the reader helping the rescuers and did not know if he was alive and was too frightened to ask anyone below because she was afraid they would say he was not, and she was afraid to think of carrying the child of a dead man. She heard the chain saws and saw the flame of the acetylene torches and thought, to be in there, entombed, waiting to be cut out, God, can you be any poorer than that?

Then she recognized the reader, black as his face was, a pink rim around his mouth, nostrils and eyes like a minstrel scrambling up the hill toward her. She tried to run down the hill to him, but those next to her held her and told her, "Mind the baby, now, mind the baby." He finally reached the summit and held her close, rubbing the black of his cheeks onto hers. He said only, "Pack our stuff. I'm a poet," and then he slid back down the hill on his bottom to continue the digging. He had noticed all the women working their rosaries and envied the Catholics their beads, their something-to-say in every situation.

"Keep an eye on the scraper line! Careful with those chain saws!"

There was still enough of the breaker attached to the scraper line to cause a second disaster should it fall.

"Don't get too close to it! Be able to run if it falls!"

The Philadelphia and Reading Company's first-aid team arrived in individual cars and relieved the miners who were half-cooked from the hot sun.

Every cop in town was there, primarily for traffic and crowd control, but Shakey in his civilian clothes was digging for Thunder and calling his name. It was Shakey who had got Thunder the job. It was not because Thunder couldn't keep up his half of the rent—Shakey had nothing else to spend his pay on—it was because a job brings self-respect and self-respect is the first kind. Otherwise, there is respect for nothing. But a job is not supposed to bring this.

Shakey looked at the people on the hill. Me too, he thought, me too. I got family in here, too. I'm worried, too. I'd be lonely, too. I don't know what I'll do, too.

Smoke was rising from the rubble and the firemen strategically sent in streams of water, fearing a small fire or two inside which could suffocate the survivors still trapped.

I got family in there, too, thought Shakey. Me, too.

One does not have to be a sailor to realize that the next tack is going to capsize the boat. Likewise, when Thunder felt a jarring beneath his feet, he knew that the breaker would collapse with the next, and he fell to his knees and covered his head with his arms and let himself float with the falling breaker.

When the collapse was over, Thunder was trapped in this position of supplication. He tried to tuck his face against his shirt to avoid breathing in the dust and soot that filled his shell. An agony that ran from his neck to the base of his spine told him that something necessary for motion had been broken. He groaned to relieve the pressure. He was unable to move anything.

He heard someone call, "Who's that moaning?"

"Who's that askin'?" replied Thunder.

"Manny Pratt," came the answer.

They were no more than a few feet apart in the wreckage, but they seemed to be calling to each other through miles of buried waste.

"How're you doin', kiddo," called Thunder.

"Not so hot."

"You shoulda took the old man's business."

"I took enough of the old man's business."

"Dark in here, ain't? Like in a pocket."

Thunder heard no answer.

"You still livin', Pratt kid?"

"Yeah, I'm tired, is all. Boy, am I ever tired."

He was never more tired. The fingers of his right hand were squeezed between a pipe and a timber, and although he didn't know this he knew something was wrong there because his fingers were numb and his hand was fast. I shoulda been a goddam lip-syncher, he thought. I *was* a lip-syncher, that was the problem. But I shoulda been a *professional* lip-syncher.

He felt himself ease into unconsciousness and thought, if this is dyin' it ain't all that bad, really.

"Hey, Pratt kid," shouted Thunder.

It woke him up.

"Hey!"

"Yeah, I'm still here," said Manny.

"You know Shakey the Cop?"

"Sure, who don't," said Manny.

"What's his last name, you know?"

Manny thought for a moment and answered, "I never heard it once in all my life."

"Well, ain't that a helluva note."

"Some Polack name, I think."

"Okay, I'll call him Shakey Woyaku. Give the bastard a name at least."

"What's the difference?"

"We're big-ass buddies."

"Yeah, I heard."

"Shakey Woyaku the Cop. Who the hell's gonna give 'im his medicine when he's bad?"

"You hear the sirens?" asked Manny.

"Yeah."

"Won't be long now, we'll be out of here."

"Don't hold your breath," said Thunder.

"They can get us out, can't they?"

"Oh, sure, they don't spare the cost. First they'll get out the mules, then they'll get out the men."

"What mules?"

"That's what we said in the old days 'cause when there was a cave-in or explosion and the boss heard about it, the first ting he'd always say was, 'How are the mules?' "

"The old days, huh?"

"Which are now," said Thunder.

"Huh?"

"Hell, we'll be out in time for dinner. How long can it take to clear everyting?"

"Can you move?" asked Manny.

"Naw. You?"

"I could move an arm 'cept I got my hand stuck in somethin'."

"If we had some beer, we could have a shot 'n a beer, if we had a shot."

"I'm afraid for my fingers."

"Huh?"

"I've always been scared of losin' my fingers."

"How come?"

" 'Cause everybody around here is missin' some."

"I lost three onct."

"Jesus God . . ."

"It ain't that bad. You don't feel nuttin' till later. Anyway, ten fingers is more than anybody needs. All you need is two, to eat, scratch your ass, pick your nose, play wit yourself . . ."

"I don't know," said Manny. "Sometimes I get the feelin' that I just wasn't cut out for life."

"Who *was?*"

"And this only proves it."

"You're only down 'cause it's so dark in here. Pretty soon we'll be seein' the sun and then it'll be different. Hell, you'll get your picture in the paper tonight. We all will. Second time for me."

"Do you suppose anybody died here today?"

"We didn't."

"Not yet."

"Dyin' ain't so tough. Hell, I could do it wit me eyes closed," said Thunder.

"I'm just afraid for my fingers," said Manny.

"Don't worry. Tink about pretty young girls wit nice long legs. Tink about vanilla ice cream wit big whole strawberries on top of it."

"I'm also afraid somethin's busted inside of me."

"Hey, listen!"

"What?"

"Listen. I tink I hear old Shakey Woyaku the Cop yelling for me."

Manny began to hallucinate, seeing old men and young men in baggy patched drawers dancing to accordions, waving finger stumps in front of their faces.

"Listen!" yelled Thunder.

Manny came to again and tried to listen and thought he did hear someone call from a great distance, "Thunder! Thunder! Thunder!"

"Ain't that somethin'? I knew he'd be down here lookin' for me."

"You're big-ass buddies."

"He got me the job. That's why he's bustin' his gut lookin' for me. Big flatfoot yonko jerk."

"He must feel terrible now."

Thunder laughed. "If I found the job for him, which I wouldn't anyway, and he wuz here and I wuz dere, I'd tink that wuz a helluva good joke on Shakey Woyaku."

"No, you wouldn't."

"Yeah, I would. Guess that's what makes some people saints and some people walkin' divils."

"Some people never find out what they are."

"I'm no good. Ask anybody. I'm gonna go to hell."

"It only takes one person to redeem you."

"Yeah? One too many, like they say."

"Shakey must think you're a good man."

"Shakey don't know fish from pork chops."

"I think you're a good man, Thunder."

"Yeah? Does dis mean I'll get to heaven?"

"I'll tell you this. Since time began there's only one guy who knew for sure he'd get to heaven. Only one. And he wasn't a pope and he wasn't a king. He was a son-of-a-bitch, always was. Like you think you are. But at the end he wound up hanging next to Jesus, Who gave him the guarantee: you're goin' with me, Ace. That's what He told him."

"I'll be damned."

"You never know."

Thunder felt his knees become cool and wet. Water was running into his boots.

"Hey, Pratt kid, you feel something wet?"

"Yeah, my whole ass is soaked. There's water coming in here!"

"I know what it is."

"What?"

"Gunner Walsh mannin' a hose for the Good Friends and Neighbors Fire House. The bastards are tryin' to drown us like cats."

"We must be on fire in here. Jesus God . . ."

"If the breaker don't get you, then sittin' still wit the pain will, and if that don't get you, then the fire will, and if that don't get you, the water will. Goddam, Gunner, blow it out the other end!" he yelled.

"Turn off the water! Turn off the water!" shouted Manny, who was on his back, his head a little higher than his feet. He felt the water wash over his waist. Thunder could feel it at his hair and forehead, and if it did not run off any faster it would take only a few more inches to drown him.

Outside, the trestle and scraper line shook and everyone was ordered back. Those on the hill wailed at the possibility.

"Did you hear that?" asked Manny.

"Yeah. The water's goin' down, too."

"What do you figure?"

"I ain't even gonna tink about it," said Thunder.

"Somebody died here today."

"We'll go to the wake and chip in for the widow."

"All this just so you can say you have a stinkin' job. It's stupid. It's ridiculous," said Manny.

"People are always hell about someone else havin' a job."

"So here we wind up, Manny and Thunder, workin' for a livin'. I wish I had it to do over again."

"Once is plenty," said Thunder.

"There's a phrase the miners use . . . 'robbing the pillar' . . ."

"Sure."

"What's it mean exactly?"

"When you're minin' a coal hole you leave yourself a stanchion, a pillar of coal to hold up the roof of the hole. Only trouble is some greedy-guts always wants to chip away at the pillar and carry off the easy coal, and when they do that it's called robbin' the pillar, and the goddam roof comes down on your head."

"Jesus."

"Why?"

"You start off life with a pillar like that. Somethin' in you that keeps you upright, that supports you. And then as you get older you chip away at it until you wind up robbing the pillar, consumin' what supports you. And all to keep warm. Until it's finger stumps 'n the goddam roof on your head."

"Tink about pretty young girls with nice smooth long legs. It's only 'cause it's so dark in here."

"I don't hear anythin' outside."

Outside they were silent, watching the teetering trestle, waiting for it to fall.

"Me neither," said Thunder.

"We're both dead."

"Stick wit me, kid, I'll take care of you. It's easy once you get the knack of it."

Manny tried to pull his hand loose. It gave a little. He rested a moment and tried again, giving it what strength he had left. It came free. It was sublime to be able to move his arm. He brought it to his chest so that he could clasp his hands together. With the fingers of his left hand he discovered that those of his right hand were gone.

"This, just to be working," he said.

It made his dying less difficult.

"What, Pratt kid? You're only down 'cause of the darkness. It gets you that way. Keep the spirits up. Sunshine's on the way. I'll sing a little song for you.

> *"There's poTAToes in the OV—en,*
> *They are ROASTing nice 'n BROWN—*
> *There's a JUIcy waterMELon,*
> *When the SEAson rolls aROUND—*
> *In the PANtry there's a CHICKen,*
> *In the SMOKEhouse there's a HAM,*
> *And I'd ruther be Shakey WoYAKu,*
> *Than a poooor WHITE man."*

The crowd screamed together when the trestle fell. The dust once again envelóped the wreckage. By the time it cleared only those spectators whose men were unaccounted for were properly entitled to stay. They came down from the rim to the site and gathered together, sitting on the ground next to a fire truck. Shakey the Cop was among them.

Dear Son,

Do you remember all the funerals after the breaker came down? Who ever saw so many of them at one time? The church bells were bonging all day til it got on everybody's nerves. And the long lines of cars in the different funerals winding up Peddler's Hill to the cemeteries, with the Amvets and the firemen and who-all in their uniforms marching ahead of the hearses.

Shakey the Cop was supposed to be on directing traffic, but he got the night man to switch shifts so he could be at Thunder's funeral, Lord knows nobody else was. Shakey had to ride to the cemetery with the hearse. The boys from Brolly's gathered around the grave, making the rounds of all the boys that hung out at Brolly's, but Shakey stayed til everyone was gone and they covered Thunder up.

They said that at the wake Shakey reached under the closed half of the coffin to make sure that the undertaker put on the new shoes Shakey bought for Thunder. He was afraid the undertaker would steal them and bury Thunder in his stocking feet. Guess Shakey didn't want old Thunder burning his toes on the hot coals of hell.

You know, Brolly had to remodel his bar because nobody would sit in the favorite stools of the men who were killed. Even if the place was crowded they'd stand around the empty stools and look at them and say, "That was where he always sat." So finally Brolly had to change everything around so they would sit down again. How a man can sit at a bar for five hours at a time will always be a mystery to me.

Anyway, Shakey's retired now. He sits all day on the bench in front of our store. He's mellowed, I think, and often a few of the kids from the Slovak school sit with him during recess or lunch and talk to him. Remember how no kid used to get within a block of Shakey?

I'll send you the recipe for kiskis.

Be sure to write about the time our ceiling caved in. That will be the funniest part of the book.

Love,
Mom & Pop

CPSIA information can be obtained
at www.ICGtesting.com
Printed in the USA
LVHW102340050722
722842LV00005B/92